Until the Last Breath

NEW YORK TIMES & USA TODAY BESTSELLING AUTHOR

SHANORA WILLIAMS

Copyright © 2020 Shanora Williams

All rights reserved. This eBook is licensed for your personal enjoyment only. This eBook is copyright material and must not be copied, reproduced, transferred, distributed, leased, licensed or publicly performed or used in any form without prior written permission of the publisher, as allowed under the terms and conditions under which it was purchased or as strictly permitted by applicable copyright law. Any unauthorized distribution, circulation or use of this text may be a direct infringement of the author's rights, and those responsible may be liable in law accordingly.

Thank you for respecting the work of this author.

Cover Design by By Hang Le

Trademarks: This book identifies product names and services known to be trademarks, registered trademarks, or service marks of their respective holders. The author acknowledges the trademarked status in this work of fiction. The publication and use of these trademarks is not authorized, associated with, or sponsored by the trademark owners.

NOTE FROM THE AUTHOR

Hey there!

Before you dive in, I just want to let you know that the disease used in this novel, Onyx Pleura Disease, is not a real disease. It is a fictional one, however diseases and health conditions from real life (like cancer, asthma, etc) were used to create and, in a way, inspire this fictional disease.

I hope you enjoy reading this book as much as I enjoyed writing it.

Much love,

Shanora

ONE

Many people are afraid of darkness. To them darkness creates an instant fear in their minds, but what people don't realize is that that fear is only a figment of their imagination. If you're afraid of darkness, it's because you're terrified of what hides within it.

Monsters.

Demons.

The Boogie Man. Whatever it is you're afraid of, it's because you've allowed yourself to become afraid of that dark unknown.

To me, the darkness is my life. I dwell in it. Bask in it.

I enjoy the coolness. The quiet. The peace. Staring into nothingness. I don't mind darkness. I'm not afraid of it either. In fact, I love it because it hides my appearance and who I really am.

I spent most of my childhood cloaked in shadows, which is why it brings me comfort. In the pitch black, I can hide my face, my eyes, my guilt. No one can see me. No one can read my face and tell how I'm feeling.

It's a pleasure honestly.

And it's why John and I are sitting in this room in the dark. I'm staring up at the blank ceiling and he's watching the rain slide down the windowpane across from him as if it's some wet, constantly altering masterpiece.

He's quiet. *Too quiet.*

I shouldn't feel so relieved about his silence but the truth is I don't want to talk right now. The rain, along with the steady beeping of the monitor beside me, have become sounds of comfort—noises my hollow mind can drown in.

John's head turns as I sigh.

"You okay?" he asks, leaning forward. Though it is dark, there is a sliver of moonlight pouring in through the window, allowing me to see him. The dark circles around his blue eyes causes a tug around my heart.

My lip twitches as I nod for him.

He places a hand on my arm. His touch is always warm. Comforting. I try to smile, but my cracked lips prevent a full one.

"You've been quiet today," John murmurs, running his fingers down my arm. He lifts my hand in his and kisses the back of it, his shimmering blue eyes finding mine. They flash from the lights filtering in through the window. "You should try and sleep."

I slowly pull my hand away. "You know you don't have to keep telling me to sleep, John," I sigh.

"I'm just worried about you, Shannon. I have every reason to be worried." And he's still upset about the argument we had earlier over me not wanting to be sedated again because I felt just an *inkling* of pain. I was fine. I swear I was. He was just being his usual overbearing self.

I mumble something beneath my breath and hear him shift in his chair.

"What?" he asks.

I don't respond.

My silence clearly bothers him, and, seconds later, I hear the legs of his chair scrape across the linoleum and the lights flicker on above me. I shield my eyes, feeling like a vampire caught in the sun.

"John! Seriously?"

"What did you say?" he asks, ignoring my slight overreaction to the light.

"Nothing," I mumble, dropping my hands.

"You did say something. Would you be kind enough to repeat it?" John stands tall, chin high, his chestnut hair floppy and messy around his ears and forehead.

I remember the first time I saw my husband. I was struck by his beauty. He's so handsome but so serious all the time. He's got a chiseled face, strong with sharp angles. His lips are full and supple, and with a body like his, it's as if he were built to be a god.

At one point I loved everything about John and all his seriousness because, to me, seriousness meant dedication and stability, but after I was diagnosed, that seriousness slowly began to annoy me. I know, I know. I'm a horrible wife for thinking that.

I blow a breath. "John, let's just forget it, okay? I really don't want to waste my energy arguing right now." I adjust the tubes running from my nostrils.

He sighs. "Repeat yourself, please."

"Why? What do you think I said?"

"I don't know!" he snaps, and I flinch. "That's why I'm asking you, Shannon!"

Our eyes lock, the hostility like static in the air. We go through this so much—*too much*, in fact. I'm starting to get sick of the same old thing, arguing over my health, something he wishes he could control. He's the kind of man who wants to be in control of *everything* in his life but with my situation, it can't be that way and he knows it, and that makes him angry sometimes. Irritable.

"You need to stop kidding yourself. Stop playing so many games when it comes to your health, Shannon," he snaps.

Anger strikes me, and before I can think about it, I spit out the words I was once afraid of him hearing. "Fine. You want to know what I said? I said I want you to stop worrying about me, John! I don't need you to worry so much about every little thing, okay? Sitting here like this is hard enough. I want you to move on before it's too late! Forget about me and this fucking hospital already and just prepare yourself for what's next. We both know I'm not going anywhere—well, actually, no. I take that back. If I do go anywhere, it will be because my dead body is carried out of this room and buried six feet underground. You'll get to go home, and I'll be gone."

His hostility disappears and in an instant his eyes are filled with both agony and guilt—guilt that he shouldn't feel.

"No." He marches forward, standing above me. "Why would I forget about you? *How* can I forget about someone like you, Shannon?"

"You'll have to one day." I look up into his watering eyes, trying to fight the ache in my chest, but of course I feel everything. I hurt for him because I don't like to see him upset. I don't like to think that he'll have to live without me. "I'm...I'm going to die, John. Don't you see that?" My voice cracks when I speak. It's unintentional. I don't want to cry. Not right now, but I can't *not* cry with him. He's my husband —my everything—and the fact that this is happening to him guts me. It's not his fault, yet he constantly blames himself.

John's red-rimmed eyes line with tears and he tries

reaching for my face, but I turn away, sinking back against the hard hospital bed.

"Shannon..." His head drops and shakes. "Babe, please don't talk like that. Anything can happen. A miracle—a chance. You can still fight this. You're the strongest woman I know."

"Can you just turn the lights back off, please?" I can't take his encouraging words right now. We both know there are no miracles coming my way.

"No. I know what you're trying to do and I'm tired of it. You can't hide from me. You're still beautiful to me. You're perfect." He pulls my hands away before I can shield my face with my palms. Running the tips of his fingers along the soft spot behind my ear, he whispers, "You're gorgeous, babe. My beautiful wife. Don't *ever* tell me to forget you."

My lips press thin, my eyes flashing hot. "John," I whisper.

"Yeah, babe?"

I'm going to crush him. That hope in his eyes? That faith? It's already crushed, and I know it. "I. Am. Going. To. Die." I utter each word slowly. "Why haven't you accepted that yet?"

Slowly, John's large hands pull away from me and he stares long and hard, looking at me from the top of my head and down to my chin.

I know what you're thinking. That was wrong of me to say. I shouldn't have said it. I agree that I am hard on John, but only because he deserves better than this—going through the depressing life-altering experience of watching his wife wither away on a hospital bed.

He's a popular chef in North Carolina who has received many, many rewards and helps run a top-rated restaurant in the heart of Charlotte, but he'd rather spend his precious time in the hospital with a dying woman, slowly losing his grip on reality and even his creativity.

I shouldn't be so unfair. I mean, I am his wife and if he was the one dying, I wouldn't dare leave the hospital for a second, no matter what kind of career I had, but I'm stubborn and I admit, I can be a bitch sometimes, especially when I'm depressed. I lash out at the people I love when I'm unhappy and that is one thing I hate about myself.

I just want a better life for him. If I'd known *this* was going to happen to me, I never would have agreed to marry him, and he could have invested his time elsewhere.

Though it seems unfair, it's simply because I love him.

There's nothing I want more than for him to get back to work, go back to what he's so passionate about. Keep building his life. I've told him plenty of times that it's okay to go to work during the day—that I'll be fine with the nurses and doctors around.

He paid for the best, after all, but he refuses. He says that he could lose me at any given moment—which happens to be true—and if I do end up passing while he's not around, he'll regret it for the rest of his life.

While I'm in the midst of my thoughts, John is walking to the door.

"Where are you going?" I ask.

"I need some air."

The door flies open and is shut in an instant, the slam making the inside of my chest rattle.

I blink my tears away, watching that god-awful greyish-green curtain on the door flap before it finally settles.

What's worse is he left the light on, leaving me to stare into the mirror across from me. I study my frizzy, dark, split-ended hair, the glazed over look in my dark-brown eyes. The way my lips pout, as if I want him to come back right away and forgive me—well, I do, but he needs space and I don't blame him.

I lift my hand and run the tips of my fingers across the widow's peak that meets at my forehead. It's the best part of me in my opinion. It suits me, the way it's directed at my features, enhancing what's left of me.

My button nose and thin, cat-like eyes.

My full lips that John couldn't seem to get enough of back when I was healthy. They're chapped now but before all of this—the sedations, the pills, and the medicines—they were perfect.

Always glossed for John.

Always kissable.

Now they're like fucking sandpaper.

My eyes sting with tears.

I turn my head away, staring at the blank white wall to my right. Pressing the big speaker button on the bed, I call for the nurse.

Vickie pops her head in seconds later, eyes tired, but curious.

"Everything okay, Shannon?" she asks. I'm assuming she witnessed the slam of the door that happened moments ago, or heard it at the least.

"Yes. Do you mind turning the lights off? John forgot to turn them off before he walked out."

"Of course." Her smile is faint as she reaches for the switch. When it's off she turns for the door again. "Let me know if you need anything else, okay?"

"I will. Thanks."

When she's gone, I exhale, allowing the darkness to wrap around me. I grab a pillow and tuck it behind my head, pressing the back of my head against it, and closing my eyes.

What kind of ungrateful wife am I? I should be pleased to know that a man like John doesn't want to lose me. He could easily move on to a newer, healthier woman with a great body. Someone who doesn't have a timer ticking on her forehead.

When the disease returned three months ago, Dr. David said I only had eight months left, if that. Well, it's been five out of those eight months and the chances have slimmed a lot more.

My health fluctuates.

One day I feel like I could stay up for hours, watch some TV and even eat the lunch John cooks for me whenever he decides to go home and make something, but the next day I will hardly be able to move. My body will ache, and my head will throb. It always feels like needles are stabbing my brain.

I spiral and can never get enough rest, and that's when Dr. David will sedate me. Because it's the only thing that can take the pain away. Not even the pills work to take the edge off.

I'm not satisfied with the life I've lived. In fact, for the most part, I hated my life until I and my sister were taken away from our drug-dealing mother to live with our grandmother.

We did well—stayed with my grandmother until she passed away four and a half years later. By that point, I'd found a job at a nice bar in uptown Charlotte called Capri and worked long night shifts. Sleep was seldom, but I loved working at that bar. I loved the aura. The music. The lights. That bar was my freedom.

I loved the drinks, tips, and the pure excitement from the patrons. Plus, it was rare for a twenty-one-year-old to be working at such an upscale, trendy place. I considered myself lucky to have even landed the job and refused to take it for granted.

So, maybe I did love my life just a little more after I became a woman and accepted myself. I guess what I'm saying is I'm not satisfied with a *certain* part of my life and some of the decisions I made years ago. To this day it still haunts me.

Allow me to explain how this particular part of my life began.

TWO

PAST

FOUR YEARS AGO

Five months into working full-time at Capri, an upscale bar of freedom in uptown Charlotte, Eugene hired a new bartender and his name was Maximilian Grant.

Everyone called him Max. At first, I hated Max. When Eugene hired him, I worked fewer hours, which resulted in less money and tips.

Plus, well, Max was hot as hell so everyone wanted his face behind the counter much more than mine.

Max had smooth, russet skin. Short, wavy black hair. Piercing almond-shaped eyes the color of honey, and dimples to fucking die for. He was tall and broad. Toned and muscular in all the right places, like those NBA players you can't help staring at while they're on screen.

The way he worked up a light sweat while bartending...

my God, it was amazing. There were moments when I wanted to angrily lick that sweat away—angrily because for some reason I envied him. He was my competition and he was in *my* way.

The girls came just for him and even the hot guys thought he was a cool enough dude to ask for a drink from. They paid him extra, which meant I was stuck in my crappy corner getting cheap tips from perverts and loners.

Max had no problem with me at all. I mean, why would he? He was getting paid well. He was nice-looking and everyone knew it. He owned a nice car, had a hot girlfriend —he had it all. The list could go on for days. He may as well have been living the life of a professional ball player.

And me...well, I shared a two-bedroom apartment with a roommate. I drove a black 1999 2-door Beetle that didn't have a functioning radio and was in dire need of a paint job, and I didn't have a boyfriend or men chasing after me.

Not that I was ugly or anything, I just wasn't very involved with the dating life. The fast zone wasn't really my place.

But one night...it all changed, and I was no longer a stranger to Max.

Eugene called me back to his office with a sullen look on his face. And the words he shared were *not* words I wanted to hear.

"We just can't afford two full-time bartenders right now. You said you don't want to be a waiter and there are no other positions. I'm sorry, Shannon, but I have to let you go."

I argued with Eugene for ten minutes straight but, eventually, I gave up and stormed out of his office, on the verge of tears. There was no point in arguing or even crying. First thing the next morning, I was determined to go job hunting.

I couldn't be without one. Despite Tessa being in college now, we still needed money.

I entered the backroom and yanked down my leather jacket, scowling as I spotted Max sitting in the corner with one of the waitresses on his lap. She giggled, ran her hand down his chest, but his eyes were on me, one brow cocked.

I kept my eyes on him, tugging on my jacket and watching as he dismissed himself from the girl and walked my way.

"Hey." His voice was sin. Pure sin. If I weren't so pissed at him, I would have begged him to talk more.

I ignored him, going for my locker and taking out my belongings. I felt him watching me as I stuffed my bag angrily, then he turned on his heels, entering Eugene's office and closing the door behind him.

After pulling out my keys from my satchel, I stormed for the exit and rushed across the parking lot to get to my car. As I tried to get the piece of shit to start, I heard someone yelling my name.

Max was jogging across the parking lot and coming in my direction. When he met up to my car, he smiled down at me, his honey-colored eyes flashing from the streetlights.

I flared my nostrils, eyebrows furrowed, and rolled my window down. "What the hell do you want, *job thief?*"

He blinked, stunned. "Job thief? Why do you call me that?"

I clutched the wheel, ignoring that faint smirk and small gleam in his eyes. "What do you want?"

"Just a word."

"Well?" My eyebrows lifted and I waved an impatient hand before sitting back against my seat and folding my arms.

"I heard Eugene was letting you go and, uh..." he

scratched the top of his head, "well, I told him that if you go, it would be a really stupid move. He didn't take my statement lightly, of course. You know how that asshole is. I thought he would end up firing my ass, but instead I made him think it over and he's offering you your job back. In return I will work less hours. Makes it fair for everyone."

I stared up at him, dumbfounded. And here I was thinking he was going to try and get my number and then brag about it later. "Wait—what?"

"You're *not* fired," he said, laughing.

"What do you mean I'm *not* fired? He just told me I was—wait, why are you even helping me?"

Max pressed a hand on my car, leaning forward. "Because I know every single female employee in *Capri*, except you. Since I've been here, I've never gotten a word from you."

"So what?"

He passed a crooked smile. "Okay, maybe a part of it is also because Eugene is my uncle-in-law and I told him it would be really foolish to let someone like you go. I mean, you work hard. You have fun. You're really good at what you do—hell, I think you get the most appreciation for your drinks. People love you. You're a necessity here and this is my father's business. He'd hate to see it go down because of a dumb mistake like this one. He'd also hate to hear that I'm jobless in a new city while in school, all because my uncle wanted to be an idiot. So, Shannon, you are *not* fired."

My breathing stifled a moment. For one, Max was leaning against *my* beat-up car, arm flexed, and body toned beneath a black muscle tank, and two, I wasn't fired! I'd never felt so relieved in all my life.

Max cocked a brow, probably confused by my silence and blank stare. "That is, unless you don't want to work here anymore..." His voice was not as confident as before.

"No—no," I quickly defended my silence. "Trust me, I do. I need this job. So much more than you think. I'm just…just shocked is all."

"Alright then. If that's the case, get your shocked ass back in there and start serving up some drinks. We've got customers waiting."

I grinned, lowering my head, my dark, unruly curls curtaining my face. Sighing, I rolled my window up and he stepped back as I pushed the car door open. "You didn't have to do that, you know," I murmured, stepping out of the car and shutting the door behind me.

"I know, but I wanted to. Consider it a favor." He started walking backwards. "One day you'll owe me and you can't say no." His smile grew bigger and then he turned around and jogged to the back door.

He glanced over his shoulder once before disappearing. I stared ahead, huffing a laugh in utter disbelief.

Max had just saved me from being jobless. Hell yeah I owed him a favor. I owed him a thousand favors. I loved working at Capri. I loved getting creative and making over five hundred dollars every night of the weekend. If we're being honest, that was close to stripper money, only I didn't have to take off my clothes in order to get paid. I could keep my pride and dignity and still make more than enough money to provide for myself and my sister. A job like this was rare for someone my age.

But that favor Max was asking for? It turned out it wasn't a simple one. He really meant that I *owed* him, and not with work, or covering a shift for him one night so he could take his girlfriend or some random chick out on a date, but something else entirely.

Something that completely blindsided me.

THREE

The room door creaks open.

Light footsteps pad across the floor after the door shuts and I hear a long, weary sigh as the couch in the corner crunches beneath the weight of a body.

I wait for him to speak, but I know that he won't. He probably thinks I'm asleep.

"John?" I call.

I can see him in my peripheral, just his silhouette. He perks up, his hair glistening from droplets of rain. "Yeah?"

Silence again. My mouth works hard to form words…an apology. I am sorry, but I also meant every word that I said. He has to move on sooner or later.

"I'm sorry," I whisper, and my voice cracks. Tears immediately spring to my eyes.

John stands immediately and walks to my bed, sitting on the edge. The moonlight reveals his smooth face. "No. I'm sorry, baby," he murmurs. "I shouldn't have stormed out like that."

"No. I shouldn't have said that to you." I turn over a bit,

grabbing his hand. "I just…I want you to understand where I'm coming from when I say that. You're only thirty-one, John. You have so much ahead of you. It would hurt me as an angel, or a ghost, or whatever I turn out to be to see that you're depressed and no longer doing what you love." I force a smile and he laughs, and I'm so glad to see the smile actually touch his tired eyes.

"A ghost?" he repeats, teasing. He leans forward and kisses my forehead. "I'd prefer an angel over a ghost any day. Don't need you haunting me."

I giggle.

"You're a goof, you know that?" he says, stroking the pad of his thumb over my cheek.

I grin. "I know."

His mouth works hard to form the next set of words. "But you know how I am, Shannon. It's not an easy pill for me to swallow, knowing there's a chance of losing you."

"I know." I pause and twist my lips. "Just promise me you won't be extremely depressed because I don't want that," I plead, still trying to keep the mood light.

"No way I can promise that. I'll be in so much unbearable pain and heartache."

"Well, promise me you won't turn into an alcoholic or druggy or anything like that."

"I can guarantee you that will never happen." And I'm sure of it. John's father was an alcoholic and, sadly, his mother used drugs and pills, which resulted in her spending countless months in rehab, demolishing her perfect career as a news anchor. She overdosed when John was fifteen. It destroyed him.

In high school he was teased and bullied about his mother, seeing as the whole town knew her, so he dropped out. Fortunately, he got his GED, went to a community college, and then decided to go to culinary school to do what he loved most. Cook.

He's never wanted anything to do with drugs and to this day you'll hardly ever catch him drinking hard liquor. He revolves around red and white wines and even a craft beer here and there.

Our pasts are very similar, which is why I think we connect so much. We can relate to one another and understand each other's struggles and stubbornness, and yet when we're together we are the most vulnerable.

"I love you." He leans forward, kissing my cheek.

"I love you too, Johnny." He kisses my lips next, sweet and tender. Soft and warm. I melt inside, my tummy rumbling with those flutters I love feeling whenever he's close.

"Let's not argue anymore, okay? I hate arguing with you."

"Okay. But only if we can make a deal."

His brows draw together. "What kind of deal?"

"I promise to avoid arguments if, and *only* if, you promise to start going back to work—at least during the day."

His face stiffens and I can already tell he's ready to storm out the room again.

"Please, John? Just consider it."

I know him. He's ready to tell me no, but he knows saying no right now will result in another argument and no deal, so he says, "I'll think about it." He scratches his brow. "But I won't be too happy about being away from you—and if I do go back, I'm only staying for a couple hours. Not all day." By his tone, I can tell he's been thinking about work a lot. He misses it. That kitchen is his second home.

I grin. "Good enough for me."

He brings the blanket near my feet up to cover me. "Get some sleep. I'll be right over there."

"Kay."

After placing one last kiss on my lips, he goes to the sofa and lies flat on his back. Several minutes later and he's out like a light, snoring with the ferocity of a lion's roar.

I nuzzle my cheek on my blanket and shut my eyes, but as I get comfortable, my phone vibrates on the table next to me.

A text message.

I pick it up and my heartbeat almost comes to standstill.

Max: I need to see you.

I read the message several times. I haven't heard from Max in months—not since I told him I was sick and that he needed to stay away. Not since I'd chosen John to be the one by my side as I laid on my sickbed.

If John witnesses him staring at me the way he used to, with eyes so full of passion and care and tenderness, it would ruin everything.

Our marriage. My final days here on earth. Our love. *Everything.* I can't afford hurting him during my last few weeks with him. Because it is getting close to the end. I feel it in my body, my soul.

I swallow thickly, dropping the phone and shutting it off. I won't respond. Maybe he'll take the hint that I don't want him to see me—that he shouldn't come see me. Not while I'm like this.

Maybe when I'm lifeless in a casket, then he can come, and at least by then, I won't have to confront him about anything.

FOUR

PAST

FOUR YEARS AGO

I wanted to strangle Eugene for having me think I was fired. Three days after Max told me I wasn't, Eugene had hired two waiters. Quincy and Brenda. Granted, they were part-time employees, but it annoyed me to no end that he'd had the audacity to fire me just to hire two more people.

I heard from Max that he had to convince Eugene to hire more people because summer was coming and college kids would be out of school and looking for a place to hang out. The workload would be too much for the current employees, so it was best to be prepared ahead of time. He was right and, luckily, he saved Eugene's ass from getting a serious talk with me when I saw I had more hours on my schedule.

"So, listen," Max said after downing a swig of his beer. We were standing at the counter of the bar. It was a slow

Thursday night. I turned my attention to him, sipping on a peach margarita while smiling behind the straw. "Remember that favor I said you'd owe me?"

I released my straw, placing my glass down as my smile slowly evaporated. He focused on my eyes. They didn't dare shift, not even as I stared back. "Yeah?"

"I'd like to ask for that favor now."

I adjusted on my stool, straightening my back. After clearing my throat, I said, "Okay...what is it? Need me to cover a shift for you? I don't mind tackling a whole night if I need to. After all, that's how it was before *Maximilian the Great* was hired." I grinned.

He grinned back, his eyes relaxing. He turned in his seat to face me, giving me all of his attention. Even as the other female employees walked past in their black shirts, revealing flat bellies and rocking their low-rise jeans, he could only look at me. Me, with my sleeveless tee knotted in the back, my ripped jeans, and black ankle boots. I never felt the need to dress like the other girls.

Leaning forward, his chest close to mine, Max murmured, "Covering a shift isn't exactly what I had in mind as a favor."

"No? Then what did you have in mind?"

"Come on, Shannon. This is a free pass for me. Not that I feel like you really 'owe me' or anything, but I know you appreciate me for helping you keep your job."

My face warped with confusion. "I don't know what you're getting at."

Max's eyes softened as he reached up, running the back of his hand down my jawline. When he reached my chin, he pressed the pad of his thumb on the center of it and then held it firmly between his fingers.

My breath hitched from the sudden movement, my arms

sweeping with goosebumps. He'd never touched me before. There were plenty of times when I saw in his eyes that he wanted to do something to me, touch me somewhere, but he never actually went through with it. There were many instances behind the bar on busy nights when he'd come close to pressing a hand to the small of my back to get by, but never did. But tonight, he was up close and personal.

"Come out with me Friday night. Brenda and Quincy are working the night shift," he said. "Melanie and Jace have the bar."

"How do you know I don't have to work in VIP?"

His lips flattened, the look he gave me sarcastically asking *seriously?* "Because I checked. And because you hate VIP. Saw it on a sticky note in E's office."

"Geez. Stalker," I laughed.

"One night, Little Shakes. That's all I ask of you." He was still holding onto my chin, like he didn't want me to look elsewhere but into his eyes.

"Little Shakes?" I breathed.

"Yes."

"What is that supposed to mean?"

"The way you shake those hips to the music when you whip up those drinks..." He shook his head and ran his tongue over his bottom lip. "You have no idea how many times I've wanted to come up behind to join you in a dance. Luckily I know how to keep things professional around here."

My heart sped up a notch as I imagined us on the dance floor.

Grinding.

Touching.

Making out until our bodies could no longer endure the ache or need. I brushed the idea aside.

"Why have you never tried making a move before?" I asked, my voice barely a whisper.

"Because it just so happens that when I watch you, it's too hard for me to move—too hard for me to function."

I laughed, removing my chin from his soft grasp and picking up my margarita again. "You have a response for everything, don't you, Playboy?"

"What?" He chuckled. "I'm telling the truth." He picked up his bottle to finish off his beer. When he was done, he asked, "So what do you say? Will I be given one night with you, Shakes?"

I blinked up at him as my lips wrapped around the black straw again. His eyes immediately darted down to my mouth. His nostrils flared, his large body no longer relaxed. Instead of holding in what he had to say—because, lets face it, Maximilian never bit his tongue—he said, "Your lips are so fucking perfect."

I pulled away from my drink as a song by *X Ambassadors* poured out of the speakers. I wanted to say yes to going out with him right in that moment. I wanted to pounce right on top of him, have him carry me to his 2-door Audi and drive me to that apartment that I heard so much about from the girls who came to the bar every night just to see him.

But I was a smart girl. I admit I was interested, but he wasn't going to get me that easily.

"Your girlfriend?" I asked over my drink.

"Don't have one."

"Hmm."

"You're stalling. You must be cuffed to someone already."

"Nope. Single. No cuffs. It's been that way for a while now."

"Hmm," he mimicked. I narrowed my eyes at him playfully, conjuring a silent laugh from his end.

"If I tell you I'll think about it, will that work for you?"

Max's head tilted a little, then he pressed his lips and stood from the stool smoothly. "Sure," he said as he stepped behind me, planting his large, warm hands on my shoulders. His chest brushed across my back and he leaned closer, his lips touching the shell of my ear. Up close, he smelled good, his scent reminding me of a warm, spring day. "But don't think for too long, Shakes. I'm not a very patient man."

I fought a smile, sucking on my straw again as he walked toward the backroom. When he disappeared, I sighed, trying my best to ignore the racing of my heart. I wiped the sweat off my palms as if it would help. It didn't. My heart was still racing.

"Well, well," Quincy said as he came to my end of the bar. I whipped my head up as he grabbed my empty glass and rattled the ice. "What?" I asked, my cheeks ablaze.

"You have *never* finished a drink at this bar, Shannon Hales. Someone must've made you a little hot and thirsty, huh?" Quincy smirked.

"Oh, please. I just really needed one." I wave him off.

"That's what you say. Girl, you know you can't deny that man. He already has you wrapped around his finger."

"He does not." I fiddled with the edge of a black napkin.

I looked up as Quincy placed his elbows on the countertop, bringing his face closer to me. "I hear that once he has you, there is no way you can stop thinking about him. I hear that man is a *god* in the bedroom. By the end of it you'll be worshipping him." He fanned himself with exaggeration. "Too bad he isn't into fine men like me." Quincy lifted his hand and pretended to flip invisible hair over his shoulder as he turned for the drinks. I giggled as he twisted his eyebrow piercing and pursed his lips. "Take it from him, Shannon. *Take it* and never let it go! You know you want to!" His outburst caused a few of the waitresses to look our way with frowns. I avoided their eyes, giving him a *shut up before I kill you* look.

It was close to closing now and since the night was slow, I knew Eugene would send me home. As I cleaned the bar counter, the door of the employee lounge swung open and out walked Max. As he walked out, my smile completely faded.

His arm was wrapped around Brenda's shoulders and he had her way too close to his body for my liking. His eyes flickered over to mine, only briefly, and then he looked down at Brenda who was going on about something I'm sure was irrelevant.

What the hell? Was he doing this on purpose? Trying to make me jealous so that I could come running to him?

Well, fuck that. He had me all wrong. I wasn't that type of girl. I didn't go running to any man. I had dignity and sometimes a little too much pride.

I wasn't Brenda, the redhead who was a pro at giving blowjobs in the men's bathroom. I deserved patience and respect, and that damn sure wasn't what Max was willing to give me.

Quincy shook his head with a hand on his hip, a look of pure disgust on his face as he watched them walk by. "You know what," he mumbled as they passed by and Max completely disregarded me, "I take what I said back. Don't take shit from him. Make his player-ass work for what you've got."

FIVE

My head spins, my body going through the same routine it does every couple of mornings.

Aching bones.

Fatigue.

Breathlessness.

Sometimes the OPX treatments help me forget where I am, until I allow myself a chance to remember. In a hospital, on a wing full of other sick patients.

It's depressing as hell, waking up to a plain white ceiling or hearing someone cough so hard it seems their lung might pop.

I groan, forgetting just how much of a pain in the ass it is to wake up and get comfortable.

My ass is numb, my fingers too. The IV in my arm digs deeper but I turn a bit, relaxing it.

Yesterday's round of OPX isn't working in my favor. It's pointless anyway. The only reason I've continued it is because John wants me doing everything I can to survive, even if that means sitting for almost an hour while I allow the OPX to swim through my veins, then allowing the unbearable body aches and skull-splitting headaches to set in. It makes him feel better, so be it.

I already know it's too late. The OPX isn't working like it should and soon the doctors will stop wasting it and save it for someone that might actually be saved.

After all, this medicine is expensive, mainly because Onyx Pleura, the disease I carry, is rare and not much of the OPX has to be made to cure it.

I hate the disease.

It's destroying me. It's caused me to lose a lot of weight and for my hair to shed—so much to the point that Tessa had to take me to cut it a few months ago.

My hair has grown back some, but it is very thin and brittle. I've lost some color to my umber skin, my lips are always dry, and I can't forget to mention the permanent dark circles around my eyes.

Onyx Pleura Disorder.

It is definitely not my best friend, yet it's been with me every day since the age of twenty-three. Never have I touched a cigarette. I may have smoked some weed here and there, but that surely isn't the cause of the diagnosis.

They say, for people with this disease, that it is formed in our lungs when we are born, but it is so rare that doctors don't check unless there are symptoms of it when you're a child.

It gets worse as you age, especially when you partake in a lot of strenuous activities that pump the lungs. I guess all of my stressing, working two jobs at one point, and keeping up with Tessa, had finally caught up to me.

I loathe this disease. *No*, I hate it—hate it so much for ruining my life. Without a lung transplant, there is an 8% survival rate. And it can't just be any kind of lung. Besides matching blood types, there is a certain section of the lung that has to be taken in order for it to be replaced. We are on a long waiting list. It's been months. I've given up hope.

A knock sounds on the door and Leah, my day nurse, walks in, singing "Good morning!" as she makes her way for the window. She draws the curtains open dramatically, like the moms do in all the teenage movies, and then sighs as the sunlight hits her face.

Leah is perfect and so highly underestimated as a nurse. They all take her for granted but when it comes down to me staying at the hospital, she is the woman I want taking care of me. Not Vickie, not Ronda, but Leah. She's almost like a sister, and she actually cares about my sanity, happiness, and health. There are no cat fights or arguing included, like Tessa and I tend to do.

"Why are you still trying to sleep in on this glorious day?" she asks, spinning around to look at me. "All that rain last night... you should be happy we have this. Are you hungry?"

I sit up groggily. "Hell no. I feel like I'm about to throw up already."

She rushes for the purple bucket beside the bed. "Here," she places it on my lap. "Take it out on the *Fuck-It Bucket*."

I shake my head, laughing a little. "I think I'm okay. Some water would be nice, though."

Her head nods and she goes for the pitcher on the table, carrying it to the door. "I'll go get you some." She takes a look around the room as if something is missing. When it finally registers to her, she asks, "Where's John?"

"I convinced him to go back to work for a few hours."

Her brown eyes expand, the sunlight highlighting her brown skin. The shade of her skin reminds me of my dad's.

"Are you serious? He actually listened?" She props a hand on her hip with a smug smile.

"Well," I shrug, "I told him he has to live before I stop living. He can't keep putting his life on hold for someone that won't make it."

Leah's smile evaporates. "You know I hate when you talk like that, Shannon."

I shrug. "It's the truth."

She grips the door handle a little tighter. "I'll go get the water." She's out of the door in less than a second.

I sigh.

Leah and I are close, so she knows I hate it when she tries to coddle me or show sympathy. That's why she walked out.

To me, sympathy equals pity.

This is my life—what I've been served—and I've finally accepted it. Although it hasn't been a very long life, I've tried making the most I can out of it, though there are some things I wish I'd done and places I wish I'd gone before ending up on my deathbed.

My phone buzzes on the table next to me. I look over and spot Max's name again. He's calling this time. I don't answer.

Leah walks in again with the pitcher, pouring me a cup of water as she nears me. That moment of sadness we shared less than two minutes ago has passed because a full smile is on her lips again, contagious enough to make anyone's day.

"Let's get some food in that belly of yours," she chimes.

And I nod.

This is the way it has to be.

SIX

PAST

"Fine." I stepped up to Max, one eyebrow raised, and a hand on my hip. I slammed the other hand down on the counter.

He turned my way, adjusting himself on the barstool, his warm, manly scent making me slightly weak in the knees. He never wore too much cologne. It was always just enough. Subtle and tempting, making a girl wish she could move in closer for a deeper smell.

"What's that now?" He put on a smug grin, eyes widening as he lowered his cellphone.

I narrowed my eyes, stepping closer to him. I was almost between his legs, but I kept a good, safe distance. Showing any sign of weakness while around him was *not* an option. "I will give you *one* night, but *only* one," I said, holding up a single finger. "And we have to go to a place that I really want to go to."

"Alright." He ran a hand over the top of his head. His hair

was wavy, like ocean waves at night. "You name the time and place."

"Tomorrow night. Eight o'clock at Crave on West 5th." I stepped back, tucking my hair behind my ear. "And please," I said over my shoulder as I turned away, "don't be late."

I gave him a faint smile. To me, this was a game of cat and mouse and he'd finally caught me, but he hadn't tried to eat me just yet. I had to tamper with his ego—get under his skin just a little bit.

Only it didn't work.

The legs of his stool scratched across the floor and Max caught me before I could make a break for it out the back door. I spun around and was between his arms, my lips parting as I met his honey eyes.

His skin, up close like this, looked like it was made of satin. I wanted to touch his face, trace my fingertips down his firm, chiseled jawline. But I refrained.

"You think you're fucking with my head, don't you?" He asked, his voice a murmur beneath the music.

"Not at all," I challenged.

"What made you give in?"

"Nothing. I just think I owe you this much…"

He frowned. "I told you, you don't really owe me anything."

"I kinda do…"

"No, you don't, Little Shakes. You don't have to do this. I'm not forcing you."

"Whatever," I said, deliberately maneuvering out of his arms and pulling my satchel on top of my shoulder. "It's just one night. Can't cause too much harm, right? Might as well get it over with."

Max scoffed, which made me frown. He was giving me a

dubious stare, and that stare alone proved that maybe I didn't know what he was capable of.

"Shakes," he said. "When I'm done with you, you'll be begging for more than just one night." He took a step toward me again, holding onto my wrist and reeling me back into his rock-hard body. I clashed softly with him, my head tipped up, and our eyes bolting. "I don't fuck around," he murmured, leaning forward to place his lips near the shell of my ear. "I want you. *Bad*. Now that you've given me this chance, I'm going to make sure this one-night turns into many, many more."

I could hardly breathe. Every word ran over me like hot lava. His voice was so orgasmic and deep. His body, so hard and smooth and warm on mine. It was no wonder the girls couldn't resist him. I was trying hard not to be *that* girl, but with him so close, it was damn near impossible.

Max knew what he was doing, and I shouldn't have tested his ego, considering I hadn't been laid up in over five months.

I admit I was a little desperate for him. I mean, he was the finest man I'd been around in months. I saw him almost every night, and he was into me. Really, *really* into me.

The way he held me, his hand on the small of my back and purposely near my ass, exhibited more than enough proof of how much he craved me. He was silently teasing me and slowly but surely unraveling every stubborn fiber in my body.

I wondered why, however. I was the dullest girl working at *Capri* and, I admit, I wasn't the most attractive of the bunch. What was it about me that made him want the chase?

I straightened up, smiling softly as I pulled away from him and walked to the door. I felt him watching me go, and when I looked over my shoulder, a hint of a smile was tugging at the corners of those perfectly sculpted lips.

As I pushed the door open, I casually said, "We'll see about that, Max the Great."

Then I walked away, glad the door shut behind me quickly. I bet it made me, dull old Shannon, even more enticing to him. A door slamming in his face—cutting off his view.

What topped the night off was the text I received from him later that night.

> Max: Can't stop thinking about you

The message thrilled me. To be running around in the wild mind of Maximilian Grant was a great way to end the night.

So, before I fell asleep, I sent him a text back.

> Me: Can't stop thinking about the cupcakes and drinks we'll be sharing at Crave. The carrot cake cupcake, I heard it is to fucking die for.

> Max: LOL. Potty mouth

Yeah, I was still testing his ego, but this was fun, and for the first time in a long time, I felt alive. Flirting didn't come naturally to me, but playing hard to get did, and for some reason he liked that. And I liked that he liked that.

I liked where this one-night thing was headed already, and it hadn't even happened yet.

With this story, I am going to go deeper—explain to you exactly how I ended up falling for Max. Judging by the story so far, a person can probably assume that I love him more than my husband. Well, that person would be incorrect. I love my husband with every fiber of my being. But my love for Max is...different. It's a raw kind of love—a love a woman will never, ever forget, no matter how bad some of it may have been.

Although he's cocky, arrogant, and so full of shit sometimes, there is so much about Max that people don't really get to see.

The history between Max and me runs deep, and I hate that I'm even telling it because for one, most of it is not my story to tell, and two, John would hate that I'm thinking about another man while on my sickbed.

But I have to. Why? Because being with Max was probably one of the best times of my life, even if it was a big eye-opener in the end.

I actually felt *alive* with him, and not in the corny sense, where people constantly party and travel and jump off of cliffs. No. That's not what feeling alive is to me.

Feeling alive to me, is being around someone who can make you feel things you never thought possible. A person who can help you cherish every small moment, even the bad ones. Feeling alive is when your heart beats madly as you watch the person you love approach.

That person lights your soul on fire and ignites the better parts of you—makes you see the good in yourself when you look in the mirror every day. And when you do look at yourself, you just...*shine*.

You shine bright and bold like the sun on the first few days of summer. You're beautiful. You feel like you can take over the world with just that inkling of love in your heart.

Perhaps I shouldn't just call it feeling alive. Maybe I should call it happiness as well. Without a doubt, there was a time when I could say Max made me the happiest woman on earth, but sometimes things happen that are out of our control, and that happiness morphs into something else—something depressing and heartbreaking.

Sometimes things change and before we can work hard to get it all back, it's too late. It's done, and deep down we regret not fighting for the one thing that completed us.

The night that I agreed to go on that date with Max, I knew what I was in for. I knew I would most likely get hooked, start looking forward to his text messages every day, and even look forward to seeing him at work.

I knew I would fall for him…but what I didn't know was how unprepared I was going to be when it all happened.

SEVEN

PAST

It was nearing eight the night of our date and Max still hadn't arrived. I stepped in front of the mirror, plucking the clumpy pieces of mascara off my eyelashes and cursing beneath my breath.

Emilia, my roommate, walked into my room, flipping her wrist and checking her waterproof watch.

She was retro, with silver braces, pigtails in her hair and rainbow pajamas. I loved her for it, though. She was unique, the very reason I allowed her to become my roommate. She never pretended to be anyone but herself.

"Wow…you finally score a once in a lifetime date and he doesn't show? That's gotta burn," said Emilia.

I looked at her reflection in the mirror, narrowing my eyes at her. "He'll show. He has to." *Because he would be stupid to cancel on me when we work together.*

"He'd better." Someone knocked on the door as soon as

she said that. I already knew who that *someone* was, and my heart pounded in my chest.

Emilia's eyes stretched, as if she had some big idea. "Hey, I'm gonna peek around the corner to see him, alright?" It was funny how she could ask a question and be serious, but also completely oblivious of how corny she sounded.

"Em," I laughed, "you don't have to sneak to see him. Just come out and meet him."

"Looking like this?" she shrieked. "No. Fuck that. I'm wearing my mom's favorite pajamas every night until Aunt Flo passes. I'm bloated and craving nothing but sweets—oh, make sure you get my chocolate cupcake, too!" She skipped off to her room, cracking the door and I shook my head with a laugh as I grabbed the doorknob and twisted it open.

Max had a hand pressed on the wall outside the door, towering above me with a smirk on his lips. His nearness caught me off guard and I took a step back, brows furrowing.

"What are you doing?" I laughed.

"Eavesdropping." He looked around the room. "Where's your friend?"

"Oh my goodness!" I laughed. "Don't worry about it!"

He shrugged, pulling his hand down and sliding his fingertips into the front pockets of his black pants. "Tell her there's nothing wrong with a woman in pajamas on a Friday night."

"Yeah." I scoffed, picking my satchel up off the table. "Keep it in your pants, Playboy."

He chuckled, stepping back to let me out the door. As I pulled out my keys and started to close the door, I spotted Emilia rushing to the living room and mouthing the words, *"Oh. My. Fucking. God!"*

I fought a grin, shutting it rapidly before Max could see her.

"So," I sighed, looking at him after locking up. "You ready?"

"Been ready."

"I actually don't think you were," I said as we walked down the stairs. "It's ten minutes after eight."

"Oh, I wasn't late." He pressed his lips. "I was sitting in my car at eight, watching you mess with your face. You checked your phone about six times, then you sighed as you looked into the mirror."

I stopped walking, frowning at the back of his head as he took a step down before me. "You have a lot of nerve watching me, Max." I was hesitant as he fought a laugh. I wasn't sure whether to be weirded out or excited that he was. "So, you were purposely late to come up?"

"Just wanted to see if you were prepared for tonight."

My lips pressed thin.

He continued. "Don't think anything of it. Your curtains were wide open. Kinda hard to miss a woman that looks like *you*, walking back and forth on the second floor." He laughed. "Trust me, I'm no stalker, Shakes."

I gave him a look full of doubt. "Could've fooled me."

I went for the passenger side of his black and silver Audi. I waited for him to unlock the doors, but he stood a few steps away from the vehicle, looking sexier than ever as he scanned me with his eyes.

I hadn't paid much attention before, but he wore a casual white dress shirt with the sleeves rolled up to his elbows, his black jeans not too loose or too tight of a fit.

He'd gotten his hair cut too. His beard was lined up. The sight of him made my mouth want to water like a waterfall. He was gorgeous, and I was sure he knew it. So casual and still so damn beautiful.

"We're going to be late, Max," I said, switching on my heels.

"I don't think it's Crave you're really looking forward to having tonight." He walked around the car, diminishing the gap between us.

My heart raced. "How would you know?"

"Seems you want what comes *after* it." He was right in front of me now. "You want me, right? 'Cause I want you."

He held my upper arms gently, pressing my back against the passenger door.

"You're such a cocky bastard, you know that?" My voice had betrayed me. It didn't come out in the condescending tone I wanted it to. It came out feeble and husky instead. "I told you what I want."

"Yeah? What's that?" His mouth came closer to mine.

"Carrot cupcakes," I whispered. I was losing this battle.

His body vibrated with laughter. "For dinner?"

"After dinner…"

"And what else do you want after dinner?"

He was trying to trap me. The answer was right on the tip of my tongue, but I didn't want to give in…at least, not yet.

"Answer me, Shannon." God, the way he said my name. The way his voice changed from low and deep, to gruff and demanding made my knees weak. He lowered his hands and the absence of his touch created an ache within me.

"You already know what you're getting after dinner," I responded.

"But is dinner what you want right now?"

I bit into my bottom lip, feeling the heat of his mouth radiating above mine. "Maybe."

"All you have to do is tell me what you really want right now and I'll give it to you. Just say it."

"What are you talking about?" *That's right, Shannon. Keep playing dumb.*

After releasing a slow sigh, his mouth came down on mine and I stumbled on my heels. He caught me in his grasp, holding on tight with one hand, his other coming up to my cheek, his lips never leaving mine.

My body caught in a blaze, burning, hungry, demanding more. And more is what I got. His tongue danced with mine when my lips parted, allowing him access to a place that hadn't been shared with anyone else in months.

He groaned, pushing against me even more. My back arched against the window. My arms came up and locked around his neck and he picked me up in his large hands. Immediately, my legs draped around his narrow waist and a soft moan traveled from me to him. This was our first kiss and it was turning out to be way hotter than I thought it would be.

I melted into a puddle in his arms, feeling every frenzied sensation, every ounce of need, and most of all, how much his body was enjoying all of this. He was straining in his jeans now, his erection thrusting between my thighs.

"Fuck," Max breathed when our kiss broke.

Our lips reunited once more, molding, but then the kiss broke again when I asked, "What?" in a breathy whisper.

"You are damage, Shakes."

"Damage?"

"You're going to destroy me. I can already feel it."

I smiled as he tipped his head back to meet my eyes. "Why do you say that?"

"Look at us." He laughed and took a glance around the parking lot. "This wasn't supposed to happen like this. At least not so soon. It was only supposed to be a simple kiss."

"Says the man who started it."

"Trust me, I'll finish it, but first I owe you a carrot cupcake."

He carefully placed my feet on the ground, and I adjusted my seaweed green dress, smiling hard as I looked up at him. "How about you owe me a fruity drink instead. I could use one…no, actually let's make it two."

He laughed. "Whatever you want, Shakes."

I groaned, facing the passenger door. "I swear that name is gonna kill me," I muttered as he walked to the driver's side.

He unlocked the doors and after we climbed inside and he brought the engine to life he said, "Get used to it. You'll be hearing that name a lot from now on. As a matter of fact…" He extended his arm, turning the volume of his radio up and then pushing a button on the screen to get to satellite radio. "Do a little dance for me. Right now."

I burst out laughing, looking at him as if he was insane. "Why?" I squealed.

"Come on! You want those drinks, don't you?" he said with a laugh.

I tried giving him the stink-eye but it wasn't working. I was too busy grinning like an idiot and still dazed from that kiss—our *first* kiss. "Wait—you're serious right now?" I exclaimed.

"Yes. Come on! Give me life, Little Shakes! I need you to dance for me!"

I released another uncontrollable laugh, which made him do the same, then I lowered my head, shook it, and he brought his forefinger over to tip my chin. Our eyes met, his gaze soft and mellow.

Those damn eyes.

"Alright, fine," I said. "But this is for the drinks, not you."

He nodded, eagerly waiting.

I raised my hands to the roof and shook my body to *L.A.*

Love by Fergie. Why his radio was suddenly playing Fergie, I don't know, but I wasn't embarrassed while dancing for him.

Don't get me wrong, he did laugh his ass off at me, stating that the dance I did wasn't nearly as sexy as the ones I did at the bar, but that was okay.

Joking around with Max seemed to be a rarity with him —a part of himself that he didn't reveal to too many people. With me, it came out of him naturally and I appreciated that.

If only things between us could have stayed this way.

EIGHT

A bouquet of pink peonies appears at the doorway and a large smile spreads across my lips as John's head pops up behind them. He's smiling and I can't stand how handsome he is.

"You didn't," I gasp sarcastically, placing a hand on my chest.

"I damn sure did." He returns the sarcasm, placing the vase of flowers on the countertop across from me. The area he places them in blocks me from seeing myself in the mirror. Apart of me is pleased about that, then again, the other half is upset. I brush the feeling aside and smile at my husband as he walks closer to me.

I try sitting up but a sharp pain hits me under my ribs. I wince and John rushes for me but I stop him before he can grab me.

"I'm okay," I assure him.

"You sure?"

I nod. "Just some body aches. Haven't taken anything for it yet."

"I take it the OPX didn't go so well this time," he sighs.

"Not. At. All." I blow out a breath.

"It's a new type, babe. Supposed to be stronger." He walks to me, cupping the back of my head and kissing the top of it. Heat courses through my veins, and I'm instantly comforted. "Dr. David said it'd take a while for you to get used to it."

"Yeah. I guess." I look up at him and instead of letting the mood get spoiled, I crank it back up again. I take the attention off of me and focus on him. "So," I start again, grabbing the blue pillow Tessa knitted for me and hugging it to my chest. "How was work? Did you create a lot of new meals? New customers? Tell me everything!"

John takes the chair next to the bed with a sigh. "Work was fucking terrible."

My smile drops. "Why? What happened?"

"I couldn't focus. I burned three plates of fish. Got one of the main specials for a large party completely wrong and had to start from scratch. They weren't pleased about the wait, so they ended up eating with a discount. Lorenzo isn't too pleased about that. That was a big chunk of money we lost out on. We would've gotten it just fine if I wasn't being such an airhead chef."

"John, stop it." I grab his hand, stroking the back of it with the pad of my thumb. "You're just stressed and worried, baby. Everything will be fine once this is all over—" I clamp my mouth shut and John's head lifts, his eyes instantly locking on mine. Tears line the rims of his eyes.

"You say that…" His voice cracks. "You say stuff like that constantly, like you're ready to be gone."

The air in the room thickens around me, damn near suffocating. I want to look away so he won't see the truth in my eyes, but I don't. I just watch his glistening eyes in hopes that he'll finally understand.

But, of course, he doesn't. He never will.

"Why?" He snatches his hand away from me. "I don't understand why you won't fight anymore. There's a chance you can still beat this thing, Shannon."

"A very slim chance, John."

"Slim or not, it's a chance." He scoots his chair forward, grabbing my hand again and squeezing it. "You know what I believe?"

"What?" I whisper, my voice now thick with unshed tears.

"I believe you came into my life for a reason. You weren't meant to come into it and then leave after only a couple years. That can't be right. God wouldn't punish me like this, not after all I've been through. He knows I wouldn't be able to handle it."

"He sacrificed his own son, John. What makes you think we're any special?"

He gives me a serious look, sitting back and releasing my hand. "What are you saying?"

"I'm just saying maybe this is happening to you because he knows you *can* handle it..."

"No. I truly don't think I can."

"That's because you haven't experienced it before...not with someone you're *in love* with."

"Exactly," he says hurriedly, sitting forward again with desperate blue eyes. "You're my *wife*. We just got married—we're still considered newlyweds. Why take that away from me? Why make me suffer after suffering for so many years before? My parents were enough of a loss. Shannon, baby, if you keep fighting, anything can happen. Any kind of chance shouldn't be taken for granted."

His eyes are hopeful and it kills me. I can't bear knowing that he won't be able to let go. What's going to happen to him when I do pass? Will he give up? Will he spiral into depression? Will he ever love again or will he end up an old, bitter man who doesn't believe in the word *love* or God anymore?

"I'm not meant to be here, Johnny." My voice is barely a whisper. I can barely hear it myself over the machines, but I know what I said.

And, clearly, he heard it as well because he sighs, shutting his eyes for a very brief moment and then popping them open again. A slow tear skids down his cheek.

Sitting back, my husband drags a palm down his face and then blows out a breath, dropping his hands in his lap. "I don't care what you say. I'm not giving up on you."

"I know," I murmur. And I do. I know he won't until he has no choice but to.

He stares at me, long and hard. "I know what you're trying to do. You're trying to push me away, but I won't let it happen. I'm here to stay, and if you believe you're not meant to be here then I will sit right beside this bed every single day and night until you reach your last—" His sentence ends abruptly. Look at him. He can't even say it. "Your…last breath."

His hesitation is understandable. He's trying to accept what the future may hold, but also preserve a little hope. John, he's a firm believer in God. I like that about him because it's kept him humble and in the right state of mind.

This is why I know I *will* be gone soon. Because although he thinks he can't handle my loss, I know that he can. He will move on eventually. Become stronger. Wiser. Better. He will accept it and move forward with his life, maybe not during the first few months, but he will.

He'll find ways to cope and he'll love harder. He's stronger than he thinks. They say God never puts us through anything we can't handle. That, I believe.

I will admit that I lost some of my faith a long time ago, especially when my disease attacked right after me and John's honeymoon.

When I was first diagnosed, it went away a month later. Almost like there were never any black spots on my lungs. It was like I was perfectly healthy. But then the Onyx Pleura came back with a vengeance. I was coughing hard in my living room that night, so hard I had to be rushed to the hospital.

The third and final time was way worse. I coughed during the middle of the night and John had to take me to the ER. The good I got out of it was John's loyalty. His faith and positive attitude during it all. It progressed to a worse stage after only ten months, but he still held onto hope.

Now I look at my husband and the hope that was bright in his eyes when this all first started has dulled. It's still there, but with each day, I watch the hope fade more and more.

And every day, I wish this agony would end. Not for my sake, but for his.

NINE

PAST

TWO YEARS AGO – JOHN & ME

"John, come on!" I gestured for him to hurry as I pulled open the glass door on the cruise ship.

John fixed the silver watch on his wrist, shuffling forward as fast as possible in his dress pants and white button-down shirt. He was doing his best to keep up with me.

Not that our age difference mattered—we were only four years apart and he kept himself in great shape—but he had more of a mature mindset than I did, plus I had way more energy.

After dating for two wonderful years, we decided to get hitched. The cruise we planned was a spur of the moment kind of thing and I didn't have many friends that were free, so I chose Tessa and her boyfriend to tag along. I didn't want a regular honeymoon and neither did John surprisingly. We were okay with having company with us.

At the age of twenty-four, I thought I was too young for marriage—that I needed more time—but John was with me through it all, fighting for me, paying off some of my debts (though I'd rejected his help on many, many occasions), and being my comfort whenever I needed him. Plus, he cooked the most *amazing* meals for me, always feeding me without me ever having to ask.

I knew he was the one who could truly make me happy and support me no matter what, and that's what I needed most after all I'd been through before—a support system. It's what we both needed, which is why I didn't hesitate saying yes when he knelt down on one knee on a ferry ride in New York City to ask me to marry him.

"Babe, you've gotta slow down." He met me at the door, slipping an arm around my waist and reeling me into him, his warm lips pressing on my cheek. My body warmed up and I felt a flutter at the pit of my belly as he whispered in my ear, "Save some of that energy for later when we're back in the room."

I blushed ridiculously hard, avoiding the conversation of the events that we both knew would take place later on that night.

"Come on. The fire dancing is about to start." I gripped his hand, rushing forward.

A crowd greeted us after we took the long corridor down, and I pushed through, making sure to hold onto John's hand.

When we finally got close to the front of the deck, I met up to Tessa and Danny and released John's hand to clap mine together, bouncing on my toes as a man spewed a fierce ball of fire in the air. "Finally!" Tessa shouted over the music. She stepped to my side, cupping my face in her hands. "Guess what?"

"What?" I asked as her face turned serious.

She released my hand and held out hers, and when I spotted the large diamond on her ring finger, I squealed.

"Holy shit!"

A few people looked our way, some with rude glares and some laughing, but I was only one or two more tequila shots away from being drunk so, of course, caring about anyone's opinion on my honeymoon was futile.

"Tessa! Is that what I think it is?" I met her green eyes.

She nodded, ecstatic. "It is! Danny just proposed right at the table!" She pointed over me to the table we sat at for dinner only an hour ago.

I looked over her at Danny who smiled bashfully. He was so shy, and a bit of an introvert, but he was perfect for Tessa.

Tessa is the outgoing one—the type of person who will defend her own honor as well as the honor of everyone else she loves in a heartbeat. She's loyal as long as you are loyal to her and she doesn't take any shit from anyone, which is why Danny was good for her. He respected and loved her for who she truly was, despite her loud mouth and crazy attitude.

"Congrats!" John appeared over my shoulder, studying her stunning cushion-cut diamond. "Man," he said, looking at Danny who stepped to Tessa's side. "You did good! It's beautiful!"

Tessa nodded, holding her hand out, letting the strobe lights reflect on it. "It's almost better than yours, Shannon." She busted out laughing and I pursed my lips, sticking up my ring finger as if it was my middle one.

John belted out a laugh, then looked down at me and said, "I'm gonna grab us something to drink." He dropped a kiss on my cheek. "You two want anything while I'm there?" he asked Tessa and Danny.

"Yeah. I'll come with you." Danny walked with John and Tessa and I watched them go.

When they were out of earshot, Tessa asked, "You think it's too soon?" She turned to face me. She had three inches of height on me, her body perfect for the modeling career she wanted to pursue after college. "I mean, I know I only just turned twenty-one and have my *whole life* ahead of me, but I love him, Shannon. I really do. I see so much of my future with him."

"Then you don't need my approval, sis." I held her shoulders. "If Danny is who you can see yourself sharing a future with, hold onto that. Do whatever makes *you* happy."

She nodded, twisting the new ring around her finger. "You're right. God! Look at this ring!" She held her hand out, studying it in awe. "He did a good job. My Danny. At least he has good taste."

"He does! Now come on, love bug." I tugged on her hand, turning for the dance floor. "Let's go dance and show them why they really married us."

Tessa grinned like a Cheshire cat, holding onto my hand and hurrying to the floor with me. We danced to a song by Rihanna, laughing and grooving. The beat pulsed through my heels, and I absorbed the music like it was fuel for my drunken soul.

John came up behind me several seconds later, dancing with me as I shook my hips. I threw my arms up to clasp them around the back of his neck, then rested the back of my head on his upper chest. He kept the drinks steady in the air.

Suddenly, I had the urge to cough. At first I thought nothing of it. It was only one cough, right?

Wrong.

That one cough turned into two and then four.

After six coughs I lost count. It was a continuous cough, one I couldn't control no matter how hard I tried. I feared the outcome, not because I wasn't sure what it was, but because I knew *exactly* what it was.

Panicked, John handed me a water bottle after rushing to the bar, and I downed it. It didn't help. In fact, I think it made it worse. Gripping my arm, he pulled me away from the dance floor, away from the watching crowd, and rushed out the glass doors and to the bodiless corridor.

"Shannon, are you okay?" I heard him ask, but I couldn't respond.

It felt like something had been lodged deep in my throat and it wouldn't budge. The water wasn't loosening the stone stuck in my throat, nor was the way John patted my back and then lifted my hands above my head in hopes that it'd stop.

I held on tight to his arm, seeing the terror swirling deep in his eyes, the horror etched all over his now pale face. I wanted to tell him that everything was okay, but that would have been a lie. And even though I wanted to, speaking was inevitable.

A moment passed before Tessa's face appeared in front of me, her eyes filled with just as much worry as John's, quite possibly more.

"She won't stop coughing!" John shouted, panicking.

"Shannon, honey, take deep breaths," Tessa said to me, holding my shoulders.

I nodded, doing my best to draw in those much-needed breaths. It felt like it was working. I just needed to calm down.

I released one last round of coughs and it was the worst of them all. My throat, sore and tight, felt like the claws of a tiger had scratched through it. But, finally, the coughing came to a cease. I gathered a breath, but when I looked down at my hand, I saw red specks.

Tessa gasped, looking down at my hand and then back up at me. Her eyes darted to the corner of my mouth, to the blood that'd collected there too.

"Oh my God, Shannon." Her eyes were the widest I'd ever seen them. "A-are you okay?" Never had I seen Tessa so speechless, and never had I seen John move so quickly when he saw the blood too.

He picked me up in his arms and jetted down the corridor, bursting through the door that led to the medical office and getting me to a doctor on board.

We stayed in a small, cramped up room with one window the whole night. Other than a sore throat I felt fine. But the results showed differently. The doctor felt it was something much worse—something he couldn't diagnose on a moving boat.

We landed in Cancun and I was sent to a hospital immediately. John requested for me to see the best doctor. That doctor, of course, had no clue what was happening to me either, but he had an idea.

Assuming it was cancer, he suggested I go to an oncologist and John requested to see the best one around. He never settled for less, which was a good thing sometimes.

It turned out it wasn't cancer either, so I went back to the previous doctor who sought help from doctors that specialized in various fields of work.

After spending five nights at the hospital and hating that I was the reason we'd missed the rest of our cruise, I was finally diagnosed.

Doctor Juarez walked into the room with a clipboard in hand, shutting the door behind him as he greeted us. John hopped up, way too anxious for results. Tessa remained seated in the chair beside me, squeezing my hand as Danny rubbed her back.

"Do we have good news?" John asked.

Doctor Juarez's smile faded and to avoid having to say it out right—rip it off like a Band-Aid—he picked up his clipboard, read something on it, and then lowered it, meeting my eyes.

"After running a few tests on the black masses we found on your right lung, we've come to the conclusion that you have what is called Onyx Pleura Disease," said Doctor Juarez. "It is very hard to cure here, but there are treatments available."

Tessa gasped dramatically and I'm sure she was squeezing my hand tighter, but I couldn't feel it.

In that moment, as Doctor Juarez explained the blood I'd coughed up on the cruise and informed me that this type of disease was extremely rare, I felt like I was drowning right there in that hospital room. Not just metaphorically, but with Tessa's tears, John's tears, and even Danny's tears, I was drowning.

My life, just like that, seemed to be snatched right away from me. All that I had fought for…all that I'd gone through. It felt as if it was all for nothing.

My childhood wasn't the best and I thought the chaos of that had finally passed and life would automatically be better, easier.

Boy, was I wrong.

I'd just married the most wonderful man—just gotten hitched and ready to take on the world, bear his children, even, and then this happens?

All of it—the future and all that felt promised to us—disappeared just like that. The floor may as well have swallowed me whole.

Although Doctor Juarez said repeatedly that there was a chance of it going away, I didn't believe it. All hope for me was lost and it was obvious. I began to question my existence. Why be created just to die at the age of twenty-five?

Why try and live the life I deserved if there was no life to look forward to?

As I sat on that bed, spaced out and on the verge of tears, I couldn't help thinking about all the things I had yet to experience. I'd just started getting into traveling and that was because of John. He made a way for me and Tessa to live—to be happy for once—and even so, it'd taken me a while to accept this leisure, the bliss. It all seemed too good to be true, and I realized this was why. All of that bliss was to soften the blow.

I wished then that I wouldn't have hesitated. Paris. That was a goal of mine. We were supposed to travel there next. Clearly, that wasn't going to happen anymore.

Mine and my sister's lives as children and even teenagers was dark, lonely, and horrible and to finally have some light shone on us—to be pulled out of the darkness—was a blessing. We deserved it.

I'd pretty much become a mom to a sister that was only four years younger than me. I sacrificed so much, not only for myself, but for Tessa. I did so much so she could have a better future. I worked my ass off day and night, fought for her and myself until I bled. I worked so she could go to school and get an education.

I could've given up and not done any of that, but I wasn't selfish enough to leave her in this world alone. I was all she had left, and she knew that.

It almost seemed she was thinking the same as I was because in that moment our heads turned, our attention averting from Doctor Juarez to each other.

I fought hard to hold back my tears—to be strong for her—but it didn't even last a second. Because it wasn't pity that I saw in her eyes that day. It was *fear*.

I broke down as she climbed on the bed and held me in her arms. I still wanted to play my role as big sister—as her guardian and protector—but in that moment, she was mine.

As I wept, she placed my forehead to her chest and let me cry without saying a word, only giving tears in return. This was way worse than when we found our mother on the kitchen floor with needles in her arms. Worse than when we found out our father was dead, the man who took care of us most because of Mom's absence. He looked out for us and guided us, teaching us right from wrong, but losing to his demons in the process. He had a lot of good in him. Unfortunately, the bad overshadowed his kind heart.

That night, my strength dwindled and hung by a thread. Tessa and Danny eventually booked a hotel and left to catch some sleep, but John sat in a chair in the corner, not speaking any words for hours. His elbows were perched on the top of his thighs, his hands covering his face.

It hurt my heart to realize the pain he was in. I couldn't see his eyes, but when I called his name, he lowered his hands, finally revealing them. He was a mess.

Seeing him like that, so pale and distressed, brought the tears right back out of me.

He stood and walked to the bed side. Taking the chair next to it, he leaned forward, a slow tear sliding down his cheek. He was trying to stay calm and, luckily, he wasn't failing at it because I needed it. Like I'd said, he was my support system.

"I can't believe this," he murmured. "You. Not you. Why you? Why?" He asked *why* so many times that night, and I knew he wasn't just talking to me. He was asking the big man upstairs.

That night, I knew John felt betrayed.

He was hurting. Angry. He didn't want to accept the truth, so he made sure that as soon as we landed in North Carolina, I went straight into taking OPX treatments. No surgeries could be done without a donated lung and no one wanted to risk wasting one for a girl with a ten percent survival rate.

The disease took a toll on my body. My emotional well-being. My mind. My insecurities grew in size. I no longer felt like the free-spirited girl that was marrying the love of her life. I felt trapped in a glass box as many eyes showed sympathy that I didn't want. Every person that I ever cared for seemed to be pressing or leaning on the glass, wanting to help, wanting to get closer and I always held up my hands to resist them.

I knew that if they kept pressing—kept pushing and closing in and telling me to fight—that the glass would break and I'd be cut and bruised, surrounded by shattered glass and bloody broken hearts.

And with a piece of that broken glass, the thought to use it and slit my own wrists was always at the forefront of my mind. It would make the process faster, easier. I'd do it so they wouldn't keep waiting around for me to die.

But instead, I clung to what was left of my life.

I stayed alive for John.

For Tessa.

It was for them, because I knew they would never forgive me for giving up—for ending it and not giving them more time to prepare.

I loved them, and if staying alive for now was making

them happy then so be it. I'd hang on just to see another smile on their faces. I'd fight just enough.

"I will be here with you," John whispered during one of the first nights of my treatment, his breath warm as it ran over my ear. He was on the bed with me, my head on his chest and his arms wrapped around me. "I promise you, Shannon, while you fight, I will fight. I will be with you no matter what."

"Even when I'm walking around looking like Dobby?" The thought of it made my body shudder with the sobs. No matter the situation, no matter how many tears I shed, I had to make the situation light and playful somehow.

He let out a small huff, holding me tighter. "That doesn't matter to me, baby. None of that has ever mattered to me. You're a beautiful woman inside and out." He lifted my head, forcing me to meet his eyes. "I will *never* give up on you. You hear me?" His voice was stern, causing a tug in my chest. It was a good feeling. Hard to describe, but good.

"You won't be fighting alone. You don't have to pretend this isn't happening. You don't have to joke about it or even take this situation lightly. I know you're scared. I know you're hurting. You can cry with me. You can be angry, and if you need to lash out, do so with me. I'm angry too but we're here together through thick and thin, for better or for worse. Always and forever." He lowered his head, pressing his lips to mine, causing the furnace in my belly to blaze.

"Always and forever," he whispered.

"Until the last breath," I murmured.

He kissed the top of my head and sighed as he hugged me, but my smile had faded, and my face had stiffened as I remembered the last person who'd used the words I'd just used.

Max.

By this point, he knew I was sick, but he didn't know where I was and had no clue that I'd progressed to such a horrible stage in such a short amount of time. I was losing this battle and he had no idea.

I told him white lies, like how the OPX was working—because at one point it *was* working, and I was beginning to feel so much better—but I didn't tell him that after two months of it I began to feel worse than ever before.

Terrible body aches.

Migraines.

Forgetting the simplest things.

And worse, coughing up heaps of blood and soon finding out that the black masses were spreading to my left lung.

I was running out of time, and when I finally told Max the truth—that I was going to die—he demanded to know where I was. I told him and he came to me.

And to his face, I told him that we could no longer see or talk to each other. It seems a selfish thing to do, but I did it so he wouldn't worry and so he wouldn't be like John—clinging to false hope. Although he kept his distance for the most part, Max never accepted it.

I've always regretted telling him that, but for me it was a choice between Max or John. John is my husband and he was dedicated to keeping me as healthy as possible and nothing more. Back then I needed that.

But the worse I got, however, the more I knew I'd made a mistake. I wasn't getting any better. I was slowly but surely decomposing due to my damaged lungs and nothing could stop it. There was someone who could make me feel better just by being himself and I knew that person was Max. Even a simple visit would have made me feel better.

John was too afraid to touch me. Too afraid to even kiss me. He was afraid that any kind of affection would cause me to lose breath and die right in front of him. He was overreacting, but that was my John. My Worry Bot. I loved that he cared so much at first, but now I can't stand it.

His smothering and pestering me to take my OPX seriously. The way he tells me not to eat this or that like I'm a child. I know he's only looking out for me, but to me it no longer matters. I am going to die regardless of what I eat or say or do, so I might as well eat, say, or do it.

John eventually focused less on our relationship and happiness and more on keeping me alive, which wasn't bad, but it wasn't a great feeling either.

He lost the true meaning of the partnership we agreed to keep and reprimanded everything I did. This disease, it changed him—but only because he couldn't stand the thought of losing me. He had to sacrifice some part of himself for that, I suppose.

The Onyx Pleura changed our connection with each other… made me question our love. It changed every single thing, and for that I hated that I'd ever bothered hacking up blood on our perfect honeymoon cruise.

Why couldn't everything stay peaceful? Why couldn't I just be healthy?

Out of the billions of people in this world why did I have to be one of them to go through this? I wouldn't wish this disease on my worst enemy, so all I ask is why me?

What did I do? Why do I have to keep suffering? Why do I have to be the one to die?

Why?

Just tell me what I did wrong…
Just tell me why…
Why, God? Why?

TEN

The OPX isn't working today.

I feel horrible. Nauseous.

My eyes flutter open and I spot John watching me, most likely contemplating whether I should continue taking the treatment or finally call it quits. But he's stubborn. He won't give up. *One of these bags will be the cure I need,* he says. *It just has to be. One of them will work.*

But I know they won't.

I want to tell him…

Baby, I'm dying. Baby, let me go. Baby, forget about me. You deserve better than this.

But he won't. Not John. Not ever.

My eyes close. I don't know when I'll have the energy or the will to wake up and face him again, so I give myself a quick prayer:

Allow me to die in my sleep, Lord. Let it be easy. I'd rather not suffocate, if you will. Make it easy on everyone, so they won't have to look into my eyes and witness my last breath.

Please, God, that's all I ask.

ELEVEN

PAST – FIRST DATE WITH MAX

Crave was crowded, as expected. I was surprised Max and I had even gotten a table.

Taking a look around the bar, I noticed all of the waitresses, in their short black dresses, passed by us and gave Max *the look*.

One girl with mocha skin and bleach on the tips of her curly hair smiled at him. Before I knew it, she was at our table with a notepad in hand and a wide smile on her lips.

"Hi," she sang, looking into Max's eyes. "I'm Janelle and I will be your server tonight. Anything you need," she murmured, looking from his eyes to his lap, "and I will be *more* than happy to provide whatever it is for you."

I scoffed and Max looked at her, astounded by her audacity, but didn't say a word—at least not about the way she was flirting with him right in my face. "Right. Yeah, let me get a coke and rum."

She nodded, glancing at me unwillingly. "And you, ma'am?"

The word *ma'am* came out rude and sarcastically. "Strawberry margarita with crushed ice. Also, I'd prefer top shelf tequila, none of the cheap stuff." I beamed at her, my voice dripping with sarcasm.

Her eyes narrowed just enough for me to notice and I placed a fist beneath my chin, still looking at her.

"Mmm-hmm." She took off in an instant, zip lining toward the bar and requesting our first round of drinks. As she did, she glanced over her shoulder at me before snatching her gaze away.

"She's fucking kidding, right?" I looked at Max, huffing a laugh.

He shrugged. "I suppose some women can't help it."

"Yeah, well, she's just rude."

"I can agree with that. You're different, rude in your own way." He smirked, most likely at the immaturity of it.

I blew his comment off, shaking my head and sitting up. "It's clear that this is supposed to be intimate time shared between two people. She shouldn't be trying to ruin that."

"Hold on. So you're actually calling this a date?" His eyes widened with amusement.

"No," I corrected him quickly. "I just mean...well, if I saw a guy dressed like you at a table with a girl dressed like me, I would assume it's a date and I *definitely* wouldn't flirt with the guy."

"Shannon," Max murmured, and as he did, the waitress was back at our table with our drinks, placing them on the table. "It's girls like her—the girls who constantly seek drama and attention—that I don't care to make time for. Do you want me to prove just how little her comment meant to me, and how much more this night spent with you does?"

I cocked a brow and the waitress stepped back, fiddling with the napkins in her apron. She was listening, exactly what Max wanted. "How?" I whispered, hesitant.

His head moved to a slight tilt and, after taking a sip of his drink, he turned toward the waitress and said, "Listen, Janelle, my lady doesn't like the fact that you're flirting with me on our date. Now, considering I've wanted this night to happen for quite a while now, I think it's best if you just stick with doing your job, and keep things professional. The last thing I want is for her to be upset with me by the end of the night. I have way too much planned for us after we leave this place and I simply can't allow *you* to ruin that for me."

The waitress' bright brown eyes expanded beneath the dim lights and her throat bobbed. I drew in a shocked breath, my eyes just as wide as hers.

Did he really just say that to her? And did he really just call me his *lady*?

"I...understand," the waitress said, avoiding his eyes. "Can I start you two with an appetizer or would you like to go straight into dinner?"

She was embarrassed. I could tell by the flushed look on her face and the way sweat prickled at her hairline. Max, as if nothing had ever happened, ordered what he wanted to eat and since he was taking the moment lightly, I did as well. I wasn't expecting an apology from her. It would've just made things even more embarrassing for her.

Believe me, dinner was unbelievably awkward every time she came back to the table to check on us, pretending to be in a cheery mood. She wasn't quite sure how to handle us anymore, but I couldn't fight off the smile that lingered on my lips when I looked at Max.

Max turned a girl down for me. Not that she was ugly or anything—she was *very* pretty actually—but he did it for *me*.

"That was so mean by the way," I whispered to him after we finished dinner.

"It wasn't mean. It was the truth and sometimes truth hurts." He reached across the table to grab my hand, using his other to scoop up some of the icing that fell off my carrot cake.

Using the finger with the icing on the tip, he brought it to my lips and I smirked. Some competitive part of me wanted him to know I wasn't just some boring girl. I had to keep him guessing throughout the night, so I spread my lips apart and sucked the icing off his finger until every drop of sweetness was gone. As I did, his eyes pooled with heat and desire.

"Goddamn," he breathed, slowly pulling his finger away.

I licked my lips before picking up my drink and taking a small sip, trying so hard not to smile.

"I hope you realize that just made me want to fuck the shit out of you." His eyes were still heated.

I smiled. "I know. That was the plan."

"No," he continued in a murmur, "I don't think you understand how hard it's going to be for me to hold back, Shannon."

"I'm sure it won't be that bad," I teased.

"It wouldn't be wise to test my ego right now."

I fought a smile.

Okay, so I may have been a riled up, horny mess, and surely the drinks weren't helping in making this situation any better, but I loved this. Teasing him. Building up to the moment we both were impatient for.

"Go on," Max urged, pointing at my cupcake. "Don't stall. Finish your cake so I can get you the hell out of here."

I laughed and picked up my fork. I couldn't ignore the warmth that coursed through me as I finished off my cake.

I could've left it there or even taken it to go, but I knew I wouldn't eat it while with Max—not once we were alone again. I was also a strong believer in not wasting food. After spending weeks without food, hoping to scratch the surface by finding a job at sixteen, I vowed never to waste a crumb again in my life. Starving was no joke.

"Here." I cut the cupcake in two pieces with my fork then handed him one half. "If you help me eat we can get out of here a little faster."

He accepted his half with a cocky grin tugging at the corners of his lips. He needn't say anymore. All he had to do was show me what he wanted once we left...and I was eager for that to happen.

Max's studio apartment was nice—more like a bachelor pad, really. *Figures.*

So this was Mr. Grant. The twenty-four year old every girl wanted in her bed. He'd take them on dates, to places like Crave or a quaint, upscale bar uptown like Capri and he'd get them a little tipsy.

I knew because that was the state I was in as we barged into his place, lip-locked, and my arms tight around his neck.

As I snatched off his shirt and started unbuttoning his pants, I couldn't help taking in his place. It was tidy, chrome and Carolina blue as his signature colors. The bar stools in front of the island counter were blue, the counters a smooth gray marble. His L-shaped sofa looked beyond comfortable, good enough for him to explore my body on.

But I preferred the bed.

"Where's your room?" I asked as his lips landed on my cheek.

"Back there," he groaned. He didn't point in any direction, which caused me to giggle.

"Take me there," I whispered.

He stopped kissing me, nodding as he reluctantly released me. Grabbing my hand and leading the way toward a beige door, he pushed it open and went in the direction of the bed, freeing my hand.

"Sit here," he murmured. "Wait for me." He placed me at the edge of the bed, and I sat, looking up into his eyes.

He turned away and walked out of the room. Cabinets squeaked opened and then closed from a distance, glasses clanking.

Laughing, I asked, "What are you doing?"

"Give me a sec," he called with mischief in his voice.

I sat back, placing my palms on the comfortable blue comforter and smoothing it out. Moments later and music sounded from hidden speakers in the room, catching me by total surprise. One of my favorites by Miguel played and in walked Max with two glasses of some sort of pink drink.

My heart pounded as he appeared between the frames of his bedroom door with no shirt on. I couldn't help carrying my line of sight down the length of his body, focusing on that delicious V that never failed a man. So cut and lean in all the right places.

"Here," he murmured, stepping closer and handing me one of the glasses.

"Pink?" I questioned, studying it.

"Pink moscato. The best. Got it for you. You don't like it?"

"I like pink moscato." He took the spot beside me as I took a sip. "I hope you didn't put anything in this…"

He laughed out loud, finding my remark utterly humorous. "Like what?" he asked, cocking a brow, highly amused.

"Date rape drug, ecstasy or something to get me to willingly sleep with you."

"Pshh." He shook his head, fighting a grin. "I don't need a drug to get you to sleep with me. And, for the record, I would *never* do that to a woman."

"Hey," I took a look around his rather large bedroom, "with a place like this, I'm sure something's gotta give."

He swapped glasses with me and quirked a brow, taking a sip from my previous glass and proving nothing was in my drink.

"Normally the ladies see this place and it's all they need. As soon as they're in here the panties come off like they're visiting the gynecologist."

"Oh my God!" I snorted. "You are so disgusting! Do you know that?"

He leaned closer to me, placing a kiss on my shoulder and murmuring, "You like me though."

My eyebrows shifted up as I drank some of my wine. Max downed his in one solid gulp, then stood to place his glass on top of the dresser.

After dimming the lights, he turned to fix his eyes on me. They glittered down my body, softening as he stepped close again. And as he did, my body weakened for him.

He slowly spread my legs apart and moved between them in a matter of seconds, grabbing my glass and stretching his arm past me to place it on the nightstand.

"I don't think I can wait for you to finish that," he breathed, the tip of his nose running down my jawline.

"But it was so good though," I murmured.

"I'll let you finish as soon as I'm finished with you."

"By that time it'll be all warm and gross."

He chuckled. "I'm glad you think we'll be at it long enough for your drink to get warm. Smart not to underestimate me."

Finally, it had arrived. The very thing I'd been waiting for.

In that moment we were like magnets. Connected. Unable to be pulled apart unless someone dragged us out and sent us our separate ways.

He held me tight, his lips molding with mine as he rocked against me. My back hit the cool pillows and Max slid upward, rocking his groin on mine.

In an instant he flipped me over and I was on top of him. He took off my dress, tossing it aside when he had gathered the material in his hands.

I positioned myself on the center of his lap, tipsy, uncaring. I'm sure he wanted it that way. Not that I hadn't taken it into consideration. Max wanted me as loose and free as possible, considering the terms we were on. I could've postponed this—held off—but I could no longer deny him.

He knew I was into him.

And I knew he was into me.

The way his eyes roamed my body, how he strained in his boxers and held me close proved that we both had a desire that needed fulfilling. No longer able to hold back, I leaned down and kissed him, cupping his face in my hands and bringing him upright with me

Groaning, he cupped my ass in his hands, and I sighed. My tongue immediately explored his mouth and I got a taste of the pink moscato he'd just drank.

Hungrily I kissed him, grinding on his lap, wanting him to feel how badly I wanted this moment. In seconds my bra was off, my breasts pressing on the warmth of his chest.

I didn't think I'd cave so easily to the idea of being almost naked on top of him, but it was hard not to. I'd been attracted to Max since the beginning. Ever since he set foot in Capri.

His chiseled face, sculpted lips, and a body to fucking die

for—Maximilian Grant had it all and not even the girl that pretended he didn't exist could deny him.

Back then, he was everything I'd longed for. Someone I knew I would be permanently attracted to, someone who actually listened. Someone who defended my honor and stood up for me. Someone who found me just as beautiful as I did him. Someone who was just a tiny bit aggressive and a little rough around the edges, but genuinely sweet on the inside.

Well, I guess I should say at the time he was what I wanted—what I craved. I needed fun after all I'd dealt with, I just didn't think I deserved it. I felt taking care of my sister and myself was all that mattered—working hard to provide for her and myself—but Max quickly proved that theory to be false.

As I continued kissing Max, trailing my lips down his bare chest, he stiffened beneath me and I looked up. He was already looking down at me, eyes hard, face somber in the dim lighting.

I stopped immediately, asking, "What's wrong?"

He was quiet a moment, studying me. "I...*fuck*." He released a heavy breath. "I thought I could go through with this, but I can't. I can't do this. Not to you."

I sat up, offended by his words. "What do you mean? Isn't this what you wanted from me tonight?" I collected my bra and then folded my arms to cover my chest.

He grabbed my wrists and gently removed my arms one by one. "No," he whispered, bringing his lips close to one of my nipples. "I mean it *is* what I want, don't get me wrong," he said, defending himself. "It's just...I can't take you on these terms. This can't be just because I wanted it. And it can't just be one time. I don't want it to happen like this—because you think you owe me. A girl like you is hard to find. I don't want to lose out on someone like you."

"I want to," I assured him. "I mean at first I didn't but...*shit*. Max, how can I resist you right now?" I looked him over, studying the flat planes and muscles of his body. "Besides, it doesn't have to be just this once."

"How many times, then?" He smirked.

"I don't know," I breathed, pressing my forehead to his. "But I won't keep count if you don't."

"So this'll be a fling then? Nothing more?"

"Is that what you want?"

"Not really."

I sat back. "Well, it can be whatever we make it. For now, we can just go with the flow and whatever happens, happens."

He nodded, bringing me closer, his fingers spreading across my hips. "That sounds nice."

"So, can we go back to what we were doing before you so rudely interrupted with this sob fest?" I teased.

"Yeah," he murmured. "I'll give it to you." He ran the tip of his nose up the crook of my neck, placing a tiny bite on my shoulder. "But not tonight, Shakes."

His head moved down, those warm lips of his gradually wrapping around my taut brown nipple. I moaned as he circled his tongue around it. When he pulled his mouth away, I climbed on his lap again.

"Are you kidding me?" I asked, breathless. "What do I get tonight then?" I adjusted my hips as I moved forward on his lap, purposely grinding on his erection.

In an instant, Max grabbed my wrists and flipped me onto my back, pinning my hands above my head on the bed. I yelped as he hungrily sucked on my exposed breasts, just enough for me to feel how serious he was in this moment.

My back arched and he seized the opportunity, clasping the waistband of my panties and tugging them down. When they were off, he went lower and lower, planting kisses on my stomach, above my navel and then below it, until he was right there. *Right fucking there*, where I needed him to be most.

His mouth hovered above my sex, so close that it was unbearable. I was panty-less and writhed as his tongue ran through the lips of my sex. A soft cry rushed out of me as his tongue pressed down on my aching nub. My back arched, and he whispered, "Be still for me, baby. You'll get this, but nothing more tonight."

"Why can't I have more?" I asked breathily.

"Because." He brought his hands down to spread my legs further apart. Resting my thighs on his shoulders, he centered his face between them and continued with, "You aren't ready for me just yet, Shakes. I have to get you there. I have to make sure that when it finally happens, you're ready. I can tell it's been a while since you've had some. Gotta make sure I'm well worth it."

He grinned up at me and before I could say another word, he was devouring me like I was the best thing he'd ever tasted.

I was vulnerable to Maximilian, his for the taking. I felt like a queen on top of the world. On top of King Max.

Soon, my thoughts came to a hush, and I'd reached my peak. I came from his mouth alone, back arching, crying out so hard and loud there was a bang on the wall across from us.

I gasped, nearly breathless as my body tried to settle itself. "Did someone just bang on the wall?" I ask, panting.

When Max lowered my hips and sat up, glancing over his

shoulder, he said, "Oh, yeah. Don't worry about that. It's just Francine. She's a little upset that I don't do cougars."

My eyes widened. "She wants you to have sex with her?"

He stood up, laughing. "Who doesn't?"

My lips pressed together as I drew my legs in. "Don't be so full of yourself, Playboy."

He laughed, holding his hands out and gesturing to me.

"What?" I ask, biting a smile as he looks me over.

"I just can't believe Shannon Hales is sitting on my bed completely naked and I just made her come all over my mouth." His palms pressed on the bed as he planted a deep, warm kiss on my burning cheeks. I turned my head a little and our mouths connected. The kiss was deep, passionate, and perfect. "You still think you're ready for me, Shakes?"

"I'm not intimidated."

"A girl like you shouldn't be…"

"So why can't we right now?" I whispered in his ear.

"Because," he said, kissing the crook of my neck. "I want you to *beg* me for it."

"Well, good luck with that because I don't beg."

"Says the woman who just let me eat her out on *my* bed."

That smoldering look in his eyes, the nearness, and knowing deep down that I would surely be begging for him to be inside me, drove me wild, but I was never going to tell him that. I was stubborn that way.

"I won't beg," I said smugly as he laid me back and rested his erection on my lower belly. He wanted me to feel him—feel how hard he was.

He smiled, then ran the tip of his nose over my cheek. He was about to kiss me and I prepared my lips for it, but then he jerked back enough so that my mouth couldn't reach his. "Yeah," he said, a deep chuckle leaving him. "We'll just see about that.

TWELVE

"Tessa called this morning." John's tired voice rises, taking my attention away from the words in my romance novel.

"She did?" I drop the book, snatching up my cellphone. "Why didn't you tell me sooner?"

"Because it's the first time you've been okay in a while. And earlier you were resting. She understands."

"What did she say?"

"Not much. She said she had something to tell you but that she'd wait to tell you when you felt better. She sounded excited." He smiles.

I pick up my phone and go to my list of favorites, calling her right away. She answers on the second ring, her voice chipper. "Shanny!"

"Tessy!" I sing.

"Guess what?"

"What?"

"I'm done with exams and Danny will be in Louisville for the next week and a half so I'm coming to Charlotte!"

"What?" I gasp. "Seriously?"

"Yep! I miss you and can't wait to come see you." She breaks away, saying something to someone in the background before addressing me again. "Sorry, I'm getting coffee. Long night. Anyway, listen, I'm going back in a few to finish packing and should be on the road within the hour. I promise to sneak you lots of chocolate." She whispers the last sentence, knowing John is around and most likely trying to hear everything she's saying.

I laugh. "Alright. I'll see you soon."

I hang up and John looks at me, his eyes inquisitive. "What was that about?"

"She's coming to Charlotte."

"Oh." He fidgets in his chair, scratching the top of his head. "You think that's a good idea right now?"

I frown. "What do you mean?"

"Tessa stresses you out sometimes. You two argue about the silliest things. The last thing you need is stress...and her sneaking you chocolate. Dr. David said to avoid sweets if you can."

"John," I laugh dryly. "Are you serious right now? Why were you listening so hard? She literally whispered the chocolate thing."

"I'm just looking out for you, babe. That's all." He raises his hands in the air, pleading innocence.

I look away from him, blowing out a sigh as I focus on my lap. "Whether she stresses me out or not, I need to see her right now. I miss her."

"I understand."

"You can't be selfish with me, Johnny."

"I'm not." He moves closer, holding my hand. "I just want what's best for *you* right now."

"I'm fine," I insist. "I swear."

He squeezes my hand, pressing his lips, as if he doubts

every word I'm saying. Silence showers down on us, and I blow out a breath, slowly pulling my hand away.

"Who is Max?" He asks the question as if he's been waiting hours to—like it's been heavy on his mind and he's finally getting it out there.

My heart nearly stops beating as I pick my head up to focus on my husband. That name is one that should never come out of John's mouth. He knows nothing about what Max was to me.

"I saw him say that he's coming by," John goes on, trying to pretend he's curious but clearly bothered.

"Max is a friend. Someone I knew a long time ago. He knows I'm sick."

"Have I ever met him?"

"No. I knew him years ago. We worked together and were really good friends." I wave a hand, hoping to dismiss the subject.

"Oh." He looks down at the hand he has resting on the bed. "Well, I can't wait to meet him whenever he visits."

"You know what I want?" I say quickly, changing the subject.

"What's that?"

"To go home. Back to our cozy, quiet place."

John's face tightens and his eyebrows draw together. "Home?"

"Yeah. I just think I should be home right now. You know, comfortable?" I smile weakly, looking around the room. "I don't feel comfortable here. I feel like a part of the number."

"But it's better here. More convenient for you. You have the best doctor in the city. You get the best care. You even said you love Leah—that she's your favorite nurse."

"Yes, all of that is true, but nothing beats being at home, John."

"No, Shannon." John's voice is firm as he sits back and folds his arms. "No. We won't have this discussion. You're too sick. Attempting to even transport you from the hospital to our house is a risk."

"For God's sake, John. Stop treating me like I'm your child!" My voice is louder, the anger transparent. "I am your wife. Not your baby. Not your daughter. Your *wife*. Don't you understand that? You should be supporting me, not scolding me about things like this."

"I know you're my wife, Shannon, but as your husband and your life partner I need to remind you of what's best. Being here, surrounded by people that can help you, is best. I would feel much better knowing you're here during the times that I can't be around."

"But you fail to realize that this is not just about you. And you also fail to realize that these people—these doctors that you are treating like gods—cannot bring back the dead. When I die, they won't be able to revive me. They won't be able to do jack-shit." My eyes burn with tears, and not from sadness or pain. Anger. Raw, heart-shattering anger.

He shoves out of his chair, pacing back and forth and muttering under his breath. Pressing my back to the bed, I shut my eyes and fight the tears. I fail miserably.

"I just...I mean, I don't know what to do here, Shannon," he sighs.

"Just forget it," I mutter, swiping hard at my eyes. "Let's just pretend I never brought it up, okay? I don't want to argue. Not right now. Not with you." John stops pacing to look at me. His eyes immediately filling with regret.

I put my head down, whispering for him to turn the lights off. I no longer want to be looked at. Plus, it's getting late. The sun is just setting but my blinds are closed. It's dark enough for me to get some rest.

"Babe, come on," he pleads.

"The lights please, John." My voice is firm. I avoid his eyes.

He hesitates, but with a heavy, reluctant sigh, he walks away, flipping the light switch on the wall to shut the lights off. My body relaxes as the comforting darkness fills the room. I can see John standing in his white T-shirt. I can also see his eyes, and everything else, but at least it's not every single detail of his face, like that small dip I know is between his eyebrows as he pouts.

John blows out a breath as I turn on my side and pull the blanket over me. The machine beeps a little faster before settling to a steady rhythm again. Several minutes pass before I feel John's hand on the small of my back, rubbing in slow circles.

"Shannon," he whispers, his voice faint and remorseful.

I don't respond. The tears stream, dampening the pillow my head rests on.

"Baby, please tell me what to do here. Please tell me what you want that makes sense." His voice cracks, deepening the pain I feel in my chest.

"I already told you what I want."

"Something realistic."

I swipe at my eyes with the little energy I have and then sit up to look at him. "Fine. You want realistic? I'll be real with you right now." He sits back, eyes wide as they lock on mine. "I don't want to die in this place, Jonathan. I don't want to spend my final days on this rock hard bed, staring up at the white ceiling or at the mirror across from me, contemplating my life and all I should have done differently. I don't want to hurt anymore. I don't want to be on three fucking IV drips of OPX a week. I don't want to keep doing this to myself—to us—going through the same routine *every single day*. I want to spend the final days of my life doing things that I love and being where I deserve. I don't deserve to be on this bed with this fucking tube in my nose and needles in my arms. I don't deserve not to be able to stand and kiss you. To cuddle with my husband in our fucking bed."

He closes his eyes, tears falling, and I stroke his cheek, using the pad of my thumb to swipe some of his tears away. I hate seeing him cry. "I don't deserve to be here. Don't you see that?" I whisper. "Whenever it's meant for me to be gone, I'll be gone. But I hate that I have to be restrained—trapped in this cold, depressing hospital—all because you think it's best for me. Maybe, for once, I want what *I* think is best for me. Maybe you should take that into consideration. I am your wife, John. *Your wife.* For once, can you please just support my decisions during all of this? Listen to me about my needs. I'm calling out to you and it's like you're not even listening."

His mouth parts and I can tell he wants to say so much, but is unsure of how to go about it. Instead of speaking, he stands up and sits on the edge of the bed, holding me but not too tightly.

I miss his tight hugs. His warm embrace. I miss the carefree John. The one who didn't worry so much about my health and what I could handle. I miss us, and it's sad to see it all going down the drain because of a stupid disease that refuses to go away.

We know we deserve more, but how do we get it when our destiny has already been written?

"I hear you, baby," he whispers in my hair. "I hear you and I understand." He tips my chin, kissing my lips gently. Oh, how I've missed his touch, his mouth on mine, greedy and soft. I lean into his hold, wrapping my arms around him and sighing as the kiss deepens. My tongue begins to part his lips, but he stops me, head shaking.

"We'd better not," he murmurs.

"But I miss it," I whisper. "Kissing you. Being with you."

"I miss it too, trust me." He plants his lips on the top of my forehead and stands. Defeated, I slouch back, staring ahead. "Get some rest," he tells me, sitting on the chair. But I don't need it. I am a little tired, but I slept for nearly twelve hours straight yesterday. The last thing I want to do is sleep but I know that weary feeling will soon set in, so I slide beneath the blanket and turn my back to him.

I want to be angry, but I have to put myself in his shoes. He doesn't know what to do. He just knows he doesn't want to lose me. Trust me, I get it. Our life as one had just begun and now it's coming to an end.

I don't know when I fall asleep but when I wake up, the windows are open, the sun is shining through the window, and John is sitting next to my bed with a smile and fresh clothes on.

At the door is my expected surprise, Tessa. She unfolds her arms as she comes rushing my way.

"Shanny!" She eases her arms around me, making sure not to cause any pain or harm. She hugs me a little harder than expected, most likely assuming I'm the same weight I was during her last visit.

Wrong.

I've lost so much more. I don't even look like myself anymore. By the way she pulls back and looks me over as casually as possible, her eyes slightly worried, I know that's exactly what she's thinking. Strange, we have many differences but I can always read her mind.

"Hey! When did you get in town?" I ask as she pulls a chair up to sit next to me.

"I got here around midnight. John met me so I could drop my things off at the house."

"I'm so glad you're here. How do you think you did on finals?"

"Ugh." She rolls her eyes. "I don't know. I just know I studied my ass off and did my best. Can't be too bad, right?" She shrugs, biting into her bottom lip.

"I'm sure you did great."

"Where's Danny?" John asks, as if he doesn't already know.

"Louisville for work. He'll be back next Saturday." She beams at him, almost like she's waiting for him to say or ask something else. John looks at her, unable to hide his smile.

My forehead creases. "Um…is there something I'm missing right now?" I ask, laughing a little. "Why are you two smiling like that?"

"Go ahead, John! Tell her!" Tessa insists, waving her hand in his direction.

I look at John who seems hesitant.

"Oh for goodness sake," Tessa gripes. "Do you want me to tell her? It's no big deal—I mean it is a big deal, but I can tell her if you want me to."

"No." He shakes his head. "I got it."

My eyebrows draw together as he looks at me and sighs. "So, I took what you said last night into consideration. When you fell asleep I went to talk to Dr. David and at first he wasn't too lenient, but after about an hour of guarantees, he's agreed to discharge you, assign you a new doctor who can visit the house, and have you spend your days at home."

My heart catches speed and my eyes pool with instant tears. "Oh my God." I sit forward. "You're serous?"

"I'm serious. I've already hired the doctor that Dr. David highly recommended. He will come by the house every day and a certified nurse will be coming a few weeks later, once we're settled."

Tessa claps like a trained seal, maybe just a tad bit more excited than I am. "Yay! You need this!" she cheers. "You deserve to be at home, a place where you're most comfortable. I'm part of the reason John went to go talk to the doctor, you know? I told him 'Listen, man, you need to do whatever my sister wants right now.' Basically slapped some sense into him."

I laugh, fighting tears. Damn my pride. "You guys...you seriously didn't have to."

"Yes, babe, we did," John murmurs. "I heard you last night and the last thing I want is for you to be unhappy. I was too worried about what I wanted and not worried enough about what you want." He cups my face, kissing the center of my forehead. When he pulls away, he says, "I'll go speak with Dr. David, let him know you're awake and that we'll need to be discharged soon."

"Damn right." Tessa purses her lips and cocks her head as John opens the door. "Tell him to hurry the hell up. Shannon really needs a manicure." She picks up my hand, looking at my cuticles with disgust.

I snatch my hand away, flipping her the bird and laughing. When John is gone, Tessa and I talk about her finals, and as we do, my phone buzzes on the table.

"Hey, can you get that for me, please?"

Tessa fetches my phone, looks at the name on the screen, and hands it to me. "What in the hell is *he* calling you for?"

I stare at the screen. *Max.* So many thoughts run through my mind—so much about him that I can't ignore. My happy thoughts about going home fade the longer the phone buzzes.

"Don't answer it." Tessa hisses. I don't even realize she's at the door. "I'm going to go grab some coffee."

I nod. When she's gone, I answer the call.

Whether I want to admit it or not, I have to see Max before I die. I have to look into his eyes at least one more time, tell him that I regret nothing that happened between us. I'm sure that's what he thinks. That I regret us and all we ever stood for, but I don't. I've accepted it.

I answer the phone and when he speaks, I get that old feeling back—the feeling I used to have when we were together. My hands become clammy, my throat thick with words unspoken. So much...there's so much I need to say but I don't say anything right away. I allow him the chance to speak.

"Hey, Shakes." His voice is smooth, casual.

"Hey." My voice is light. "I have something to tell you."

"What's that?" he asks.

"I'm going home."

"Are you? That's good. Makes it easier for me to find you."

"No," I say quickly. "You can't show up. John wouldn't appreciate knowing a stranger is hanging around me."

He laughs. "You still haven't told him what I am to you."

"No. He's already been asking questions. Besides, he doesn't need to know right now. What's the point?"

"That won't stop me from coming to see you. Your excuses have never worked on me, Shannon."

"Max," I breathe, recalling each and every time I made an excuse and he still showed up.

"I like how we always pick up where we left off," he says, changing the subject.

I ignore his statement. "We have a lot to talk about."

"Yes. And that's why I need to see you."

"I'm not how I used to be. You know that, right?"

"Listen," he starts, his voice stern, "stop telling me that. You've tried pushing me away over and over again and clearly it's not working."

My throat thickens with frustration and shame as I look at my reflection in the mirror. When I catch sight of my frizzy hair and dry lips, tears line the rims of my eyes. "It's not that I'm pushing you away I just—I mean…" *I'm ugly. I'm gross. I'm lethal. I'm damaged. I'm fucking terrified. I don't want you to hurt too.* I sniffle. "I don't want you to see me. Not like this."

Max is quiet a moment. "Don't cry." When he hears another sniffle, he says, "Stop crying, Shannon."

I clear myself up a little and then swallow hard, doing my best to fight off the wave of emotion. "Let me see you, prove to you that your looks aren't what matter to me."

"You shouldn't right now. John wouldn't be pleased."

"Well, all you have to do is let me know when he won't be around. If I have to, I'll sneak you out."

A laugh bubbles out of me. "He would kill you for that."

"Let him try."

The door creaks open and Tessa trots back into the room, blowing over a cup of coffee. "I will let you know. Okay? No need to sneak around. I'll just have to set a time."

"Promise me, Shakes."

I'm silent.

"I really need to see you," he adds.

"Okay…"

"You can't keep me away."

I don't speak. I don't know what to say.

"Afraid the good memories will resurface?" he asks, interrupting my silence.

I scoff. "They already have been."

"Which is why you're keeping me away? That and because you think I can't handle seeing you the way you are right now?"

"Maybe."

"Well, see, the funny thing is I'm looking right at you and I still think you're the most beautiful woman I've ever laid eyes on, tubes, IVs, and all."

Gasping, I look up at the open door and standing between the frames is Max.

THIRTEEN

Max stands just as tall as ever, his hair grown out more from the last time I saw it. His hair is curlier, and he no longer has the clean, shaven face he had during his bachelor days. His facial hair looks good on him.

His black T-shirt hugs his body, the muscles in his arms flexing as he pulls the phone from his ear, smiling so sweetly at me it hurts.

It hurts because I have been trying so hard to keep him away. I don't want him to see me like this. He's still so fucking gorgeous and healthy and I'm all skinny and wilted and my blood streams with toxins that are supposed to cure me.

Those old feelings come rushing back and they hit me hard, tackling whatever's left of my soul. Slowly dropping my phone, I focus solely on him. My lips part, wanting to say so much to him but unsure of where to even begin.

"You are gorgeous, Shannon," he says, taking a step into the room.

"M-max," I stutter. "What are you doing here?"

"You know why I'm here." He finally takes his eyes off of me, flicking them over to Tessa. A pang of jealousy hits me and I hate that I even feel it. She's my sister. I should never feel like I'm in competition with her. But she looks ten times better than I ever could, even more so right now. Her makeup is always great, she dresses well. She's the full package.

Though she isn't taking her modeling career as seriously anymore, she still has her model figure—the one every girl would kill for just to have. When Max's eyes bounce to mine again in less than a second, I'm glad. He doesn't think of her that way. He never has. Mainly because of their differences.

"Her *husband* is just around the corner," Tessa informs Max, placing her coffee down on the table with narrowed eyes.

"I don't care."

"He'll wonder who you are," she goes on. "You should really get out of here."

"You know how I am, Tessa. Nothing's changed."

"Yep. I know exactly how you are," she says. "Wasn't a fan of you then and I'm definitely not a fan of you now."

"And why's that?"

"Because you're an arrogant, selfish son-of-a-bitch." She folds her arms and smirks.

"Tessa," I scold, frowning.

"What?" She shrugs. "He is. And he clearly doesn't listen very well because he's still standing there."

"He's here for me, Tess. Now can I please have a moment alone with him?"

She looks at me, her brown eyes wild, bewildered. "Are you fucking serious?"

I give her a stern look, one I only give to her whenever I don't think arguing is necessary. She blows out a breath and snatches up her purse. After grabbing her coffee, she walks past Max but not without saying, "Don't you dare touch her."

Max is amused. He's always liked getting under her skin. "Can't make any promises, sis."

She points a finger at him, thinning her eyes. "You can't call me that anymore." She's out of the door, muttering the word "Asshole" before she goes.

I shake my head, fighting a smile as we watch the door click shut. "She still hates me, I see," Max sighs, running a hand over his head.

"Yeah. I don't think that's going to change." I laugh.

"She has to understand, though, right?"

I shrug. "Tessa is a very tough person. Once you lose her trust it's hard to win it back."

"I see."

"But she is right, though," I go on.

"About?"

"You shouldn't have come here. John will ask questions... wonder why you're here. Who you are..."

"And I'll tell him exactly who I am. Why keep secrets from your husband?"

"Max, please. I really don't need the drama right now."

He points at the door with his thumb. "So you want me to leave?"

"No, I don't want you to leave. I'm glad you're here but right now is really not a good time."

"Because you don't want John to see me and ask questions?"

"Exactly."

Instead of moving backwards, he walks forward, sighing and putting his hands in his front pockets. "When will I be able to see you again then?"

"I'm not sure. The first couple of days I'm home I'm sure

John will be around much more and I want to spend that time with him."

"Well, how about you call me when the *hound* has finally given you some space."

"This is my husband we're talking about. He doesn't believe in giving me space. Not when I'm in a state like this."

Max's eyes go thin, his anger transparent. "Don't throw that at me." He draws his hand back.

I frown. "Throw what at you?"

"The whole *husband* thing. I was here first."

"But he's who I'm with *now*," I retort.

His frown deepens and he steps away, looking me over thoroughly. Insecure, I bring the blanket up, shielding my frail body from his hard, penetrating gaze.

Instead of arguing with me, which I'm glad for, he digs into his back pocket and pulls out a small black box.

"I got you something." He hands it to me and I hesitate, holding it in my palm, meeting his eyes.

"This better not be a ring."

He laughs. "Would you accept it if it was?"

I roll my eyes then open the box. It's a silver necklace. The charms attached to it are the Eiffel Tower and a french bike. My heart catches speed.

"Wow, Max. I—" I don't even have the words. How does he remember?

I look up at him and he smiles.

"You remembered?"

"I never forgot." He takes the box away from me, carefully pulling out the necklace and then coming behind me to clasp it around my neck. "I think it was worth the buy. You still want to go there, right? To Paris?"

"I would love to go to Paris." I smile as I pick up the tiny silver tower, twisting it between my fingers.

"So why don't you?"

I frown up at him. "Are you serious? What kind of question is that?"

"Having Onyx Pleura doesn't mean you can't travel. It's a risk, yeah, but your legs still work, and treatment can go with you. There are ways around it. I've done my research."

"I have maybe three months or less to do that very thing called living, Max. Traveling would most likely shorten my days. Plus, my doctor would never approve."

"Never say never, Shakes." Max steps back, pointing his thumb at the door. "I'll get out of here before the hound shows back up, but I'll be expecting a call from you soon."

"How long will you be in town?" I ask.

"For as long as you need me to be."

He starts to walk out, but I call after him and he stops, peering over his shoulder at me. "What made you come today?"

He shrugs, a smirk on his lips. "I couldn't go another day without seeing you."

I fight a smile, looking down at my lap instead. I missed him too, but I won't admit it. I can't lead him on or have him sticking around more than he needs to. It'll just be leading him into a dark oblivion.

Several seconds later and Max is near the bed again, standing right above me. Fastening my face in his hands, he tilts my head, planting a warm kiss on my forehead and then my cheek. Warmth courses through my veins, bringing back feelings I haven't felt in years. Looking into my eyes, he asks, "I'll see you soon?"

I nod. "Yes. Soon."

And then he pulls away and walks out of the door, smiling over his shoulder at me before disappearing around the corner.

FOURTEEN

I never thought I'd miss the sun. I'm more of a cool nights, fall weather kind of girl, but as I ride in the car, absorbing the warmth of the sun on my skin, I'm almost certain I can get used to the Spring. I bathe my face in the rays, pointing it up at the sky as a song by Laura Welsh flows through the speakers. For the first time in months, I don't desire darkness. I finally have light.

John created a playlist for me last night for our ride home. All last night, I kept thinking about walking through the house, wondering if John changed the paint in the dining room like I'd asked. Swept the deck every week like I used to? Watered the plants? Changed the pillows on the bed and covered the patio furniture?

A few minutes later and John finally takes the turn I've been waiting for, pulling into the stone driveway of our home. As I shift in my seat, I smile, and John looks over and picks my hand up to squeeze it. When he's at the top of the driveway, I release his hand and grab the door handle.

"Babe," he calls before I can get out.

"Yeah?" I look back at him before I can climb out.

"Let me get that," he says, getting out of the car. I sigh, sitting back against the leather seat and watching him round the front of the car. He pulls my door open and smiles down at me. Helping me out, he wraps his arm around my waist and I wrap mine around his. "I know you're eager to be home but you have to take it easy. No strenuous activity, remember?"

"It's hard to be calm when my big comfy bed is waiting for me upstairs. Plus, I get to touch my house again, all the little trinkets and stuff."

"Well, now you can do all the touching you want...as long as your doctor says it's alright for you to be up."

"Oh, please, John," I mutter as we take the stone steps up to the front door. "I'm a rebel. You know this." I grin up at him.

He laughs, taking out his keys and unlocking the door. Once it's open, he guides me down the hallway, his arm still tightly wound around me.

We step around the corner, John flips a light switch, and as soon as the light is on, a loud, "WELCOME HOME, SHANNON!" fills the room.

I gasp and place a hand to my chest, smiling wide as confetti is tossed in the air and kazoos are blown. Everyone I know and love is here, most of them sporting silly, colorful cone hats.

"Oh my God!" I gasp as John releases me. I look up at him but there is a solid frown on his face. It catches me by total surprise and my smile fades a bit. I thought this was all his idea but as he looks across the room at Tessa, his frown deepening, I realize this was not his idea at all. This was hers.

Instead of causing a scene, he puts on a forced smile and greets our guests as they approach us.

Tessa rushes to me, hugging me for what has to be the twentieth time in the past twenty-four hours. "I'm so glad you're home," she sighs.

"You did all this?" I ask, taking a look around the room flooded with party favors, finger-foods, and décor.

"I did!" Her brown eyes sparkle as she looks around. "You like it?"

I nod. "I love it. And I appreciate it. Thank you. I'm just not so sure John approves."

"Tessa," John steps beside me, looking her hard in the eyes. "Can I have a word with you in the kitchen, please?"

"For what?" she demands.

"John," I sigh. "Please, not right now. At least wait for everyone to leave."

He looks at me before giving her a stern onceover, knowing I'm right. "Fine. Later." He walks away, forcing a smile at Emilia and Quincy as he passes by them.

"Tessa," I hiss, pulling her toward the window draped with copper curtains. "You should've asked him before doing all of this."

"I wanted to but he didn't come home and he wasn't answering his phone! I thought you deserved it, and that he would at least support the idea." She rolls her eyes. "Didn't realize he'd freak out like this."

"I understand, but you know John is far from spontaneous so next time you do something like this make sure you ask him." I press my hands together in prayer mode. "Please?" I beg. "I want my time home to be comfortable, no stress."

She nods and releases a slow breath. "Okay, okay. Fine. I'm sorry I overstepped. It won't happen again, I promise and I'll tell John the same once he's cooled down."

"Thank you."

She turns and wraps an arm around my shoulders, facing

everyone in the room. "Guys! Can I have your attention please?" she yells.

The murmurs and laughter come to a hush as all eyes point to Tessa. She grins, surprised it works. "Hi," she squeaks and blushes, but we all know Tessa is far from timid. "So, most of you are closer to Shannon than you are to me, but if you hang with Shannon then you probably have heard her complain about her crazy, dramatic baby sister before, I'm sure."

Everyone laughs, including John, who stands in the corner, sipping on a glass of red wine and nodding his head with way too much enthusiasm.

"Anyway, I just wanted to say that I'm so glad my sister is home. If you know Shannon, you know she's a fighter and has been one her whole life. She's never given up on me, never given up on herself, and although she could give up right now, she hasn't. She inspires me and pushes me to become a better person and I love her so much." Her eyes land on mine, damp and red now. My eyes are full of tears at this point. "Tonight is for you, Shannon!" She smiles hard, clasping her hands together. The tears I'm trying hard to fight finally escape me.

"I love you to death Shanny. You're an amazing person with an amazing heart and I'm so glad to have you as my sister." Tessa steps down from her soapbox, walking straight into my open arms.

"I love you, sis," I murmur over her shoulder.

"I love you more."

Everyone smiles and croons. I bubble a laugh, enjoying her embrace. After all, I know to cherish every waking moment now. I don't have many days left, nor do I know when the time will come, but nothing will stop me from living it up. Being home is just the start. There's so much more I'd love to do.

"Okay," Quincy says, walking up to us and splitting us apart. He swipes at his eyes, laughing as he goes for the stereo. "I can't handle these crocodile tears and Shannon is home, right? Let's turn up the music and have a little fun!" Quincy moves in front of me and cups my face in his hands. "I know you can't have alcohol so I made some Shirley Temple's for you. They're in the fridge whenever you want them. I didn't add a lot of grenadine, though. Tessa told me not too much sugar."

"Thank you, Q." I hold his face and kiss his cheek. After letting him go and chatting with a few old friends that worked at Capri, and my former roommate Emilia, who can still crack me up to this day, I politely dismiss myself from the gathering. A small part of me wonders if Max was invited to come tonight.

Entering the kitchen, I open the fridge and take out one of the virgin drinks. "Here's to living," I whisper to myself, bringing the drink to my lips and sipping it. It's been a while since I've had something so full of flavor. Although the grenadine would've perfected it, I know I don't need it.

Footsteps sound a short distance away and John walks into the kitchen. I force a smile at him. "You okay? You tired?" he asks.

For the first time I don't put the feeling off. I'm a little lightheaded and weary. Rest is needed. It's been so long since I've moved around and socialized. I can't afford to pass out in front of my friends, ruin the night for the people I love most.

"Yeah. I should probably lay down."

Without hesitation, John holds my hand and takes the other exit, the one that leads to the den. We walk through the den, and from there he picks me up in his arms, carrying me up the staircase. Pressing my ear to his chest I listen to his steady heartbeat, feeling the warmth of him radiate through me.

"Let's get you some rest," he whispers as we make it to the bedroom. The way this happens puts my mind at ease. I know John won't go back downstairs to argue with Tessa when everyone is gone—at least not tonight.

"I don't want anyone to worry," I tell him.

"They won't. I'll send Tessa a text so she can let them know."

John closes and locks our bedroom door, giving me complete assurance that he won't be downstairs again. After taking off my shoes and putting on my pajamas, I lay on our king-sized bed and groan with delight at the feel of the feather pillows.

"Oh, how I've missed these pillows," I sing.

He lifts the sheets with a smile, tucking me beneath them and then bringing the comforter on top of me.

When I'm nice and cozy, I watch as he moves to the other side of the bed to tug his shirt over his head, revealing six rows of abs. I haven't seen those abs in months and it's just now occurring to me. He steps out of his jeans next. Moments later and he's in bed with me, sighing with his palms relaxed behind his head.

"It's been a long day, huh?" I whisper with a smile. I can still hear the music downstairs, my friends laughing and chatting.

He looks at me with tired eyes. "It has." Moving closer, he pulls me to him and I rest my head on his chest. "You're okay, though, right?"

"I'm okay."

"Your breathing?"

"It's okay," I whisper. "Dr. David said I should be able to last until morning since I took that bag of OPX. I actually think it's doing what it's supposed to do and making me feel better today."

"Yeah?" His voice is hopeful. "That's good. I'm glad." He kisses the top of my head. "I'll stay in here tonight. Keep an eye on you."

"Totally unnecessary," I yawn.

He chuckles. "You can sleep."

"When will all of the stuff be here for treatments?"

"It'll be here in about an hour or so but until then, rest."

I nod, curling into him, holding on tight. "John?"

"Yeah, babe?"

"Thank you for doing this for me. And for not getting too upset with Tessa. You know how she can be."

"Yeah. I know. You warned me about her." He laughs and I laugh with him. Then he's quiet a moment. His breathing changes. It's softer.

His entire body has relaxed and I'm glad because I hate when he's so tense. "I want to be able to do whatever it takes to keep you happy, Shannon. I love you."

"I love you too."

He strokes my hair, the affection and nuzzling bringing back feelings I've truly missed. I missed lying in bed with my husband, holding him. Kissing him. Molding with his sculpted body. I missed all of John Streeter. Everything. Such small touches and actions that many people take for granted every day.

Before I know it, through the constant stroking of my hair and the gentle kisses from him on my forehead and cheek, I'm falling asleep and I can tell it's going to be the best sleep I've had in weeks.

This, I know, is the start of bliss again. I have to make the most of what I have right now. I have to do what's best for me, no matter whose feelings are hurt in the process.

Shannon Hales-Streeter can no longer be restrained. She has to soar like a bird. Fly like a plane. She has to build strength and live. She has to remember that each day is a gift waiting to be unwrapped and that life is all about what you make it. Right now, life is telling her not to hold back. To keep going. To keep fighting.

Life is waiting, and it shall be lived.

FIFTEEN

PAST

It was nearing midnight the night I met Jonathan Streeter. It was the kind of late where a twenty-three-year-old woman should not have been out alone.

I'd just blown a tire coming off the freeway. The rain poured down, thunder clapping, the lightening striking the sky in silver streaks.

It was bad timing. I was late for work and I hated being late. That night, I was supposed to be tending the bar by myself. Eugene was going to fire my ass for sure this time.

I whipped out my cellphone, dialing Max. He didn't answer. I wasn't surprised. We'd had it rough and he was playing this annoying distant game that I was becoming fed up with.

"Shit," I hissed when it went to his voicemail.

I had a spare tire and remembered my father showing me how to change one once, but as I sat inside my beat-up

Punch Buggy, I had no clue where to start with the rain and thunder.

Instead of sitting around waiting for Max to answer, I hopped out of the car and rushed to the trunk, rain beating down on me. Popping the trunk, I bent down to take a look inside. I had a lug wrench, a spare tire...but I wasn't sure what the hell else I needed.

I stepped back, watching as cars rushed by me, the helpless girl stuck in the rain, cold and fucking pissed. I tried Emilia but there was no answer. I knew she was asleep. It was after ten. She was an early bird, plus she'd been stressed and overloaded with studying and finals.

"Damn it!" I shouted, and as if things couldn't have gotten any worse, a large gush of water hit my face, soaking the entire front half of my body.

I gasped and, unsure how to react, just stood there on the side of the road, arms up in the air, dumbfounded as I watched the white Mercedes Benz keep driving.

I would never forget that snazzy car. It was one I knew I'd never be able to afford. It sped toward the exit and I cursed after it, yelling every bad name in the book as if the person could hear me. I was sure they had no clue I was even there.

To my surprise, after my ranting and waving a fist in the Mercedes's direction, the car came to a stop, the red brake lights bright.

Soon, the reverse lights came on and the car zoomed backwards, maneuvering to the right and stopping a few yards in front my car.

Oh, shit. I'd done it now.

I stood in place, slowly reaching for the wrench in my trunk. I couldn't clearly make out the person as they climbed out of the car, but the person was definitely tall and sporting a black coat. The person walked with a slow stride, the stride of a killer, I'd say, or maybe I was just thinking that because I was stranded on the side of the road in the rain.

The closer the person got, however, the more I realized how absolutely beautiful he was. Because of my headlights, I could see the raindrops that had collected on his long eyelashes. It had dampened his messy bed of auburn hair and his eyes were so blue and mesmerizing.

He narrowed his gaze as he came closer, moving around the passenger side of my car with his hands in the air, a defenseless gesture.

"Hey!" he called over the noise of the passing cars and rain. "You alright?"

I nodded, taking a step back, tightening my grip around the metal. "I'm fine!"

His eyes moved down to my anaconda grip around the wrench. "Do you need some help?"

"No." I shook my head, shooing him away. "I'm fine, *sir*. Please, just go back to your fancy car and soak another person standing on the side of the road with a puddle."

He scanned me with his eyes. "I sincerely apologize for that. I had no idea anyone was standing by the car." He took a step forward. I stepped away. He stopped in his tracks. "I'm not here to hurt you. Here—" He marched ahead, reaching for the wrench in my hands.

Defensive, I held it up, warding him off. "I told you I'm fine! I have friends coming to help me!" What a lie. All of my friends were too busy ignoring my calls. His hands shot up to the air quickly as he backed away, stunned. But in a matter of seconds, he was shaking his head and walking away, back to his Mercedes. "Yeah," I called after him. "Just go!"

Only, he didn't go. He popped his trunk, dug some items out, and then rushed back. I gasped, my heart racing, thinking he was coming to kill me.

I figured in that moment I was going to die. Maybe he had anger issues and didn't like the way I was talking to him. Or maybe he hated rejection. Either way I'd just gotten on his bad side and was bound to die now.

I wouldn't have been able to make it far if I tried to run, and he seemed fit enough to catch me if I dared. Open roads with fast cars surrounded me and going for the woods was a definite no-go. I stood still, stuck in my tracks as he met up to my car again.

I watched as he dropped the objects and bent down on one knee, the rain beating down on him.

He wasn't coming back with a gun or a knife to kill me. He had his own lug wrench, a jack, and lug nuts. Once he cranked the car up a few levels with the jack, he took the wheel off with the wrench and then stood, digging in my trunk for the tire.

He glanced at me as he took it out, putting on a subtle smile before returning to the job. In a matter of minutes, he was finished, collecting his tools and making his way back to his car again.

Flabbergasted, I walked around my car, watching as he dropped his tools in his trunk and then slammed it closed.

"Hey!" I called, rushing after him.

He stopped before climbing into the safety of his car, looking back in my direction. The rain had transitioned to a light drizzle.

When I finally met up to him, I cleared my throat and drew in a breath. "Umm...thank you for that back there."

Rain trickled down his chiseled face, making the stubble around his mouth sparkle. It looked like he hadn't slept in weeks. Up close he looked different. Still hot, still beautiful, but different. There was sadness in his eyes—a sadness I assumed was unexplainable. It seemed to have been buried deep in those eyes of his for years.

"I wasn't going to hurt you," he informs me.

"I...well, I mean you never know with people these days. This world is crazy, ya know?"

"That, I know. I get it." He put on a boyish smile.

"Well, again, thank you. As you can probably tell, I've never changed a tire before."

"Yeah." He got a kick out of that one, grinning like a schoolboy. "I can definitely tell."

It was then that I noticed he had food stains on the white shirt underneath his jacket. The look didn't quite fit the car he drove, and neither did his dirty black slacks and sneakers. "Just getting off work?"

He looked down at his attire, sighing as he tugged on the hem of his shirt. "Oh, uh, yeah. I'm a chef. I promise I'm not always this filthy." He gave me another goofy, crooked smile. I laughed and it felt nice to laugh.

"Well, anyway you're welcome. But I advise you to go to YouTube or something and watch how to change a tire. It's not as hard as you think it is. There are tons of videos out there."

I nodded, and I could have told him I already knew the basics, but I was completely mesmerized by the way his lips moved, how straight and perfect his teeth were. "I will."

He turned for his car. "Have a good night, strange girl."

My lips pressed as he started the car, shutting his door behind him. I turned around, walking back to mine and scooting in, starting the ignition. The guy sat on the side of the road for a while, way too long for me to wait for him to pull off. My car was fixed and I was already late for work. I wasn't sure how I was going to get through my shift with wet clothes on but I had to make do.

I pulled off and went off the exit, going down another freeway until I was uptown. It wasn't until I parked in the back and gathered my things that I noticed that same white Mercedes parking a few spots away from me.

"What the hell?" I breathed. *Did he really just follow me? Now this guy was really creeping me the hell out. What was it for him? Change a girl's tire, flirt a little, and then kill her whenever he was ready? No, it had to be: change the tire, pretend to be a nice, innocent guy, follow her, and then slaughter her ass as soon as she thinks she's safe. He was a Ted Bundy case for sure.*

I hurried for the back door of the club but he called after me. I opened the door halfway just to make it easier for me to escape if I needed to, but looked over my shoulder at him anyway.

"Are you following me?" I asked, narrowing my brows at him.

"No—I... okay, don't laugh," he said, laughing himself, "but I thought when I stopped on the highway to be a good Samaritan, that I would end up helping some helpless old lady." He paused, eyes turning serious. "But when I saw you... I...well..." He hesitated and I looked at him, doing my best to contain my laughter. Running his fingers through his wet hair, he said, "I just didn't think you'd be *so* damn beautiful, is all."

I softened for him right away.

Okay. So, I admit that although he was corny about it, it was the sweetest thing I'd heard in a long time. He wasn't too forward like Max, but he also wasn't afraid of letting me know his truth either.

"I know you think I'm crazy for following you here, but if I could just have your first name it would really put my mind at ease. A name with your face will make my entire night, and then I swear I will leave you alone." He held his hands up in an innocent way before dropping them gradually.

Releasing the door, I walked his direction with my arms crossed. "My name? You sure that's all you want, *crazy man?*"

He nodded, smiling. "That's all I want, strange girl."

I bit into my bottom lip, taking a look around the parking lot before meeting his sparkling blue irises again. "Alright. It's Shannon."

"Ehh," his nose scrunched up, "I think I like Strange Girl better."

I giggled, and it was natural and it felt amazing. I hadn't laughed so naturally in so long. He was teasing me, joking around. It was cute. Still corny, but cute. "Take it or leave it, bucko."

"Well, I'm Jonathan Streeter. I go by John." He extended his arm, his hand held out for me to shake.

I reached forward and shook it firmly. "It's nice to know the name of the man who saved my Punch Buggy. I don't have a name for my car but maybe I'll start calling it Streeter now."

"That's hilarious. You should try and get a new one, though. Doesn't seem like Streeter back there will last you much longer. Eventually it'll be more than just a tire that needs fixing."

"Yeah, well," I sighed, raking my fingers through my hair, "I'm working on that. Hence the reason I'm about to walk into this bar."

"Hmm." He made a noise, his face inquisitive, almost like he had an idea but didn't want to say it out loud. I wasn't going to make him. He was probably thinking up cornier things to say.

Silence fell between us and, seconds later, when I looked up, he was already looking at me, his gaze soft. Beneath the streetlights I could really see him. There was so much damage in his eyes. Pain lied deep within them, but he did his best to cover it up. Don't get me wrong, his eyes were beautiful but I knew pain. I knew hurt. I could spot it in a person from a mile away.

Other than the sadness there, he was breathtaking. I wanted to hold him, tell him that whatever it was that was bothering him, it would okay. I, of all people, knew how hard life could be.

In that moment, I realized we had a lot in common. John Streeter wasn't just some random guy that changed a helpless girl's tire. We may have met accidentally but there had to be a greater reason behind it. I'm a firm believer that everyone who comes into your life is there for a reason. Back then, I didn't know what John's reason would be for coming into my life, but I wanted to find out, so I invited John into the club for a few drinks. The first one was on me.

He was free the rest of the night, so I did my best to make sure he had a good time and he had even offered me a spare black T-shirt to wear that he had in his car. I'd knotted it in the back to have a feminine appeal, but my jeans were still a little wet.

He was okay with chatting with me over the bar, bantering with me, laughing about how I thought he was coming back to kill me with a handful of tools and even how he soaked me with a random ass puddle and his car tires.

He was okay being around me and, while he was, I saw some of that sadness slowly fading from his eyes.

I saw light. Joy. I assumed that was rare for him. I wanted to keep it that way. From that moment forward, John Streeter was no longer just a stranger. He'd become a friend. Then a best friend. And then a boyfriend. And finally, my husband.

I had no clue while at the bar that night that he would be the love of my life and the man I ended up marrying.

A great man, he is. God, I still can't believe he's mine. Of course, our relationship wasn't always steady, nor was it easy.

We faced challenges, him with his job and not being able to spend as much time with me until later at night, and me with my past—the past I never settled or came to terms with.

Max was still in my heart though, and we still kept in touch here and there. It was hard to completely cut him off—get rid of him—but with John, it became a little easier to not think about him every day. Eventually, I stopped thinking about him all together, dedicating my heart and mind to John.

I knew it was bad to use my disease as a reason to not talk to him anymore, but Max had hurt me. Max went off the grid and John made me forget about the man who had broken my heart for just a little while.

That is, until he returned again.

SIXTEEN

I've been awake for hours as my new doctor, Dr. Vivek Barad, tampers with a new device I'll have to use.

As he checks vitals, marking things off the sheet on his clipboard while also asking me questions about my levels of comfort, I've been practicing his name in and out of my head.

"Vi-veck Bar-odd," I sound out the name, rolling it off my tongue.

"That is correct." He smiles down at me.

Dr. Barad is a very young and handsome Indian man. He has shoulder-length black hair and warm brown skin. His round glasses make him seem older than he really is. I'm sure he wears them purposely, probably for people like me to take him more seriously. He doesn't seem too much older than John.

I find his age a good thing. He respects my wishes a lot more, unlike Dr. David who mainly respected John's.

"Okay," he says in a heavy accent. "I've thrown out the old bag of OPX and have inserted a brand new one. You should change the bag out every six to eight hours." He lifts up my new device, the one I now have to carry everywhere with me. "John and your sister Tessa have mentioned that you are tired of being in bed all day and would like to walk around more?"

I nod. "Yep. I'd like to at least be able to go down the stairs without someone having a heart attack about it."

He laughs. "I understand, but you must realize this is a disease that can't be taken lightly, Shannon. I had to go through hula-hoops just to get this device. No one believes the small doses will work for you, but I have faith. They'll pump through the tubes in your nose and into your lungs every few minutes to keep your lungs stable. The pills I've prescribed should give you plenty of energy to get through the day. But remember, any kind of extra activity could damage your lungs even more. You've hit a critical level. You are lucky that you are even breathing right now—that the OPX is still working."

"I understand." I lower my head, avoiding his eyes.

"Trust me, I am not here to scold you," he reminds me for the third time today, "I am simply here to make sure my patient is comfortable and happy." I look up at his bright white smile, watching as he pushes his glasses up the bridge of his large nose. "So, this can be carried in a backpack." He picks up the silver jetpack looking device, twisting it around for me to get a good look. "Or just carried like this. But, regardless of how you decide to carry it, you must have it with you at all times if you don't plan on taking bags of OPX to last you through the day. It makes a small noise, but can be easily ignored. This was designed to be light and personable for the patient. That way you can go up and down the stairs and not feel as if you're carrying a two-year-old child." He places the device on the ground again. "The OPX will keep your lungs functioning properly as long as this device is running. It will beep when it needs a quick battery charge. I'd say it needs at least thirty minutes."

"Okay. Thirty minutes I can do."

"Good. Now, you must also remember to keep this tubing free from pinches and bends. Always keep an eye on it. If you can't, have someone else be on the lookout. We don't need the airways blocked."

I nod, looking down at the clear tubing running from my nose to the device. "Got it."

"So, what will you name this thing? There is some long name for this, but I won't bother with pronouncing it." He chuckles, placing his clipboard down on John's dresser and then folding his arms.

"I think I'm just going to call it my jetpack. With it, I can walk around again. Feel the sun. Go to the lake. Have a little fun at least. To be able to walk now is like being able to fly. Not all OPX patients can afford this thing, right?" I lift it up off the brown rug, resting it on top of the mattress.

"That is right. Consider yourself lucky. Your husband is a great man. He wants nothing but the very best for you, no matter what it costs."

"Yep. I know." Everyone knows.

"Well, anyway." Dr. Barad blows out a breath, unfolding his arms and grabbing his clipboard. "I will be on my way and back in another three and a half hours. Remember everything I said and please do not get carried away. It can be easy to work your body more than necessary. Try walking down half the staircase out there, sit for a few minutes, and then go back up. If that feels like too much then stop and call me. The OPX should help you maintain control of your lungs but anything could happen." He collects his things, packs them in his bag, and walks to the door.

"See you later," I call after as he gives me a small nod of his head.

I twist so my legs are over the edge of the bed, then look at the jetpack. This thing will be annoying to carry around but it's better than sitting on my ass in this bed, watching cartoons and reading books all day long.

I get off the bed, carrying the jetpack with me to my walk-in closet. When I step in, I sit in front of the black chest, fold my legs, and after collecting a few breaths, I open it, digging around and searching for my old black *Jansport* bag. When I come across it, I smile way too hard for my own good.

"There you are, old friend." I unzip it, dumping out random sheets of paper, pens, empty water bottles and even snack wrappers. When it's empty, I smooth out the tan leather on the bottom and then I tuck my jetpack neatly inside of it. I start to zip it, but then I realize the zippers might cause a pinch or bend, so I leave it halfway open.

I dig in the chest again, looking for the hand-me-down pocketknife given to me from my father. As I search, I hear footsteps coming into the bedroom. Moments later and Tessa's voice screeches, "What the hell are you doing?"

"Looking for something," I tell her, completely ignoring her overreaction.

"Well, let me do it. Looks like you're struggling. Stop." She swats me away, taking over my scavenger hunt. "What are you looking for?"

"The old blue and brown pocket knife dad gave me." I tuck the loose strands of my hair behind my ear. "It's in there somewhere."

"Oh, God." Tessa's eyes stretch, full of horror. "Please tell me you're not looking for it so you can off yourself."

I narrow my eyes, pushing her away from the chest and

getting on my knees to search again. "Suicide and Shannon don't mix," I mutter.

"I know. I'm kidding. I love you." She looks down at my backpack, fingering the levers and knobs on the jetpack. "So this is the thingamajig John spent an arm and a leg on, huh?"

"Mmm-hmm."

"Is it working?" She looks up.

"Yep. Breathing better than before. It feels ten times better to get smaller doses than having to sit and let a full bag drip into my veins."

She gives an inconspicuous look. "You're just saying that."

"No, seriously," I say, pulling out the knife and flipping the blade. "I feel great. Kind of like how I did before. I think moving around with it is actually helping, not making it worse."

"I really wish you wouldn't walk at all—at least, not so much, Shannon."

"Tessa," I mutter and she raises her hands in defense.

"I'm just saying," she mumbles. "If I were given the opportunity to lay in bed all day, I would totally take it!"

"Of course, you would." I laugh, using the knife to cut a hole above the label on the backpack. I quickly take off my tubing, slide it through the slot and then put it back on, inhaling quickly.

"How neat," she says, fiddling with the hole. "Well, anyway, I came up to tell you that I went down to that bakery you like so much and got you a gluten-free bagel and donut. The donut has chocolate icing on it." Her smile is mischievous as she stands and holds her hands out for me to grab.

I take them and she brings me up to a stand. "I'm so glad John decided to go to work today and can't see the chocolate donut," I laugh.

"Me too. I swear, Shannon," she groans, leading the way

out of the closet and bedroom, "I love John like a brother, but I don't know how you do it. He's trying so hard to control everything you do. I know it stems from love but *come on*."

"Well, that's John for you." I shrug. "He's just really overprotective. He's lost a lot in his life, so I can't really blame him."

"Yeah, I know." She sticks her bottom lip out, giving that some thought. "He's a great man though."

"I agree."

She makes her way down the staircase, but I stop before taking the first step down, realizing just how many steps I have to take before getting to the first floor.

Tessa reaches the middle of the staircase and starts to say something as she turns at an angle, but when she realizes I'm not behind her, she frowns, looking up. "Shannon? You okay?"

"Yeah." I hold up my hand, giving her reassurance. "I'm fine. It's just been so long since I've walked down the stairs by myself." I force a laugh. It's winded.

I haven't walked down any of the stairs and I'm already breathless. The crazy part about this is I'm not even afraid of the staircase, I'm afraid of my lungs racing, trying to catch up with an activity I haven't performed in months.

"You don't have to come down. I can bring the food up. It's fine—"

"No." I cut her off, head shaking. "I got this. I can do it." I take a step down and make a mental tally. *One down, at least thirteen-more to go.* I take another and Tessa remains in place as she observes me with worried eyes. When I'm four steps down I beam at her. "See," I breathe. "I got this."

"Shannon, I don't know. You already sound tired. You don't have to do this. Maybe you should start with walking down the hallway."

"No, Tess. I can do this." Although I use her nickname, my voice is harsh, and I immediately regret letting my pride rear its ugly head.

Tessa's lips seal tight and her gaze lowers. She pities me, and I hate it. She shouldn't feel pity for me, the older sister. It should be the other way around. She should be looking up to me, wondering just how I do it. But instead she fears losing me over a fucking staircase.

The doorbell rings and Tessa takes that as the perfect opportunity to break the tension.

"I'll get it," she calls softly, scurrying down the rest of the stairs. Glancing over her shoulder, she begs, "Just *please* be careful."

She walks down the hallway and I stop for a second, gripping the railing and collecting my breath. I'm already exhausted and my heart is racing. I can't believe how weak I've become.

Tessa's voice carries through the hallway. I can't make out what she's saying, but she's clearly upset.

Several seconds later and a door slams shut, shoes scuffle across the floor, and stepping around the corner and in front of the staircase is Max.

Max?

Tessa is gripping his gray, sweat-dampened T-shirt, trying her hardest to drag him back down the hallway. She grunts and growls, but it's no use. He's a brick wall. He's not going anywhere.

My heart catches even more speed as he looks up at me, then down at the hands I have tightly wrapped round the railing.

"You okay, Shakes?" he asks.

"I've been better," I admit.

Tessa releases him, rushing for the stairs to get to me but

Max, like a cheetah—swift and agile—beats her to the punch, picking me up in his arms and scooping up my backpack in the process.

"Watch out for the tubing," I tell him.

He nods.

Tessa smacks him on the back. "I can help her myself!"

"I'm pretty sure you can't carry her, little sis. Nice try, though."

She growls at him.

I shake my head. They are ridiculous.

"Going up or down?" he asks, looking me in the eyes.

"Up," Tessa says before I can respond. "Back to her bedroom."

"Down," I counter.

"Down it is." A soft smile graces those plump, pink lips of his and he walks around Tessa, taking each step one at a time. Slowly. Carefully. Just for me.

"This is insane," she sighs. "You know what? I'll be in the bathroom scrubbing the grime off my fingers. Can't believe I actually touched you. Why in the hell are you so sweaty anyway?"

"Long game of basketball and working out," Max calls over his shoulder. Tessa mutters something under her breath and then stomps up the stairs. Max laughs. "Your sister is crazy, you know that?"

"Oh, trust me. I know," I laugh.

"How are you feeling? Seemed a little stuck up there..."

"I'm good. It's just my first time using the stairs in a while. I had to prepare my body for the task."

"I can understand that. Tessa told me you got something new to help you get around. Is that what's in this bag?" He gestures over his shoulder with his eyes.

I nod. "I call it my jetpack. The thing's like magic."

He laughs. "Glad it's working for you, Shakes."

When he's a few steps away from the door, I realize that he didn't take the turn for the den.

"Max, where are you going?"

"Outside."

"No. Why? Put me down," I say hurriedly.

"Is that what you really want?"

Honestly, no. But I can't leave the house with him right now.

"Max." I struggle to get out of his arms. Realizing this will only cause harm to me, he stops walking and places me down on my feet immediately. "What are you trying to do, kidnap me?"

He cocks his head. "Can I? Just for an hour?"

"An hour?" I reach for my backpack, sliding my arms through the straps. "Where will we go?"

"Wherever you want to go."

"Paris?"

He sinks his teeth into his bottom lip, trying to fight a laugh. "I still want to take you there one day."

"And you'll get me a bike with a basket?"

"I'll pedal that baby for you."

"Then where will I sit?" I ask, keeping the mood light and playful.

"You can ride on my lap. You can either face me or the handles. You know I don't mind either of the views."

I fight a laugh. "You're gross. That is never going to happen." I look back and sigh. "Okay. I guess an hour is okay. Where are you trying to go?"

"That's a surprise."

"No games today, alright? I have to be back before John gets home, Max."

"Tessa said he wouldn't be off until after ten tonight."

"Yeah, but knowing John, he'll try to get off earlier just to check in on me."

"Man," Max said, chuckling, "that guy doesn't let up, does he? Maybe he's the reason you can't breathe. All that damn smothering."

Max continues his laugh, walking ahead of me.

Normally I would join in with him, but this time I don't. I'm quiet for a long time, staring at him as he unlocks his car doors. When he's inside the car, I'm still standing outside, stepping back with my thumbs tucked beneath the straps of my backpack.

Realizing my hesitancy, Max hops out of the car again and looks over the top of it at me. "Shannon? What's wrong?"

"You're making me think that I should just stay home." I turn back for my house.

I hear his car door slam shut and his feet carrying across the pavement. He catches me, spinning me around to face him. "Did I offend you?"

"It would have offended him too."

"I...that wasn't my intention. It was a joke."

"I don't think me not being able to breathe is something to joke about. That was a horrible thing to say—a very ignorant thing to fucking say, Max. John does not smother me."

He swallows hard, scratching the top of his head. "I'm sorry." His eyes are full of shame, guilt.

I sigh, shifting on my feet. That look. I remember that damn look. Those eyes and how they instantly make you feel sorry for him, even when he's in the wrong.

The sad thing about this is I'm still weak for Max in some ways. I'm mostly weak for him because we've been through so much. There's so much that people don't know about us. Yes, we split up years ago, but there are reasons behind it —*big* reasons that are hard to talk about.

"Let me make it up to you," Max offers, stepping back.

"How?"

"By taking you somewhere special. Somewhere I'm sure you haven't been in a while."

I thin my eyes at him. "I'm pretty sure I already have an idea of where that place might be."

"Maybe you do. Maybe you don't. You wanna find out?"

I look back at my house, studying the forest green door, and then putting my attention on him. "Fine." I point a finger at him. "But no funny business, Mister Grant, and I mean it."

"Yeah, I know," he says, smiling over his shoulder. He walks to his car and pulls the passenger door open for me. I move past him in my sandals, sliding onto the warm leather seats. When he's behind the steering wheel, buckling up and starting the ignition I can't help noticing the mischievous smile on his lips.

What is this man up to?

SEVENTEEN

PAST

FOUR YEARS AGO

It was June 16th, Max's twenty-fifth birthday and we were five months into dating. Everything was perfect, from him showing up at my doorstep with boxes of popcorn, chocolate and wine (because I didn't care for flowers back then), to me showing up at his place, wearing nothing but a foxy trench coat with sexy lingerie underneath.

I'd just clocked out of Capri. Of course Max was off, taking the night lightly. Although he was spending his Tuesday night at home, I knew he was most likely getting drunk with a few friends, having a ball in his so called bachelor pad.

"What are you gonna do for him tonight?" Quincy asked as I slid my arms into my jacket at the bar.

I shrugged, tossing my hair over my shoulder. "I'm not

sure. I bought a cake and some movies. He claims he doesn't want to do much but watch them with me." I pick up my satchel. "I guess that's the plan."

"That's all, huh?" Quincy looked sideways at me as he topped off a martini with a swirled lemon peel.

"Yep. I think we're past the constant sex phase. We've reached a new milestone. Eating junk food, cuddling, watching movies, and if it so happens that our clothes end up being tossed aside and we're naked, so be it."

Quincy sighs, pouting his bottom lip. "You have no idea how much I wish for that. The men I meet are so fucking inconsistent."

He rolls his eyes at the thought, handing his drink to the young woman waiting at the end of the bar with a twenty-dollar bill in hand. He accepts the bill graciously and she prances off.

"It'll come," I tell him. "Don't rush it."

He groaned. "Oh, I'm rushing it. I need a man. Like, right now."

I turned and laughed. "I'll see you tomorrow, Q."

"See ya, babe!"

I pushed out of the back door, unlocking my car manually and climbing in. After stopping by my apartment to pick up the cake, balloons, and movies, I gave Max a call. He didn't answer so I left a quick voicemail.

"Hey, you're probably completely wasted—which you have an exception for since it's your birthday and all—but I just want to let you know that I am on the way. Hope you don't need anything else tonight."

Ending the call, I took the freeway, driving for fifteen anxious minutes and pulling off the ramp, coming into Max's rather expensive neighborhood in Ballantyne.

I'd learned that Max's parents made really good money.

He was well taken care of by them and with the tips he got at Capri, it was an added bonus. He only worked because his parents wanted him to have some kind of responsibility.

Parking the car, I climbed out, collecting the cake and balloons first. After sliding my satchel over my shoulders and locking my doors, I was on the way up to his apartment.

I knocked several times with this silly smile plastered on my face. I couldn't believe I was so eager to see him, then again, I hadn't seen him all day. We texted throughout my shift. He wanted to stop by the bar but I told him it was better to stay home, that way he wouldn't end up too drunk to drive back. He hated leaving his car behind.

I knocked for the third time, my smile slowly fading.

"Max?" I called behind the door. "Open up. It's me." Several seconds later and the lock clinked. The door swung open and I prepared myself for an intoxicated boyfriend, only it wasn't an intoxicated boyfriend that I got.

It was a girl. A very beautiful and familiar girl.

She had long brown hair and light brown skin. Her piercing hazel eyes bolted with mine and she clung to the door, a smile threatening to take over her lips. I knew exactly who she was without even having to be told.

Max's ex-girlfriend, Evelyn. "Hi," she chirped. And my heart dropped.

"Why are you here?" I asked, stepping past her and looking around the apartment.

Everything was in place. Nothing out of order. No panties or bras lying around. I placed the cake on the countertop, releasing the balloons and letting them bump the ceiling.

Spinning around, I marched toward Evelyn and asked again, "Why. Are. You. Here?"

She held up an ugly-ass gold necklace with a pearl on the end, smirking. "I just stopped by. I needed something."

I blinked at her, disregarding the ugly fucking necklace and storming for the bedroom. I expected to see Max lying there, half-naked but he wasn't there. I checked the shower. No sign of him. "Where is he?" I asked.

"Not here." She laughed as I entered the bathroom again.

Walking out, I thinned my eyes at her, opening the door. "Get out right now, please."

She held her hands up in the air, picking up her *Coach* purse from the foyer table and walking past me.

"In case you're wondering," she started, digging in the purse for something, "I have a key to his place. I had it back when we were together. I told him I needed to stop by and get something and he said it was fine."

Wait. He actually talked to her? Kept up with her? And why in the hell did she still have a key and I didn't? I watched as she dangled it in the air, as if flaunting gold.

Instead of responding I slammed the door in her face, mainly so I wouldn't claw her to pieces, then I drew in a deep breath and went for my phone again. There were three missed calls from Max. He was most likely calling to inform me that he wasn't there, and probably so I wouldn't run into his ex.

Too late, jackass.

I called back. He didn't answer.

When I dialed again, the door swung open and in he walked, drunk as hell.

"Babe?" He was breathless, putting on a smile. He walked to me with his arms out but I backed away, which caused him to stumble and land on the sofa. He tried playing the fall off, but it didn't work. He was too drunk and clumsy.

"Max." I placed a hand on my hip, doing my best to keep

hold of my patience. "I'm going to ask you a question and I want the truth. Do you understand?"

He shrugged. "I always tell you the truth, don't I?"

I ignored his question because, frankly, I had no clue if he always told me the truth or not.

"Why was Evelyn in your apartment?" I asked, looking him straight in the eyes.

He looked confused for a second, but when he thought about it, he said, "Oh! She said she left some necklace here from a long time ago. Some hand-me-down traditional thing. Her mom's in town and she has to have it on while she's around or something. I don't know." He shrugged again.

"Okay," I murmur, "I have another question."

"Yeah?"

"Why in the hell does she still have a *key* to your apartment? And why in the hell do you still stay in touch with her?"

"That's two questions." He laughed.

I frowned, stepping forward and shoving him back against the cushion of the couch. "I don't give a shit how many questions it is, Max! Why does your ex-girlfriend still have a key to your apartment!?"

"I don't know, Shannon! I guess I never thought to ask for it back, damn!"

"That should've been the first thing you asked for, Max! As soon as you break up with someone, you ask for your shit back!"

"Well, I forgot about it until just now. Why are you acting like this?"

I gave him an obvious look, throwing my hands in the air with exasperation. "Because your ex has way more access to your place than I do! She could walk in here at any given moment and have her way with you! Women like her—I see through them. She's sneaky and it's clear she still wants you."

He sighed and groaned and that really made me angry. He was drunk, yes, but right now he was being a complete asshole.

"You know what?" I shook my head, huffing a laugh as I turned around and picked up my satchel. "I'm out of here. I don't have time for this."

Max hopped up, rushing for me and catching me by the elbow before I could make it out the door. "Wait—Shakes, I didn't even do anything!"

"Don't call me that," I seethed, glaring up at him. "Don't fucking use that name with me right now."

I snatched my arm out of his hand and turned away.

"Babe," he called after me as I yanked the door open. I rushed down the hallway, ignoring him. "I'll get the key back. If that's what you want, I'll get it back."

I spun around, narrowing my eyes at him. "Max, it shouldn't have even come down to what I want. I come here every fucking night and I have to *knock* on the door. She comes by and can just waltz right into your place and treat it like her own. How is that fair to me when I'm supposed to be your girlfriend now?"

He stared down at me, speechless. Max wasn't always great at explaining or defending himself. I think he'd grown accustomed to not giving a fuck and shrugging everything off in his previous relationships, but I wasn't those girls.

With me, it was different and he knew it. I was glad that he was willing to change for me, but he just wasn't quite there yet. It was his birthday and I felt horrible for ruining it, but I had too much pride and too much respect for myself to stay.

I blew out a sigh and then stood on my toes, placing a kiss on his cheek.

"Maybe you'll get where I'm coming from when you're sober. Until then, enjoy yourself, Max. Have a good night." I walked away, catching myself before I could make it to the stairs. "Oh, and happy birthday."

Still confused, he stood in the middle of the hallway, calling after me, begging me to come back. A good girlfriend would've tried to work it out the same night, but I wasn't a good girlfriend. In fact, I am ashamed to admit I was a horrible one.

I can admit that back then, I wasn't always the greatest partner to have. I figured since he was my boyfriend, that he had to do whatever it took to make me happy again. It was his job to make me happy.

Happy girl, happy world, right?

I was Max's longest relationship. We'd been at it for five months and there were hardly any dull moments.

He loved that—that feeling of being comfortable with someone. Happy with them. Adoring every aspect of them just as they do the same to you.

But the problem was he was still learning, and I was already ahead. He had a lot of catching up to do and I didn't know if I had the patience for it.

After all I'd been through, being patient for something that I wanted to happen never worked out. When I wanted or expected something I wanted or expected it in that exact moment.

Not months or years later.

Not tomorrow.

Not within the next hour.

Right fucking now.

I didn't hear from Max the rest of the night, and it kind of pissed me off. No calls or voicemails. No apology texts. Nothing. I figured he either drank himself into oblivion while eating cake and passed out or just passed out period.

I went to work the following night, agitated and on edge. I was still upset because I hadn't heard from him. He had a shift behind the bar with me and I wasn't looking forward to it because at least he'd be sober and aware while working.

I got there first. He showed up minutes later, stepping behind the counter and rubbing his hands together, ready to tackle the night.

The volume of the music cranked up, people flooded the club with dollar bills and credit cards at the ready.

For the most part, I was busy so I paid Max little mind, but during the moments when we could catch a small break I felt him staring at me. Watching like a hawk.

I may have purposely worn a short black dress with the word *Capri* across the chest. The dress flaunted all my curves and a lot of my bosom. Emilia helped me curl my hair and do my makeup so I was pretty damn sexy that night.

It didn't help that the men that came up to the bar flirted with me, and it damn sure didn't help that raunchy, skanky girls came up to flirt with *my* boyfriend.

I did my best to ignore them as they leaned over the counter, batting their eyelashes and puckering their lips at him. Some reached over the counter to tuck the money into the front pocket of his shirt, some aiming to feel how *big* and *strong* he was.

He didn't stop them, and when I happened to look in his direction, he actually held onto one of the girls' wrists, whispering something in her ear. She giggled and blushed, pulling away slowly and picking up her drink. This was something he always did and it never bothered me before (he'd explained that this move always got him more service and tips) but that night it really, really pissed me off.

I watched her disappear within the flailing arms and gyrating bodies before looking at him. He was already looking at me, arms folded, a subtle smirk on his lips.

He winked.

I flipped him off, picking up a rag and cleaning off my area.

Something warm pressed on my backside seconds later and a voice filled my ear. "You're mad?"

I turned around, meeting Max's honey eyes. "Fuck off, Max."

He wasn't surprised by my response. Instead he reeled me in before I could get away and I crashed into his hard body. All I felt was abs and muscle. All I smelled was the heavenly scent of a man.

"You never wear dresses to work," he informed me as if I didn't know.

I shrugged. "I need to wash clothes. It was all I had left in my closet."

"Liar."

"Asshole."

"I'm sorry," he murmured.

I didn't know what to say to that, so I said nothing at all.

"Guess what?" he asked.

"What?" I sighed.

"I got the key back," he murmured in my ear.

I leaned back, tilting my chin to meet his eyes. "When?"

"Told her to meet me in the parking lot before my shift. When she met me, I told her, 'Look, my girl isn't happy about you still having a key to my place. I need it back if I want her back.'"

I fought a smile. "You did not say that."

"I did. She gave it back. It came along with some fussing and bitching about wasting gas, but I got it back." He pulled it out of his pocket, dangling it in the air. I stared at it as if it were made of pure gold—like it was worth more than just a typical, manufactured key.

Max grabbed my hand, turned it over, and placed the key in my palm. "It's yours now."

I swallowed hard, whipping my head up to look at him. "Max—no, you don't have to give it to me if you're not ready—"

"I'm ready."

"Are you sure?"

"I've never been so sure about anything in my entire life. If there's anyone I want having a key to my home, it's you." His warm lips pressed to my cheek.

I clung to the key with a gleefully beating heart. I was excited, even though a part of me still wanted to be upset with him. This was all way too easy.

I needed him to work for me. So, like a petty girlfriend, I pulled away and turned to the customer walking up to the bar, asking him what he'd like.

I prepared the drinks and when the customer walked away, I looked at Max. "You don't forgive me?" he asked, his voice loud enough to be heard over the dubstep music.

"Oh, I forgive you," I said blatantly. "But you should know things aren't as simple with me like they would be with all of the other girls you've dated. You aren't winning with smooth talk. Not this time. That's way too easy for you, Mister Grant."

His head shook and dropped, and a silent laugh caused his body to vibrate.

"Hey! Excuse me!" A customer flagged Max down from

his end of the bar. He smirked at me before going back to his corner.

I leaned against the counter, watching as he took a mental note of the guys order and then went to work, grabbing whiskey and other liquors.

He moved swiftly, effortlessly, like he'd done this most of his life. When the drinks were ready he took the money and went to the cash register, giving me a quick glance.

"Too easy," he scoffed.

Max said nothing more to me after that...at least, not during the rest of our shift. Instead, he focused on his side of the bar, making drinks and collecting tips. He passed by me several times without saying a word and for a second, I thought maybe he was tired of my bitching and complaining and was realizing just how annoying I could be.

I mean, I had the key to his apartment now and he had apologized. What more did I need?

Before I knew it, it was three in the morning and our shift was ending. I cleaned the bar, counted down the register, and was out of there in no time.

"Goodnight, Max," I said as I started to walk out of the break room.

"Yeah. Goodnight," he muttered over his shoulder as he stood in front of his locker.

I started to ask him if we were hanging out the rest of the morning, but he looked away so quickly that I didn't have the chance.

I hurried out of the club, rushed to my car, and slammed my door behind me, cranking the car up.

I pulled away from Capri with tears in my eyes, and it was my own damn fault. Why did I always have to make things difficult?

I entered my apartment, slamming my bedroom door

behind me, so glad Emilia had spent the night at her boyfriend's house.

Moments later, a knock sounded on the front door and I went for it, checking the peephole. I wasn't shocked to see that it was Max. I knew he'd come, most likely to stir the brewing pot even more.

I yanked it open. "What the hell do you want, Max?"

Instead of answering, he barged right in, picking me up by the waist and bringing my back to the nearest wall after slamming the door shut behind him.

"What do I have to do to get you to realize that this is *not* easy for me? That I'm trying like hell with you?" he rasped.

I narrowed my eyes at him, refusing to respond.

He studied my eyes, every feature of my face.

"Wrap your legs around me," he ordered.

I frowned, and only did so because it was uncomfortable not having them around him while he had me pinned to the wall in his arms.

As I did, his lips came to my neck he sucked on the crook of it gently.

I fought a moan, doing my best to push him away by the shoulders. He pinned my wrists to the wall, refusing to let me fight against what he had to offer.

"You can be so damn stubborn," he grumbled on my neck.

"Whatever," I sighed.

He carried me to the bedroom and my back landed against another wall.

I gasped as the kisses continued, sensual and angry grazes of his lips, then he laid me on the bed, and I couldn't help but sigh.

In seconds he'd snatched off his belt, unbuttoned his pants, and freed his dick. Then he pushed the hem of my dress up, exposing my pink panties.

Leaning down again, he crushed my lips with his and I tasted liquor on his tongue. I sank my teeth into his bottom lip and he groaned, wanting more. He clung to me, one hand cupping my cheek, kissing me deeply, holding me, fighting and loving me at the same time.

He tore his mouth away and lowered his head, trailing small kisses down my neck, my collarbone, and my chest. I shuddered a breath.

Before I knew it, he was inside me, thrusting slow and deep, taking me like he owned every inch of me. And maybe he did.

I gasped and then moaned, no longer able to put up a fight. With each thrust, my walls were being broken down bit by bit.

"I love you, you know that?" he asked gruffly. "I fucking *love you*. I need you and I hate fighting with you. I hate that shit, Shakes. Tell me you do, too."

I could have, but I would have been lying because fighting always led to intense moments like this. Rough, pleasurable makeup sex. The type of sex I'd never gotten from anyone else.

When I didn't answer, Max dragged my body to the desk, knocking papers and other miscellaneous objects onto the floor. My stapler went flying to the carpet, crashing and splitting.

My back pressed on the cool brown wood as he spread my legs apart, slamming into me, then groaning as he clutched my thighs and my fingers clawed into his shirt.

The desk rattled, but didn't break. My body built up more and more, reaching climax.

I cried out and he let out a deep groan as he released too. We panted through the moment, and I tried so hard not to smile. Instead, I shut my eyes, taking it all in, and holding him close.

I felt his body lean backwards and opened my eyes. He was already looking at me. "You didn't say it back," he murmured.

I stroked his cheek with the pad of my thumb. "I love you too, Max," I said in a soft voice.

And he smiled, kissing me again and then picking me up in his arms, carrying me to the bed. It didn't take long for us to have sex again, and I didn't put up a fight this time because this was the first time Max had said he loved me.

"I love you, Shannon," Max said when the sun rose hours later. Neither of us could sleep, so instead we laid cuddled in each other's arms. "I won't stop saying I love you until I take my very last breath."

"Your last breath," I repeated. Those words. There was something about them. Something comforting, healing, but also, detrimental. I inhaled, lifting my head and kissing him on his perfect, sculpted lips.

He smiled at me when our lips parted, and then he rolled on top of me, taking me once more and showing me just how much he loved me. Then we fell into a deep, much needed slumber.

A moment I'd never forget.

EIGHTEEN

When Max takes a left turn, that mischievous smile still on his lips, I try and fight my own smile.

"I knew it," I say, laughing as we pull into the parking lot of Freedom Park.

He parks the Mustang backwards in a parking slot, grinning from ear-to-ear. "Don't act like you aren't excited about this."

When he kills the engine, I pull the door handle and step out as he does, taking a look around. Not much has changed about this park, other than a new playground. My head tilts up, my focus going to the towering trees above. Birds fly above with their wings spread wide. Oh, how nice it must feel to fly.

I sigh. I haven't been here in years. This park holds so many unforgettable memories. Being here now is bringing some of them back.

It's pretty vacant where we've parked, minus a few people jogging or walking to get to the trail. Not many people visit the side of the park where we are, which I've always liked.

Most people are usually attracted to the lake on the other side, where there is green grass and shady trees and benches. Perfect for picnics, or for getting lost in a good book.

"Coming?" Max asks, bringing my attention back to him.

I walk his way and he props an elbow out. I link arms with him, and he leads the way toward the trail. The feel of the rocks and gravel makes my legs rattle and my bones achy, but I ignore it because it feels nice to be walking, though I probably should have worn different shoes, not sandals.

"I can't believe you really brought me here."

"Why can't you?" He looks down at me, cocking a brow. "This place was special once."

"Yeah, once upon a time."

He looks ahead, watching as a woman turns right at the fork at the end of the trail and continues her jog. "Maybe the memories are what I want you to remember."

I nudge his rib with my elbow. "Dude, I don't need any funny business. Seriously."

"Shakes," he says, almost exasperated. "Do you think that if you meant that, you'd be walking this trail with me right now?"

Max stops walking and I rapidly pull my arm out of his. *Wow.* You know what? He's right. What in the hell was I even thinking? Going out with a man I was once in love with not too long ago. I told John I'd be out with a friend, but I didn't say *which* friend, and not mentioning it felt a little like a betrayal. But this is harmless. Friendly. Max and I, we're just friends and nothing more. The past is long gone.

"Shannon." He says my name flatly. "I was just kidding. This is just a walk. We're only catching up."

I narrow my eyes at him, tucking my thumbs beneath the strap of my backpack. "Sure. If you say so."

"I would never put you in a situation like that."

"Then why did you come back?" I counter.

"Because you only have so much time left." He pauses, lips twisting a moment. "And because I would have regretted *not* making you smile at least one more time. Getting under your skin like the old days." He smirks, and I can't fight my laugh.

I walk forward again, this time without his arm in mine. "Yeah. That was super sweet but also super cheesy."

"You're still the same," he says, meeting at my side.

"How do you mean?"

"You still act like nothing gets to you—like you aren't upset about what you're going through."

"It's the way I have to be if I want to survive it. Every day I come closer and closer to accepting it. At this point it's just my fate."

"Yeah." He runs a hand over the top his head, focused on the ground. "I see that now."

I decide to change the subject as we reach the bridge above a stream. "Hey, remember when I almost tripped and fell in the lake that one time? I was so scared. I can't swim for shit."

"Yeah I remember. And I told you I would save you—that you had nothing to worry about."

"You caught me before I could fall," I tell him, walking backwards across the wooden bridge.

He only smiles, nods.

I stop and take a moment to catch my breath, studying the fork in the trail. One trail leads to the lake, the other takes you up a short cliff to the side of a hill with a view of the city.

"You tired?" Max asks, looking down at me.

"I'm fine," I pant.

He scans the perimeter, then places a hand on my arm, leading the way down the trail that takes you to the lake on the other side of the park. We approach a bench and he tells me to sit. I take the seat because I do need a moment for my lungs to catch up. It hasn't even been five minutes and I'm losing my breath. Max sits next to me and looks sideways at my backpack.

"Can't believe I'm saying this, but maybe Tessa was right. I shouldn't have brought you out here. We should have just sat on your stoop or in the backyard or something." He looks me in the eyes. "I should take you back."

"You have to be kidding." I scoff. "*You* of all people I thought would take it a little easier on me about this." He stares at me but doesn't say a thing. "Max, I'm fine. Seriously. I just need a moment to catch my breath here and there. When I start to feel bad I will let you know, I promise you."

"I'm not trying to hold you back from anything, trust me. I'm just not sure what to expect, is all. All of this walking might take a toll on you—hell, you could barely even make it down the stairs at your house. I don't want to be the one who makes your condition worse." His face softens, and I don't believe it, but I spot a sliver of pity in his eyes.

"Ugh. Not you too, Max," I groan.

He looks at me, confused.

"I don't need your pity too. You were the only one who still looked at me like I was strong—like I'm not made of glass and can break at any moment."

I stand up and start my walk on the trail again. I hear him sigh and it takes no time for him to catch up to me with his long strides.

"Shannon," he says, but I ignore him, still walking. "Shannon, stop and look at me."

I stop, but I don't look at him.

He takes initiative, stepping in front of me and gripping the tops of my shoulders, leaving me no choice but to face him. "You are the strongest woman I know, Shannon. And it's not pity you see in me. I just care about you. I don't want anything to happen to you on my watch—hell, I don't want anything to happen to you at all. Is it so bad to care about that?"

I nod in understanding, lowering my gaze.

"I tell you what." He blows out a breath, releasing my shoulder. "You start giving me a check-in of how you're feeling every ten or so minutes and I'll layoff. I know you won't do anything to make your situation worse, but just let me know so I don't have to constantly ask myself. Alright?"

I nod and smile. "You got it, chief."

He laughs, wrapping an arm around my shoulders. We take a slow, careful stroll to the lake and stop in front of one of the benches. Before we sit, Max stops me, tugging on my arm.

"Look." He releases me, walking ahead and going to a tree just a few feet away. When I realize just what tree it is, I meet him there.

Max runs his fingers over the words carved into the bark of the thick tree trunk.

MAX + SHAKES 4EVER

Beneath the words is an infinity sign with little birds carved around it. Max carved this with a wood carving knife he'd gotten from his father. He's always been good at art, making it more of a hobby than something he takes seriously. I run my fingers over the birds' ragged wings, smiling.

"Remember that day?" he asks.

"Yeah," I murmur, laughing. "Picnic. Wine. Sunshine."

"One of our better days." I glance at him and he's focused

on the carving. "This was one of the best days I ever shared with you."

"How?"

He's quiet a moment, standing so close I feel his breath running warm across my shoulders. "Because I'd never done something like it before. A picnic? Wine? That wasn't me. I'm far from romantic."

"But you made it happen anyway," I say, breathless. Why in the hell am I breathless all of a sudden?

"I wanted to put in more effort with you. Show you that I cared." Max's hand runs down the length of my arm. I watch his fingers move down to my hand, glad my body doesn't react to his touch anymore. "What happened to us, Shakes?" His voice is low, anguished.

"Life," I say quietly, turning to face him. "Life happened, Max."

The features of his face become tight, his honey-brown gaze hardening as it drops. His jaw begins to tick and he takes a step back, looking anywhere but at me.

"Yeah." His voice is thicker. "Life can be so fucked up." He looks at me again. "Do you hate me for what I put you through?"

I answer immediately when I hear the hurt in his voice; see it in his eyes. "Max, no." I grab his hand and squeeze it. "You ask me that all the time. I don't hate you. I could *never* hate you."

"Good." He sighs, as if he's truly relieved. "I can't have you hating me."

"I don't think I can hate anyone. I don't even hate my mother, and she completely abandoned me and Tessa." I give off a sarcastic laugh, as if that will heal the pain I feel when I speak of my mom, but it doesn't. It never does.

"You got through it. That's all that matters," he says.

"But what if I hadn't?" I sit down on the bench. "What if I would have turned out to be just as careless as her? Where would I be right now? Would I even have this disease? Would Tessa be hopeless? Would I be dead?" I slide my gaze over to at him as he sits beside me.

"There's no way you can be anything like your mother, Shannon. You're too good—a fucking gem, honestly. Everything you went through happened for a reason."

I drop my head, fiddling with the strap of my backpack. "I wrote to my mother once," I say. "To tell her I had OP. She wrote back and completely avoided the conversation. Talked about her life in prison a lot, some friends she'd made. The books she'd read while in there."

Max is unsure of what to say.

"She got out early for good behavior. She came by once and I told her never to come back again. Now that I've had time to think about it, I probably shouldn't have said that to her. I mean, I would love to make amends with her, but I doubt she'll drop by after what I told her. I was just so angry and hurt and she was trying to take advantage and—" I clamp my mouth shut and bite the inside of my cheek. Then I shrug. "I guess it's better for things to stay this way, though. Let her continue not to care. That way when I die, she won't be another person who feels a ton of guilt."

"Don't say shit like that," Max snaps. "She *will* feel guilty. She's human. She'll recognize the mistakes she made with you eventually and she'll have to own up to it."

I look into his eyes. "It's true," I say. "I'm done lying to myself about the shit that's happened in my life, Max. I don't have time for that anymore. Might as well face the facts. My mother is a piece of shit and it is what it is."

He stares me right back in the eyes, lips pressed thin. "Stop making it seem like you're not worth anything."

"I'm *not* worth anything, Max. Maybe I was before, but not anymore. I'm sick. The doctors don't even want to replace any portion of my lungs because I could die right on the operating table."

Max balls his fists on his lap. Shutting his eyes, he breathes as evenly as possible through his nostrils, as if he can't believe I'm even talking this way. I guess I'm not surprised. I was never the one to talk negatively before all of this. I always kept my faith, held onto hope even during the darkest, most depressing moments of my life, but it's hard to do that anymore with death knocking at your door.

Unclenching his fists, Max straightens his back and pulls me in for a tight hug. He groans and then sighs.

"You know something?" he asks in a quiet voice.

"What?"

"If I had the opportunity to donate anything that could help you, I would."

"John says the same. Tessa too."

"Because we fucking love you and you have yet to put that through your thick skull." He presses a finger to my temple and I laugh. "When you love someone you will do *whatever* it takes to keep them happy. Safe. *Healthy.*"

He releases me and I twist my lips, sitting back and fiddling with the strap of my backpack again. "If only it were possible to do something and keep everyone alive. It's just too much of a risk."

"Anything is possible, Shakes. Besides, we don't know what'll happen. For all we know the device your using could help you, clear all of it up like magic. The medicine might work better. You could become a part of the success rate. Anything is possible, right? Especially if you keep fighting?"

Oh, boy. He sounds like Tessa and John. I snatch my eyes

away from his, changing the subject. "I'm getting hungry. Think we can go catch a bite to eat?"

I can tell he wants to go back to what we were talking about before, but I stand up, tugging him by the hand.

"Sure," he says with a sigh. "Let's get out of here."

I turn with him on the trail and we make our way back to the bridge. We're both quiet. I notice his brows are dipped and pulled together. He's thinking, but there's really not much to think about. Just like Tessa and John, he has to accept my fate.

I put my attention on the trees again, the blue sky. The wind tickles my cheeks and comfort swims through me. Nature has a way of doing that—comforting a wounded soul. If I could spend all day out here, I would.

As we cross the bridge, a cough slips out of me and that cough alone makes me stop in my tracks. Dread fills my heart as I cough again.

"You okay?" Max asks, stepping in front of me. His eyes are swimming with concern.

"I'm fine," I croak, but then another cough surfaces.

And then another. Soon, my head is spinning. I stumble backwards, trying to catch onto something before I collapse, but it's too late. I land on my side, my elbow scraping across the splintered wood of the bridge.

"Shannon!" Max's voice booms. I struggle to reach behind me, tugging at my backpack. One of the tubes must be pinched. It has to be because I now feel like I can't breathe.

"Shannon? What's going on? What's wrong?" Max drops to his knees, looking me all over, eyes swimming with worry.

"My—the pack…jetpack…I----" I roll onto my back, feeling the device digging into my back. The blue sky and puffy white clouds become one giant blur.

Fuck. Is this it? Is this how I'm going to die?

A pair of hands grip my arms to haul me up. Max is shouting something, but it's unclear.

"Shannon! Shannon!"

I work harder to breathe. He carries me in his arms and dashes across the bridge and to the parking lot.

The sky is spinning above me now, the ends of leaves and tree branches steadily going by.

My lips part.

I'm drowning. A fish out of water, that's what I am.

I want to tell him it's the tubing. It must be pinched or one of them is blocked, but when he places me in the passenger seat of the car, I watch him check my backpack to no avail.

It's not the tubing or the jetpack. It's just me. Something must have gone wrong. The OPX must not be working.

Max snatches his phone out of his pocket and then he's shouting. I hear him shout Tessa's name, the word hospital.

No, not the hospital.

Before I know it, the passenger door is closed. He's behind the wheel of his car, and starts it up, driving away immediately.

My head rolls and I look out of the window.

The trees. The sky. Nature has a way of healing a wounded soul...

He's taking me away way from this peace—away from freedom. Back to my awful, dreadful reality.

NINETEEN

I groan groggily, turning my head when I hear voices murmuring. Everything is hazy and spinning.

I look right and John, Tessa, and Dr. Barad are standing close by, talking amongst each other. Dr. Barad is explaining something as they both nod with somber faces. John takes a quick glance over at me and when he sees my eyes are open, he rushes my way.

"Shannon—baby, are you okay?" His voice is full of distress, his eyes studying my face.

I sigh as I look around, so relieved I'm not in the hospital again.

"Yeah, I'm fine." I grunt and start to sit up, but Dr. Barad walks forward, placing a gentle hand on my shoulder to caution me.

"I wouldn't try and move too much right now," he says.

"Why not?"

"Shannon, just listen to him," Tessa pleads, stepping to John's side.

I ignore her. "Dr. Barad?"

Dr. Barad exhales slowly, placing his clipboard down and picking up his stethoscope. After listening to my lungs and heartbeat, he jots something down and then looks into my eyes again.

"Shannon, the *jetpack*, as you call it, was given to you so that you could walk around leisurely—so that you wouldn't feel trapped in your own home. It was meant for you to do simple, everyday tasks, like maybe going on a grocery store trip, or a quick walk to the mailbox. It wasn't given to you so that you could go running around a park."

"But I wasn't running. I was careful," I say defensively.

"I'm sure you were as careful as you could be, but something went wrong. There was still plenty of OPX left in the tank when I checked, but your lungs seemed to have rejected it due to the physical activity. Perhaps you were a little too strenuous? Walking too much? Too fast? Either way, your lungs were working too hard, trying to absorb more oxygen than OPX. It wasn't balancing out."

I scratch my arm with uncertainty, pulling my gaze away. "I didn't realize it could happen from that."

"Shannon, you need to take this seriously," John snaps, and I whip my head up to look at him. "This isn't a game! See, this is exactly why I didn't want to leave you alone or even bring you home. I knew you would take things too far."

"Are you kidding?" Tessa's voice rises, and from the anger expressed on her face, I can tell she's taken full offense of John's remark. "Don't talk to her that way! We all agreed it would be best for her to come home—for her to take the OPX treatment with that thing." She points at the jetpack at the bottom of the bed.

"Why was this Max person in my home anyway?" John demands.

"He was visiting me. He's a friend, like I told you," I state.

John scoffs. "Yeah, well this *friend* is about to get a mouthful from me. He had no right taking you out without my permission."

"Wait a minute—I'm sorry," I snap. "I could have sworn you were my *husband*, not my father. And last I checked, this is my body and my actions are mine, not yours."

John stands tall, his shoulders squaring. He's getting defensive. I don't care.

I look at Dr. Barad who is clearly uncomfortable with the rising tension as he clings to his clipboard. "Perhaps I should allow you all some privacy."

"No way." Tessa waves a hand, dismissing herself. "I'm out of here. This is between them now." She walks out of the bedroom in a flash.

"Would you two like a moment?" Dr. Barad asks.

"Please," John says through gritted teeth.

I put my focus on him again and don't dare look away from him. Yes, I may have overdone it by going to the park, getting a little air, but he has no right treating me like this or acting like I'm his property—especially in front of my sister and doctor. If anyone is to be held accountable for my actions, it's me. Not him. Not Tessa. Not even Max. *Me*.

Dr. Barad is gone in a matter of seconds, clicking the door shut behind him, and when he is, John paces back and forth in front of the bed. "This Max guy," he seethes. "Who in the hell is he?" He stops pacing, boring his eyes into mine.

"He's a friend, Jonathan."

"What kind of friend? A best friend? A guy friend? What? I know all your friends and you've never told me about him."

I look away, folding my arms tightly across my chest. "He's just a friend." There's no way I'm telling him he's also my ex. Not while he's so angry.

"So you went to the park with your *friend*? What made

you do that, Shannon, huh? What made you want to risk your life today—and at a *park* of all places? You weren't ready for that kind of activity yet and you know it! You have to give your body time to adjust to the device and to moving again! The doctor told you that!"

"I know that! I heard what the doctor said, John!"

"Then why are you being reckless right now? Why are you going out with friends knowing you're not in a good condition to go?"

"Because Max is in town for me, John! He knows I'm sick and he wanted to catch up! What am I supposed to do? Ignore him?"

"Uh, yeah!" he says as if I'm an idiot. "Your health is more important than a trip to the park. If he wanted to catch up so badly, he should have stayed here with you in the house, not whisk you away."

I let out a frustrated laugh. "This is insane. It was just a short walk in the park, John. I've been cooped up for months and it sounded nice to go there. I didn't think it would be so bad!"

John starts to say something else, but then there's a knock on the door. We stare at each other briefly, then he goes for the door, snatching it open.

"Hey—sorry to interrupt," Max says. What the hell? What is he still doing here? "Just want to see if Shannon is okay." Max's voice is firm as he looks over John at me. He clearly heard us arguing.

"She's fine," he snaps at him, standing guard in front of the door. "Who let you in?"

"The doctor."

John stares at Max before stepping sideways and pinching the bridge of his nose.

Max takes a step in, smiling awkwardly at me. "You okay?" he asks.

"I'm fine." He needs to leave. This is not the time.

"I feel like shit," he says, looking me over. "I didn't know… didn't realize…"

"Stop blaming yourself. It's fine, Max. Seriously. It could have happened anywhere."

Max sighs then turns to face John, extending his arm and offering a hand. "I apologize for intruding. I'm Max Grant. A friend of Shannon's."

"John Streeter." He shakes Max's hand with a firm grip.

"Cool. So, uh, listen." He steps back, scratching the top of his head. "I just wanted to take Shannon out for some air. I didn't mean to cause any trouble. I stopped by to visit, check on her, and offered to take her to the park, get her out the house. I was looking out for her while we were there. I would never let anything happen to her."

John looks him over. "I would appreciate it if you ran things like that by me first. I'm sure you know that she can be a bit of a rebel. Truth is, she can't handle that lifestyle anymore."

I roll my eyes.

Max is quiet a moment, his eyes narrowing as he stares at John. "That's uh—" He hesitates, and I hope like hell he isn't about to say something rude. "Is she even allowed to go downstairs to sit on the patio? Maybe out by the pool if she wants?"

John's head shakes. "After today, it will be a while before any of that happens."

"John," I call.

"Wow." Max gives a dry laugh, turning to look at me. "I guess I wasn't overreacting about what I said before."

"Overreacting about what?" John asks, confused.

"Max." Jesus, I feel like I'm breaking up a school fight with two little boys right now.

Max disregards him. "Shannon, I'm gonna get outta here. I just wanted to make sure you were okay."

"I'm okay. Thank you for checking." Though I'm grateful he stuck around, I give him a stern look. The sooner he leaves, the better. I know how Max is. It's very hard for him to hold his tongue. I suppose I can give Max credit for his respect, though. He won't disrespect a man in his own home —especially a home he shares with a woman he cares about.

Max nods and turns away but not before giving John a quick side-eye. John watches him go, then shuts the door and looks at me.

"I'm…I mean, *fuck*, Shannon." He rubs his face, causing white streaks to appear. "Where did you even meet this guy? You've never told me about him."

I don't say anything. Instead I pluck at a loose string on the sheets beneath me.

"I'll call Dr. Barad back up," John mutters when he realizes he won't get an answer right now. "I don't even want to know what the hell that was about." He swings the door open and exits the room and I draw in a breath. I bring the blue blanket on the bed to my lap, feeling so much guilt consume me.

I shouldn't have gone out. None of this would have happened if I'd stayed home. Now, I'm going to have a hawk of a husband around until the day I die.

And Max? Well, I'm not even sure what's going to happen with him but I hope he understands and I hope he doesn't blame himself for the craziness my body goes through on a daily basis. It had nothing to do with him at all.

This is why I wanted him to stay away. I'm a ticking bomb—a threat to emotions and unstable hearts. I could break every single person in this house at any given moment and know they'll never recover from it.

I swear these rough times remind me of how much I miss the old John. The man who wasn't so hard on me or himself. The man who took life day by day, just as I did, instead of worrying about every small breath, every little movement.

Dr. Barad comes back into the room and asks me a series of questions. I answer as best as I can, and as Dr. Barad tampers with a bag of OPX for an hour-long drip treatment, I can't help thinking about my first date with John—back when things were better, happier.

We were supposed to go see an action movie that had Will Smith in it. I told John before that it would sell out because, duh, Will Smith is a superb actor and it was a Friday night.

He didn't believe me until we arrived at the theater and stood in line for nearly an hour just to be told that the showing was sold out.

"I knew I should have bought the tickets online," John said as we got back in the car.

I tried not to rub the fact that I'd already said that in his face. "We can always catch it some other time or go to another theater. It's no big deal."

"I know you really wanted to see it," he said after starting the car. "I'm sorry. Tonight is my first night free in I don't know how long and I wasted it. I suck, huh?"

"No," I said hurriedly, turning to face him as he gave a boyish smile. I knew enough to know he was always too hard on himself. "John, I swear it's fine. Stop being the crazy man I met on the highway." That made him laugh and I smiled, rubbing his arm. "It's just a movie. We can find something else to do."

He raked his fingers through his silky bed of auburn hair. "I guess so." He gripped the steering wheel. "You hungry then?"

Just as he'd asked, my stomach growled loud enough for both of us to hear. My eyes widened, embarrassment sweeping over me.

"I'll take that as a yes," he chuckled.

"Sorry," I whined playfully. "I didn't have much time for lunch today. I had to work. I was just going to binge on popcorn until after the movie."

He looked confused. "They have day shifts at Capri?"

"No. I just got a job at Green Tavern as a waitress. Part-time gig." I shrugged.

"Oh. I didn't know that."

"Yeah. I wanted to save that for an in-person conversation with you."

He gave me a warm smile and a silence swept over us. It wasn't awkward since both of us were clearly thinking hard about what to say next.

"May I ask you something?" he finally asked.

"Sure."

"What's a girl like you doing with two jobs?"

"Money is a necessity, right?" I threw my hands in the air, no big deal.

"Yeah, but I mean...well, you seem really well put together. Other than that terrible car you drive around, you seem to have it made."

"Hey, don't judge Streeter, crazy man," I laugh. "She gets me places."

"Right. But I mean you seem like a nice person, great personality, smart, clearly attractive." His face grew red when he realized what he was saying. I blushed and fought a smile. "I just mean it doesn't seem like you should have to work so hard with so many great qualities."

"Yeah, well, my life has always been very...complicated."

"How so?"

"It just has." His eyes begged for more. I couldn't believe we were going this deep already. "Bad childhood," I go on. "Taking on the role of a caregiver at a young age. I don't like to be without, so I work harder to stay ahead and to always be prepared."

"I see." He paused. "You seem like a great girl, bad childhood or not." His eyes flickered to mine for a brief moment before looking through the windshield, at the packed parking lot.

"I can tell you only reveal what you want people to see. You don't want anyone to see that you have fears. Insecurities. Weaknesses. You only want people to see you as you are now—a girl who hustles and wants for nothing...all so you don't have to go back to what you were before. I can admire that."

My forehead creased as I stared at the profile of his face. He was spot on and it was kind of scary.

"By your stunned silence, I'm pretty close, huh?" he asked, chuckling as he met my eyes again.

"Spot on, really," I whispered.

"Yeah." He dragged a hand over his forehead. "When you grow up with the same struggles, it's not hard to see that in someone else."

"You had a bad childhood too?" I ask.

"Yeah. It was pretty shitty."

"I'm so sorry."

The car was quiet again.

"You shouldn't ignore it, ya know?" he says. "Trying to act like none of it ever happened. It will only make you miserable, trust me. It's way better to acknowledge it, accept what happened, and move on from it."

"Well, I think you should be a psychiatrist," I teased him when he started the car and put it in reverse.

"Would you believe that's what I wanted to be before I became a chef?"

"No way!"

"Yep." He smiled, driving away from the theater and then stopping at a stop sign. "But I only wanted to become that after dealing with my own demons." He shrugged. "I realize I'm not quite there yet. But I'll get there."

"I'm sure you will. It's not an easy thing to let go of the past. It takes time. I know because I've been trying to heal from mine." He nodded and smiled, driving again, toward the city.

It didn't take long for him to pull up to a tall brick building. It wasn't a business-y type place. These were condos.

"This is where you live?" I asked.

"Yeah. I figured if you're hungry and since I'm a chef, I can cook for you at my place...that is, if you're okay with that? We can always go out to eat somewhere, be in public. You know since you thought I was a serial killer once?"

I broke out in a laugh. "Oh, you really just went there!"

"I did, Strange Girl!" He smirked and killed the engine, then climbed out the car.

I climbed out too and watched as he walked around the front bumper and met at my side.

"I suppose you can cook for me. After all, I am starving, and I am eager to see what you can do in a kitchen."

"Okay, then. I've got you." He had on the biggest smile as he walked with me to the building. "As long as you promise not to attack me with a wrench, I'll cook for you whenever you want."

We both laughed this time and it felt good. I liked him a lot. He was easy-going and deep and a great listener.

I could also tell he liked me too.

TWENTY

"Shannon?" Fingers snap in my face and I blink. I look down at the IV taped to my arm, then up at the bag that's nearly empty of the clear liquid, hanging on the silver pole. Tessa's face comes into view, her eyes wide. "Did you hear me?" she asks.

"Hear what?"

"John made chickpea soup. You hungry? Do you want some?"

I take a look around the room, stopping at the bathroom door. John is in there. The door is cracked open and I can see him through the gap. He's gripping the counter edge with his head hung low.

"Uh, yeah sure. I'll take some." I don't want it right now, but I need her to leave so I can talk to him alone.

"Okay. Coming right up." She saunters out of the bedroom and with the little energy I have, I take out the IV and stand up sluggishly, walking to the bathroom door.

When I push it open, John looks at me through the mirror. His eyes are red and damp. "John?"

He looks down again. "You didn't have to take out the IV, Shannon. I was going to do it for you."

I ignore him, stepping closer. "What's wrong?" I grab his arm to turn him and then cup his face in my hands. One thick tear lines his cheek and he avoids my eyes. My heart instantly aches. *Oh my God. What have I done?*

"Babe, why are you crying?" I whisper, my throat thick with tears.

He swipes at his face roughly, like a child, but I stop him. "I need to be here," he croaks. "I can't be at work while you go through all of this."

"But I'm okay, John. I swear. Today was just a small mishap. It won't happen again."

"It's not just about today. It's every day from now on." He picks me up and sits me on top of the counter. Stepping between my legs and looking at me, his arms go around my waist and he says, "I'm supposed to go out of town next week."

"Next week?" I frown. "Where?"

"Remember a few months back before all of this, I was telling you about a cooking competition. Twenty-thousand-dollar prize. Winner takes all."

"Oh." I blink, lowering my hands.

"I've been wanting to remind you about it, it just never felt like the right time to bring it up with so much going on." He lowers his head, clearly ashamed. "I'm torn about this because you were and still are going through so much and with this, it's like a once in a lifetime thing. It's hard getting accepted into these competitions."

"Yeah," I whisper. "I understand."

He tilts my chin so I can look at him. "They sent me an email a month ago. I was going to tell you that day but it wasn't a good day for you."

"Well," I say in a low, calm voice. "I think you should go."

His eyes spark, and my heart nearly skips a beat. I haven't seen a spark in his eyes like this in months "You serious?"

"I'm so serious. You don't have to stay back for me. I will be fine."

He reveals a full white smile and I want to hug him.

"Where will it be?" I ask, biting back tears.

"Vegas."

"Man. If only I could go too," I laugh.

His face warps immediately, that spark becoming dull in his eyes again. "I was just talking to Dr. Barad about that. I asked him if you could come with me. He said the flight wouldn't be a problem as long as you have your device and you're comfortable, but his concern is with the heat in Vegas. The air is dryer there. He doesn't think that's the best place for you to go...not like this."

"Oh." An ache builds in my chest.

Not being able to see my husband cook off or being able to see him have fun doing something he loves? That sucks. It's a blow straight to the gut. But when I look into his blue eyes, I know I can't be the one to hold him back. He has dreams to catch, and it's not like he'll be there forever. I'd love to go and watch him, root him on, but I can't, and that is something I have to accept, just like everything else.

"Don't worry about me, okay?" I cup his face in my hands again, smiling. "You're going to go to Vegas and kill it. Bring the money home and open up another restaurant so you can cook me even more meals."

He breaks out in a laugh, pressing his forehead to mine.

"You'll be on TV," I add, smiling as I drop my hands.

"Yeah." He sniffles.

"My sexy husband on TV. How cool is that?"

He chuckles, then brings his hands up to my face to cradle it. "I want you there more than anyone," he murmurs.

"I wish I could be there, but it will be okay. I'll watch."

"I'm taking off the rest of this week," he says. "I want to spend it with you before I go." He presses against me, holding my shoulders. "I'll only be gone for a few days for the competition. After that, I'm all yours again." The way he's saying it, I can tell he's trying to reassure himself more than me.

He reels me in for a hug, nuzzling his nose in the crook of my neck as I wrap my arms around the back of his. "Tell me you won't do anything crazy while I'm gone."

My laugh falls out, playful. Light. "I won't do anything *too* crazy."

"Nothing crazy at all." He leans back, kissing my forehead. "I want to come back to your beautiful smile. Your amazing personality. The perfect love we share." He studies my face as if he's never seen it up close like this before. I feel a surge of insecurity unfurl in my belly and instead of looking at him, I look over his shoulder at the shower. "You know I love you, right?" he asks, and his voice is deep and serious.

"Yeah." I smile. "I know."

He tips my chin with his forefinger. "I love you so much, Shannon. I don't think you realize just how much."

"I love you more, Johnny."

His teeth sink into his bottom lip, those piercing blue eyes bolting with mine. The air stills around us, but something swims deeper within his eyes.

Desire.

Longing.

A hunger I haven't seen in months.

He wedges his lower half between my legs again and bends down to kiss me. But this isn't the usual peck on the lips he gives to me, or the gentle kiss he leaves me with when he's going out for the day.

No, this time there is passion and power included. This kiss is deep and primal, and I love everything about it.

I tangle my fingers in his hair and he leans in, causing my back to press onto the cool mirror. My legs wrap around his waist and he thrusts his tongue between my lips, groaning as his erection rocks against me.

I cling to him, sighing and moaning and aching—wanting him badly, but knowing that he probably won't give it all to me.

He continues rocking between my thighs, causing a friction that gets my body heated.

I reach for the hem of his shirt and tug it up. When I manage to pull it off, I study his solid body, the wisps of hair on his broad chest. His lips part to smile and I sit there breathless, studying my husband and all of his masculine glory.

My husband. My beautiful, breathtaking husband.

"I'm sorry," he breathes. He hugs me, apologizing in my ear. "I'm sorry. I'm taking it too far."

"No," I whisper. "No, John. It's okay. I want this. I *need* it."

He watches my face, my eyes. I can see the uncertainty, his nerves trying to get the best of him, but I refuse to let him get too far in thought. Instead, I reel him back in, crushing his mouth with mine and locking my legs around his waist again.

He groans, cupping my ass, and this time, I don't think he'll stop. It's been so long. *Three* months too long. He's been so afraid to touch me, afraid of doing anything out of fear that he just might make things worse.

But we're home now. Together. Safe.

He brings me to the edge of the counter, removing his

pants and boxers and helping me out of my shorts and panties. He enters me, hard and deep, and I moan, digging my nails into the skin of his back.

He locks his fingers in my hair, thrusting recklessly, his eyes focused on mine. "Fucking love you," he growls, leaning forward so his lips are on my ear. "God, I love you so much." He kisses the crook of my neck, then sucks, clutching my ass and groaning.

Several seconds later and he stiffens and moans just as I do. I clench around him as he releases, and cry out his name. He shudders, letting out a throaty noise, releasing months of pent up frustration.

We breathe through the moment, and I'm smiling like a dazed idiot. He leans back to look at me. "You okay?" he breathes, holding my face in his hands.

I kiss his lips. "Are you kidding?" I laugh. "I've never felt better, baby."

He chuckles, wrapping me up in his arms, holding me tight, and kissing the top of my head. I hold him too, and we stay this way for a while, catching our breaths and enjoying this tiny moment of euphoria.

TWENTY-ONE

My days spent with John before his trip to Vegas go by way too quickly. Before I know it, I'm helping him pick out ties from the closet and then packing his toiletries.

In between the days spent with him, I've had many wellness checks with Dr. Barad and have spent a lot of time with Tessa.

With Tessa, we've painted our nails and tried on Korean face masks she'd bought a while back. The best part of it all was that I was able to make it up and down the stairs without passing out or tumbling down, and was even able to make breakfast once, which I consider a win.

Of course, John was by my side during every step, but I didn't mind it. He was going to be gone for four whole days. He may test my nerves from time to time, but I am going to miss him.

This is going to be the first time he's away from me for longer than twenty-four hours. As I sit on the bed with my legs crossed, folding his T-shirts and shorts, a tear escapes me when I realize that fact. John is too busy in the closet, rummaging through the racks, trying to find his favorite monogrammed chef shirts.

I swipe the frustrating tear away quickly. I can't let him be a witness to it. If he sees me crying, he won't leave. He'll find every reason to stay and I can't have that.

I want to see him make it before I'm gone, which is why I straighten myself up and smile as he rushes out of the closet, laying one of his shirts down on the bed.

"I had this one dry-cleaned today. All ready for the competition." He looks up at me, grinning from ear to ear. "You think I'll make it through the first round?"

I finish folding the final shirt. "Are you kidding? You're going to slay that first round."

"I don't know." His head shakes as he carefully folds the shirt. "I checked out the list. There are a lot of big, talented names going out there. People that I've actually learned from. It's going to be huge."

"It doesn't matter." I climb on my knees, crawling toward him. "The world isn't ready for John Streeter and that's a fact."

I hug him around the waist, tugging him down on the bed with me. He sits, smiling as he wraps an arm around me, then weaves our fingers together. "I'm going to be a wreck without you there."

"You'll be fine. Drake is going with you, right? He'll definitely be rooting you on."

He rolls his eyes. "My cousin will be too worried about drinking and strippers than he will be about my cooking. He's never understood my passion for it."

I laugh. "I'm sure he'll still be around. He wouldn't miss it."

"Yeah," he scoffed. "We'll see. Either way, I'm going to miss the hell out of you."

"I'll miss you more." I tilt my chin, allowing him to press his lips to my temple. "Don't do anything crazy," I tease.

"I'll be too busy thinking about you to do anything crazy."

"And don't go changing anyone's tires during the middle of the night," I add with a laugh.

He gets a kick out of that one, his body shaking with laughter. "I won't, Strange Girl."

The next morning, around 6:15 a.m., I'm kissing my husband goodbye. Tessa's arm wraps around me and she holds me close as we stand in the driveway, watching him leave in the backseat of an Uber.

So much emotion has been trapped inside me for the past week, so much I can't explain. I've been holding back my tears and refusing to get upset. I wish I was healthy enough to go with him. I've been strong, but I don't think I can be strong for much longer.

Now that he's leaving, it's all so real and I feel a hole in my chest—a cavity that won't be filled until he returns.

And then there's the knowing…knowing that any day now I might not be able to walk down my staircase or even to the bathroom in my bedroom.

It could happen over the weekend, while he's away, for all we know. It could happen today, while he's on his flight and can't use his phone.

That's what terrifies me most. The devastation it will bring. Sooner or later those blue and white pills won't give me energy and the OPX won't assist me.

My eyes sting with tears. I try blinking them away, batting my eyelashes wildly as I watch him wave out the window. The car's tail lights become smaller with distance. Then he's gone.

The hole is bigger now, almost like little imaginary men are digging away at my heart, shoveling whenever a wave of emotion comes over me.

My tears finally fall free and Tessa holds me tighter, turning me around and whispering that we should go back inside.

The house is quiet, and it doesn't help that the sky is gray, and rain is on the way. I sit at the kitchen table, holding a cup of green tea Tessa made me. She allows me to sit in silence as she makes breakfast.

I don't eat much when she brings the food to me, just move my fork around on the plate.

"I bet he'll do great," Tessa says after taking a bite of French toast.

I want to smile for her, but I can't bring myself to do it.

I push back in my chair, abandoning my plate. "I'm going to go take a shower."

"Okay. Do you want me to help you up?" she asks, about to stand.

"No, I'm okay." I force a smile at her.

"Kay." She sits, but I can tell she's on the fence about letting me go up the stairs alone. "I'll come check on you in a few."

I nod, leaving the kitchen and making my way to the stairs. I stare up at my ascent, and for some reason the stairs seem even more daunting than they did before. I hear Tessa placing dishes in the sink and know that if she sees me standing here, worried about a fourteen-step climb, she won't leave me alone for the rest of the day, which is what I want. I need to be alone for now.

I make my way up, taking each step slowly, steadying my

breath. When I make it to the top of the staircase, I sigh, pleased with myself.

In my bathroom, I strip myself bare, step onto the cold marble shower floor, turn on the shower head, and press my head on the wall across from me.

The warm water streams through my thin hair, down the dips of my back. Luckily, the heat of my tears blends with the water. I don't feel as helpless. The warmth comforts only a small part of me.

I remember the shower I took a few days ago with John, how he held me from behind, showered me with kisses, then twisted me around, letting water spill between our lips as we both paused for breath. Then the glass of the shower fogged, everything became steamy. I felt nothing but pure joy as we made love—as he gripped me, caressing every part of me. We were having sex again and it was magical.

I cry even harder, my core getting sore from the thick sobs. I cry until I feel I've been drained of all emotion and then I shut the shower off, carefully stepping out and wrapping my body in an oversized white towel.

I enter my bedroom, sitting on the edge of the king-sized bed. My phone rings moments later.

MAX

I ignore the call.
    He calls again.
    Ignore.
    He calls again.
    I don't answer.
    My phone vibrates next.

A text message.

> Max: I know the hound is gone.
> Pick up and talk to me.

I place my phone face down on the nightstand. I haven't spoken to Max since the day John told me he was going to Vegas. John deserved all of my attention and it's a good thing Max kept his distance during all of it.

A knock sounds on the door and Tessa trots in with a tray in her hand with cut fruit and water on top of it. Placing it on the stand beside me, she says, "John told me to make sure you eat, and you barely touched your breakfast. I expect that bowl to be empty when I come back, missy." She gives me a warm smile. I force one back, even though I know she's the one who told Max that John was leaving. It's like she wants to hate him, but she can't. She knows Max has a way of lifting my spirits. "I'm going to go call Danny. Let me know if you need me."

She's out of the door again, phone in hand, purposely avoiding looking into my puffy eyes. When I'm ready, I will talk to her. She knows this and luckily for me she respects it.

When she's long gone, my eyes land on the tray. Though food is the last thing I want right now, she cut up watermelon and strawberries, which are my favorites and I don't want it to go to waste.

Climbing off the bed, I march for my closet and take down a T-shirt and some jogging pants. When I'm dressed and have rubbed on some lotion, I grab a piece of watermelon and eat it, but I can hardly taste it.

My phone rings again and I rush for it, snatching it up and answering. "What, Max?"

"Damn." Max's voice comes through the receiver. "Am I interrupting something?"

"Why do you keep calling me?" I ask, exasperated.

"I haven't heard from you in a few days. Everything alright?"

"Yes. Everything is fine." My answer is dry.

Hesitant, he asks, "Shakes, what's going on?" His voice is full of concern. The sympathy from him feels like salt being rubbed into a deep wound. It stings.

"I'm fine." I do my best to keep my voice from breaking.

"You can talk to me. Remember that."

I sit on the edge of the bed, tapping my foot, staring down at my pink toenails to prevent tears. It doesn't work.

I'm quiet a beat, and then I sigh. "It's...John—" Finally, I break down. I break because I can't even say his name out loud without feeling an ache. "It's John." My voice is thick with tears. I want to wail but, somehow, I keep my composure.

"John? What do you mean? What happened?"

I can't speak. I have so much to say but I can't fucking speak. Never in my life have I felt so weak. So helpless. So *worthless*. Never. I can't travel, can't breathe, can hardly talk.

"Shannon?" he calls.

I crumble, dropping the phone and sobbing. When I've gathered enough composure, I bring the phone back up, gulping in air.

Max curses beneath his breath. "I'm coming to Charlotte." He hangs up and, with little effort, I drop the phone on the floor, walk to the light switches, and turn all the lights off. The sun is still out, but the black curtains help me hide.

I slide beneath the sheets, curling up in the fetal position, allowing more darkness to cover me. Tears slide across the bridge of my nose, landing on the pillows.

My body shudders and shakes for nearly twenty minutes. Before I know it, I've fallen asleep.

When I wake up, it's brighter outside. The gray clouds are long gone. I sit up, glancing around the room, expecting my husband to walk in at any given moment. But then I remember he's not here. I can't be with him because I'm worthless and sick.

I look at the alarm clock. 11:15 a.m.

Sighing, I curl beneath the sheets again. Maybe I can sleep my days away until he comes back.

TWENTY-TWO

A hand touches my shoulder, then gentle fingers run through my hair. For a moment, I think it's John...that is, until I hear the familiar voice.

"Shakes?" I look up into honey irises. Max smiles. I close my eyes again.

He lowers to a squat in front of me. "What the hell is going on with you?"

I look past him, realizing the curtains have been drawn and the sun isn't so high in the sky. "What time is it?" I croak.

Max flips his wrist to check his watch. "Nearing 5:15 in the evening." He sighs. "Tessa told me not to bother you while you sleep, but you've been in this room for two days. Your doctor has been in and out, but he says you're fine."

"He has?" Wow. I didn't even notice. I remember waking up a few times to use the bathroom, but mostly I just remember crying myself to sleep.

"Talk to me," Max pleads.

My bottom lip twitches and at this point, I'm emotionally exhausted and ready to dump it all on him. I don't think he'll be able to handle the pressure, but as he looks at me, fully concerned, I feel I have no choice but to let some of it out. "It's John," I whisper, then swallow thickly.

"You're upset that he's gone?"

"A little more than upset."

He struggles between giving me a sympathetic smile or a frown. My worries subside for the briefest moment. It's cute the way his face tries to configure to just one emotion.

"I wanted to go with him, but I can't even do that, Max. I can't even make memories with my husband anymore. I'm stuck here. I'm fucking useless."

"That's bullshit. You can still go places."

"But I couldn't go *there* because of my stupid fucking lungs."

He watches my face, studies it. "You shouldn't think of it that way. That's only one place in the world. There are more places to go."

"It's too late to go anywhere or do anything, Max." I sniffle. "I'm slowly dying. I could barely walk through a fucking park. What's the point?"

He presses his lips, placing a hand on the top of my arm. "He will be back. I'm sure he misses you already."

"How would you know?" I ask with a hint of frustration. "You don't even like him."

"Because *I* would miss you." His eyes soften as he strokes my arm. My eyes latch with his warm honey irises before moving away. Wiping a tear away, I pull my arm away from his hand and he stands to his feet, sighing. "Come on, Shannon," he murmurs, holding his hands out. "You gotta get up. We have to get you out of this house. That might be what's bringing your mood down. He's everywhere in this place. You smell him. You see pictures of him. Everything in this house probably reminds you of him."

True.

"Come on," he repeats, flicking his fingers and gesturing for me to get up.

When I don't move, he tugs me up and I groan dramatically. "And go where?"

"Anywhere."

"Not the park," I tell him.

"Doesn't have to be the park. Maybe some ice cream? We can take Tessa."

A smile touches my lips but not my eyes. "She'd love that." And the fact that he offers to bring her stuns me. They hate dealing with each other, but I see that to cheer me up, they're both willing to put up with each other. I suppose this is okay.

"Get dressed," he orders, helping me off the bed and then walking to the door. "I'll be waiting downstairs when you're ready."

I nod my head, watching the door click shut behind him. When he's gone, I sit on the edge of the bed, staring at the white wall across from me again. I check my phone, glad to see John sent me a text last night. There's even a missed call from him.

Hey, babe. Made it to Vegas and checked into the hotel. It's really hot here. Having a few meet and greets today and then getting drinks tonight with a few chefs. Don't want you to wait up. I'll call you tomorrow when I get a chance. You okay?

I start to reply, my thumb hovering over the keyboard. I could tell him that I'm not okay and that I want him home more than ever before, but I won't. John deserves to be in a place without regrets or worries.

Plus Max is right. Being here all day, locked inside a home that belongs to me and my husband will only wear me down. I could sit here and mope about John being gone and the truth that I could die at any given moment, but I won't. I have to be stronger, do something with myself. If not for them, then at least for myself.

So I text my husband back:

Glad you're having a good time already! I'm perfectly fine. Enjoy your trip and call or text whenever. No biggie. I'll have my phone around.

After sending the message off, I stand up and walk to my closet, taking down a navy-blue romper and tossing it on the bed.

In the bathroom, I brush my teeth, apply some gloss to my lips, a light coat of mascara, brush my hair down, and then I get dressed quickly, grabbing my favorite brown fedora and sandals.

I take a thorough look in the mirror when I'm done. The romper is a little big on me now, but it'll have to do. The hat is still stylish, given to me by my sister. I grab my jetpack, booting it up and adding a new bag of OPX, and carefully placing it in the black backpack.

After adjusting my tubes, I leave the bedroom, stopping at the top of the staircase. Max is already waiting at the bottom of it, sitting on the second to last step, his back to me. When he hears me coming down, he peers over his shoulder to look up at me.

Max stands and takes the stairs by twos, helping me the rest of the way down. When we're at the bottom, he steadies me, his hands on my shoulders. He looks at me for quite some time, making me feel beyond awkward.

"What?" I ask, lowering my head.

"You look nice." He steps back, looking me over again. "Go ahead," he says, flashing a crooked smile, "do a jig."

"Oh no." I wave my hands at him, laughing as I place my backpack on my shoulders. "I am not in the mood to dance."

"Come on! It's been so long since I've seen Little Shakes in action."

"Little Shakes is no longer capable of those things," I laugh.

"I'm sure she is. Come on, give me life, Shakes!"

I look up at him, fighting a smile. "You are out of your mind if you think I'm about to dance for you right now, Max."

"Come on! I bet it'll make you feel better. You always were good at a quick little shoulder-jig."

"Okay—fine. Fine." I step back and look around the house, shaking my head. I can't believe I'm about to do this. Still smiling, I do a quick bobble with my shoulders, busting out in a laugh as I look up at him. "This is so lame without music!" I shout, but it doesn't stop me from throwing my hands up and waving them in front of me.

Max breaks out in a laugh, clapping his hands twice. "Oh, man," he wheezes, swiping at the corners of his eyes when I stop dancing. "You have no idea how much I needed that laugh."

I adjust my backpack, feeling like my face is about to break from grinning so hard. "I'm done embarrassing myself for you. For that, you're paying for the ice cream."

He drapes a muscular arm around my shoulders, turning for the kitchen where I'm sure Tessa is. "Trust me, that corny shoulder bounce was worth paying for."

We pull up to an ice cream parlor close to uptown Charlotte.

I'm technically not supposed to eat ice cream, but my husband is gone and I am in need of a sweet pick me up like this. I dive into my cookies and cream ice cream as soon as it's handed to me, licking off the spoon after each bite.

"Ohmagod." My mouth is full and cold but I am not complaining. "This is so good. It's been so long since I've had ice cream."

"Do you even remember the last time you had it?" Tessa asks, biting into her strawberry shortcake sundae.

"I honestly can't even remember." I take another bite, the crunchy, chocolaty goodness of the cookies smothering my taste buds. "But I swear I can taste everything right now. You know what? Screw the chocolate, Tessa. From now on, sneak me some ice cream."

"You got it, lady," she laughs.

"Why aren't you allowed to have it anyway?" Max asks, biting into his hotdog. "Everyone deserves a little ice cream here and there."

I shrug one shoulder. "Dr. David, my old doctor, swore it would mess with how the OPX works." I glance down at my jetpack. "I think he was just being over the top. Other than not being able to do a lot of strenuous activity, no one really knows what will be okay and what won't with OPX since it's such a new treatment. Like the whole chocolate and sweets thing." I point my red spoon at Tessa but keep my eyes on him. "Dr. David swore that it would harm me—cause an upset stomach if it got mixed with the treatment. Well, Tessa snuck me a whole bar one night, I ate half of it, and I was fine. I think as long as I eat stuff in moderation, it's okay. I even asked Dr. Barad about the whole sweets and OPX thing and he said he'd never heard of such a thing."

"So, you like your new doctor, then?" Max inquires.

"Way better."

"I love him too," Tessa adds. "She has so much more energy now. Whatever prescription he gave her is fucking amazing. This is the most energy I've seen in her in weeks. He doesn't sedate her, which I like. Dr. David constantly had an IV in her arm. He's a good doctor, but he wasn't a good fit for Shannon." Tessa huffs a laugh and looks at me. "Maybe that's why John didn't want you home. Because he knew you'd be off the IV's and free to do whatever you want."

I smile. "Yeah, I bet he wishes I was on them right now. That way he'll know for sure that I'm not going to do anything crazy."

"What, did he make you promise not to do anything crazy?" Max asks, picking up his drink, smiling.

"After what happened at the park, of course, he did."

"Does he really think the worst will happen?"

Tessa is quiet as she meets my eyes. She already knows the answer to that question.

"It's not that he *thinks* the worst will happen," I mutter. "It's that he *knows* it will happen sooner or later." I look down at my nearly empty cup, pressing my lips.

It's quiet amongst us for several seconds, then Tessa's phone vibrates on the table.

"Oh—it's Danny!" She hops up and rushes away, walking to my white Lexus. I know she's glad to be saved from the awkwardness.

"Okay, so the man is protective and all, but…I suppose I get it. And that I'm a little jealous of it." Max sits by my side, exhaling as he focuses on the wooden tabletop. "We can't pretend that it won't happen. Life is fucked up. We all know that."

"Yeah…"

"So if he's afraid that his wife will pass away while he's not around, it makes sense."

"Exactly. Now you can see why I was upstairs in my bedroom soaking the sheets with my tears. That's the very thing I'm afraid of. I don't want him away, but I also don't want to hold him back from his dreams. It's not his fault I'm sick and can't go there, you know?"

"True."

I inhale, then exhale slowly and it stings my lungs.

A little girl walks by, pointing at me as she licks away at the ice cream stacked on her cone. Max frowns at the little girl as the mother hurries away with her, scolding her daughter as she puts her in the car in her booster seat.

I huff a laugh. It's hard to be offended when people point and stare anymore. I know what I look like with these tubes in my nose. "I probably look like a zombie from *The Walking Dead* right now."

"Not at all," Max says casually. "She's probably just never seen anyone with the tubes in public." He turns to look at me, sweeping his gaze up and down.

"What?" I ask quickly.

"I don't get it. I mean, have you looked in the mirror lately?"

"Yes. Plenty of times, asshole," I counter.

"Well you must not see what I see then."

I give him the stink-eye.

"Okay, fine." He lifts his hands in the air in defense. "Yes, I can tell you've lost some weight and that your hair isn't as thick as it was before. Your skin is paler too, but that doesn't mean you aren't still beautiful, Shannon." I snatch my eyes from his, focusing on my melting ice-cream. "There have been some changes, but they were expected, so you can cut it out with calling yourself ugly, hideous, gross—whatever it is you call yourself these days. Trust me, you're far from it." I look up and his eyes shimmer in the sunlight, as brown as whiskey.

"Whatever, Maxi Pad." I pick up my spoon and distract myself by finishing my ice cream.

I can still feel his eyes on me, roaming whatever's left of my frail body. He still finds me attractive, and I can't help but wonder how.

So, maybe I'm not completely hideous, but when a girl goes through such a dramatic change in such a short period of time, insecurities are bound to consume her.

"Do you wish he were here with you instead of me?" he asks.

I whip my head up, matching his stare. "W-what?"

"You heard me."

My eyebrows draw together, and my heart beats a little faster. "Why would you ask me that question?"

"It's just a question. You can be honest with me." He passes a crooked smile, then turns to look ahead at the buildings across the street from us.

I study every feature of his face. "Max, I'm glad you're here. Don't ask me stuff like that. I—I can't deal with that. Not right now."

"Okay." He holds his hands in the air. "You're right. I shouldn't be putting you in a position like that. I apologize."

Relief washes through me.

"But you're okay, though, right?"

I look up.

"I mean, I know you miss him, but you're okay? You don't feel too alone?"

"No." I reach for his hand, squeezing it. "With you and Tess around, I'll be okay until he gets back."

He nods his head and looks down at our hands. I look too, then pull mine away quickly, picking up my spoon again.

"Tessa told me she'd be leaving in a few days," he murmurs. She said you'll be stuck here with a nurse you don't even know."

"Yeah? And?"

"And I don't like the idea of that."

"Well there's not much you can do about it, Max. It's already been planned, plus I can't really go anywhere else."

"Oh, I think I can do something." Wiggling his eyebrows, he tilts his hips to pull out a sheet of paper from his back pocket, then slams it on the table in front of me. He covers the words with his hands so I can't see. "Now, before you look at what I'm about to show you, just promise me one thing?"

"What?"

"Promise me you'll think about it first before giving me any kind of answer."

I watch his face for a brief moment. He waits for me to promise, but I don't because I have no clue what I'm promising him. Max was always that way—making me promise to surprises that I often times didn't care for.

Knowing I won't respond right away, he uncovers the paper and I snatch it up, reading over it. My heart pounds when I read over the words—I can hear the beat of it in my ears now.

Shifting my eyes up to his, I start to speak, but really, what can I say? "Max...I—what is—" I can't even finish my sentence. I'm too focused on the words printed on the piece of paper in my hands. "You got flight tickets to *Paris*?"

He shrugs as if it's no big deal. "I told you I would take you one day."

"Max—I mean, this is incredible, believe me, but even if I wanted to go, how could I? This is *hours* away. John would never approve and I'm sure Dr. Barad wouldn't even give me the green light to go." I hand the tickets back to him.

"I talked to Dr. Barad the day I took you to the park," he says. "Caught him right before he left your place and asked about it. He knows there is a risk, but he didn't exactly say no. He thinks it's a good idea to take you somewhere as a final escape. He said you have at least three more months in you, maybe longer if the treatment continues to work."

I light up at his response.

"I didn't reach out to you much the past week because for one, Tessa told me to back off." He rolls his eyes playfully and I laugh. "But also because I was keeping in touch with Dr. Barad. He did some checkups on you, told me you were stable enough. He recommended a doctor that he knows in Paris that can send updates—one that you can see daily while we're there. Gave me all of her information and told me as long as you're in first class and you take your OPX tank thingy, you should be okay."

"Are you serious?" I ask, and for some reason I feel breathless. But this time it's not because of my lungs. No, it's because of this sudden realization. I could go somewhere. I could travel.

"I'm not kidding," he says, smiling smugly.

"Oh, my God!" I squeal, lunging forward to hug him. Max catches me in his arms and laughs. I want to hug him so damn hard right now, but then a rapid thought occurs.

I lean back to look him in the eyes. "What about John? Did you talk to him too?"

"Yeah...that's the hard part." He visibly winces and scratches the top of his head

My smile drops and I pull away. "You didn't talk to him?"

"No, but I wanted to. I don't know. I guess I figured you could make your own decisions." He grabs my hands, looking me hard in the eyes. "This is why I asked you to promise me you'd think about it. Because I know you will most likely ask or tell John and let him get to your head about a trip this big."

"Well, I have to tell him. If I do decide to go and I don't tell him he'll freak out."

"Trust me, I understand, Shannon. Listen, I'm not forcing you to come, and I won't be upset if you reject. I could always give the tickets to Tessa and her fiancé if I need to, or someone else I know. But for what it's worth, I think you deserve to go there. This was all you ever talked about for years and I've always wanted to be the one to take you there. Not him. *Me.* I promised it. I owe you this dream, Shannon."

Our gazes latch. "Max...I—I don't know if I can..."

"The decision is yours. Like I said, I can't force you to do anything and I won't be upset if you decide you don't want to but think about it this way—John went to fulfill a dream of a lifetime. You should be able to do the same, no matter what kind of condition you're in. You have the doctor's permission. You have a recommendation for a doctor in Paris and I will hold myself accountable and make sure you attend every single checkup. Even Tessa thinks you should go. She wants this for you." I look at the Lexus, at Tessa standing with her back against the car door, smiling with her phone glued to her ear. No wonder she's been so chipper, so okay with going back home to Danny. Most times she's putting up a fight, wishing she could stay longer. "*We* want this for you, Shakes. You deserve to have this."

I lower my gaze. *Wow.* This is so, so hard. If I go to Paris,

John will not be happy. He'll never forgive me, especially if I go with Max of all people, a man he doesn't know all too well.

"Just think about it." Max grabs my shoulders, bringing me out of my thoughts. "It's okay to be selfish for once. If anyone has the right to be selfish right now, it's you. You have to stop worrying at some point and just live your damn life."

And you want to know the crazy part? Max's words played Ping-Pong in my mind for the rest of the day. Even when he was long gone and I was left in my bedroom, sitting in the cushioned round chair in front of the bay window with my cellphone in hand, it was all I could think about.

What if I called John and told him I was flying to Paris? Then what? He would never approve. He'd probably fly here first thing just to make sure I never left. He'd miss the competition all because of me. Even if I were as healthy as a horse, he wouldn't allow me to go without him. He'd tell me to wait for him so that he could go too.

I stand, staring out the window and watching the setting sun. The splashes of pink and orange light up the sky, the clouds thick with hues of lavender.

What if I could see the sun set behind the Eiffel Tower? Up close and personal? Ride a bike in the city. Walk the city at night. *What if...*

I go to my nightstand, taking out the necklace Max gave to me and carrying it to the window. I squint one eye as I hold out the tiny tower in front of the sunset.

The necklace shimmers in the sunlight. It's pretty, but it's not the real thing. I lower my arm and sit in the chair, watching the sunset again.

Stay or go?

Leave or settle?

Live or die?

The last question is my pill of truth. Live or die. That question makes the answer so simple. I'm going to die anyway. Might as well go out with a bang.

I walk to my closet, tossing my cellphone on the bed along the way. I pull down a suitcase, trying hard not to let the guilt consume me and instead focusing on the things I'll bring.

I'm tired of holding back—tired of this dull, depressing life. I will be careful. I *know* to be careful. I can ride around in an electric wheelchair if I have to. I don't care, I just know in my gut I have to go.

It's another country—my *dream* country. I can't miss this opportunity. I have to fulfill everything I want to do with the remainder of my life and Paris is number one on my bucket list. Without going there, will I have truly lived? Will I be happy as I lay on my sickbed again, clinging to my final breaths, imagining all the ways I could have lived?

The answer is no. I won't be happy. I'll regret not going, and one thing a dying girl should never do is regret the final moments of her life because those are special.

Those moments matter the most.

TWENTY THREE

After Tessa and I eat breakfast, I watch her pack her belongings in the most unenthusiastic way as possible. Before I know it, we're outside and she's tossing her bags in the backseat of her car.

"Shannon, please be safe," she pleads, meeting up to me and wrapping her arms around my neck. She plants her chin on my shoulder, proof that she won't be letting me go for a while. "I'm glad you've decided to tell John about this."

I return a tender hug, sighing over her shoulder. "I know. I just wish he would answer his phone. I'm running out of time."

"Well, if he doesn't answer, just go. Don't let that stop you. Just be safe over there, you know?"

"I'll take care of myself. I promise."

She pulls back and holds onto the tops of my shoulders. "I wish I could go too, so I can stare at you while you sleep. Make sure you're breathing after so much adventure."

I laugh. "I wish you could too, but you have a soon-to-be

husband waiting for you at home. Plus, you know he can't stay home for too long by himself. Might burn the house down trying to cook for you."

She chokes on a laugh, head shaking as she releases me. "I can't believe you still remember that."

"How can I forget? I've never met a man that doesn't know how to grill a burger." I grab her hands, smiling. "I promise if I don't feel well you will be the first person I call. If I can't, I'll tell Max to call you."

"Okay." She releases a breath, blowing upward and causing her bangs to swing. "Tell that fucker not to do anything stupid." She lifts a fist in the air. "If he does and I find out, he'll be getting a mouth full of my fist." She waves her fist in the air, demonstrating the consequence.

I bust out in a laugh. "Trust me. He won't. We've already talked about that and came to an agreement. This is just to fulfill a promise."

"Good." She tugs me in again with a groan, hugging me hard. Then she pulls away, kissing my cheek and then walking to her car. "Well, have fun!" she calls before she climbs in. "And take lots of pictures!"

"I will!"

"And call me when you get there! I mean it!"

"You got it!" I blow her a quick air kiss as she gets into the car, starts it up, and backs out of the driveway. She waves through the window and I wave back, and just like that, she's gone.

The thing about Tessa is I wonder how she'll go on without me when the time comes. We've always been pretty tight and were practically joined at the hip until she went to college.

As I turn to go in the house, I can't help but think of our mother and how better off we have been without her.

. . .

"I got you some oatmeal." My mother walked through the door, her skinny limbs bending as she sat beside me. I scowled at her, watching as she placed the unpleasant-looking oatmeal on the table next to me. "There's raisins and brown sugar, just the way you used to eat it."

"I don't like raisins anymore," I muttered.

"Oh really?" She raised a brow, looking at me but not into my eyes. She quickly focused on the center of her lap, at her ripped jeans. Her brown skin was chalky and wrinkled, her lips chapped. She looked horrible. "I didn't know that. I guess things change after ten years, huh?" She tried laughing, making it a joke, but I sat forward, which led John to get up from the sofa in the hospital room and stand next to me.

I held my hand up, shaking my head. Yes, I was just coming off some medicine that had heavily sedated me. I was tired and cranky and had been vomiting all morning, but I wasn't letting her get by with comments like that. Not anymore.

"Why exactly did you come here?" My voice was raspy. "What in the hell gave you the nerve to just show up like this?"

I had no clue how she'd even found out where I was. I guess she'd done some digging, asked old friends, or maybe she saw an article about John in the newspaper. She read the newspaper a lot when I was younger, checking which one of her friends had been pinned or busted for some illegal shit.

My mother looked at me in shock. I hated that her eyes were so similar to mine. "I—I found out my daughter was dying."

"No, you found out that I'm married now to John. You knew I was dying when you were still in prison and didn't give a shit about it when I wrote to you. I didn't tell you anything about John, now all of a sudden I get a call about how you'd love to meet him?" I slouched back, crossing my arms across my chest tightly. "Bullshit."

She looked through the corner of her eye at John. John sighed and walked to the door. "I'll give you two a minute."

"No." I stopped him before he could make it out the door. She was no longer looking at me. Her focus had flown out of the window a long time ago. She scratched at her neck, her arms, her mangled, disgusting brown hair. She was an addict. I couldn't stand it. "Don't even bother going because she's leaving."

She finally met my eyes. "Shannon—"

"Get out, Allie. Now." I sat back, feeling a pain in my chest but for the first time it wasn't from the meds or the OPX. It was like my chest had been cracked open and all the emotion was pouring out. My mother stood, reaching for the knockoff purse beside her chair, eyes glistening.

"Okay. I'll come back tomorrow. Maybe you'll feel a little better. I heard that OP stuff they have you on gives you bad side effects, makes you feel bad or something like that."

I scoffed and sat forward again as she grabbed the door handle. "No, I don't think you're understanding," I snapped before she could go.

She blinked, turning halfway.

"You left me and Tessa to lookout for ourselves. Grandma took us in, but she was sick and couldn't do much and you knew that, yet you left her with that burden." I shook my head, tears hot in my eyes. "I was seventeen when she died, Mom. Seventeen with two fucking jobs and living in a foster home with a shitty guardian. We could have lived with Aunt Jessie, but you lied on her and said she did drugs with you too! Because of you, I got behind in school because I was taking care of my baby sister and myself. I'm lucky I even got to graduate."

She blinked again and I really, really wanted to slap her for acting so dumbfounded, as if she knew none of this. "W-what are you saying, Shannon?"

"I'm saying I never want you to come back to see me again. You weren't there for me before, when I needed you most, so I definitely *don't need you now. Tessa is finally gaining stability—finally living her life the way she should be. She doesn't even know you're here and I think it'd be best to keep it that way. If she wants to see you on her own, she can, but I won't allow you to just barge back in, acting like everything is supposed to be rainbows and fucking sunshine. I won't, Allie. I refuse. You lost that right the day you decided doing and selling drugs was more important than taking care of your daughters. And you wanna know the worst part of all this?"*

She looked at me, waiting for me to finish with glossy eyes.

"The worst part is you haven't asked about Tessa once since entering this room." I scoffed. "You're still the same. You only care about yourself. You'll never change."

Allie's face was tear-stained by the time I was done talking. I wasn't sure if she was hurt by my words, or just upset that she didn't get any money to spend on drugs, so I told John to give her the one hundred dollars I had in my night bag and then I told her never to come back—that I'd rather die in that moment than see her face for another second.

I didn't care what she did with the money, but a part of me hoped she'd use it to buy the damn drugs and forget about me. Forget that she ever even birthed me.

I can't lie.

I kind of regret it, but deep down I'm angry at my mother. I'm angry at her because I wanted to grow up with her like a normal teenage girl. There was a time when I looked up to her and respected her—before all of the drugs and near-death experiences.

My mother meant the world to me when I was a child. Like all children do, they think their parents are perfect. But as I got older, realized her flaws, I also came to realize that she loved drugs and money more than her own two daughters. She chose the party life over us, most times ignoring the fact that she was married.

Dad was great. He loved us with all his heart, but lost his job as a mall security guard, leaving himself to depend on his wife to take care of the family while he job-hunted. She resorted to the easiest moneymaking tactic when she was fired from her job—becoming a drug dealer.

We were on our own even then, spending some of our days with Aunt Jessie until my mother got jealous of how Aunt Jessie took care of us and told her never to come around again.

When my mother was sentenced to prison for ten years, she managed to have us stay with our grandmother instead of Aunt Jessie, all because of a lie she'd told about her own sister. It sparked an investigation and it wasn't pretty.

Aunt Jessie treated Tessa and me like princesses—like we were her own girls. She couldn't have kids of her own, so she took us in with open arms and did a terrific job helping us when our mother was too stoned to do anything.

She was better than my mother was, and I'm sure my mother knew that. What she did was more a spiteful act to Aunt Jessie. Aunt Jessie fought for us but, unfortunately, she died six months after our mother was sentenced. She died in her sleep. She'd gotten a really bad case of pneumonia and didn't know until it was too late. I heard it was peaceful.

When my grandmother passed away and we were shuffled into foster care, I promised Tessa I would get us out. I didn't care how I did it, but I would…and I did. As soon as I turned eighteen, I found us a one-bedroom apartment to live in that was close to Tessa's high school. I walked with her to and from school every day, and instead of going to college, I worked my ass off as a waitress at two different jobs just to make sure I could pay the bills. I did all of it so that Tessa wouldn't have to worry about anything but living a nice, fulfilling life. I didn't want her to turn out like me, angry and bitter and depressed. She deserved happiness.

Tessa is a great girl with a good head on her shoulders. She respects herself and is tough, and I love that about her, but I am aware that she watched me struggle and believes my struggles should be hers too. I don't want her to have that mindset.

I know I can be tough, and it may have been rude to tell the woman who gave birth to me to stay out of my life while she saw me on my sickbed, but I had no tolerance for her bullshit or ignorance after all I'd gone through and did to survive. Enough was enough.

Prior to becoming sick, and back when my mother was still in prison, she swore she'd get clean in the letters she sent me. The sad part about it is, deep down, some part of me believed she would. That was my mistake, though. Trusting her, that is. The only reason she'd gotten out early for good behavior is because she couldn't access any of the drugs in prison like she wanted.

Ever since the day I told her to go and not come back, I never heard from or saw her again. She was gone. Just like that. Within the blink of an eye. A snap of the fingers. Like fucking magic.

Tessa thinks she'll show up again, but I know she won't. My mother knows that she fucked up with us—that she doesn't deserve to be in our lives. She doesn't want the burden of my death on her shoulders either, so keeping her distance relieves her of that guilt.

She doesn't want to have to deal with Tessa's tears when she comes to the realization that she was never there for her

—that the only person who was ever there for her baby daughter was me.

TWENTY-FOUR

Six hours later I'm grabbing the handle of my suitcase and dragging it on its wheels as I walk to my front door. I take one final look around my home, cherishing every small fixture, every family photo.

Something familiar catches my eyes and I go to pick it up. It's a framed photo of John and me on our wedding day. We were dancing to Ed Sheeran. He's looking down at me with so much love in his eyes. I have on the perfect ivory A-line wedding gown, my hair neatly pinned up. I remember this day like it was yesterday. I was laughing as he said something to me, my hand clasped in his.

My eyes burn from unshed tears. In that moment, two years ago, I was the happiest I'd ever been. I had just married the man I was going to share the rest of my life with—have kids with. A gracious, protective man who always put *me* first.

I replace the photo and look at my phone. I've called him several times and the few times he's answered, he's either been really busy or in a loud area and can't hear me. I'm too nervous to just spring something like this on him out of nowhere and a part of me thinks I should just wait to tell him when I'm at the airport and boarding my flight, that way he can't really say anything to stop me. I'll be there and it'll be happening. *Gah, I'm so selfish.*

I take out my cellphone and give John another call. It rings several times before sending me to his voicemail. I decide to leave one for him this time. Hopefully he listens to it when things are less chaotic.

"Hey John. So…um, listen. I think I'm going to go to Paris. It's a last-minute trip, but Dr. Barad said it is okay for me to go and you can call him and double check if you want. I know you won't be too happy to hear this," I sigh. "And maybe by the time you do, I won't be able to answer your call, but either way, I'll call you as soon as I land. Please don't be upset. I need this. I love you so much and I hope you kick ass at your competition."

I hang up, guilt eating away at me for not telling him *who* I'm going to Paris with. But he'll call back and he'll ask, and I'll tell him who I'm with. He won't be pleased, but I will.

This trip is for me to get away—to stop betting on which day my life will end. Everyone dreams of doing something spontaneous in their life. Fulfilling a dream. I think I deserve at least some of that before I go.

I hang up and the front door swings open. Max charges in, picking up my suitcase as I slide my phone into my tote bag.

"You ready?" he asks.

I nod, turning to face him. He smiles down at me. "I'm really glad you're coming, Shakes."

"Yeah. Me too."

Once I have the house locked up and the alarm set, we are

in Max's car and strapping our seat belts. He pulls out of the drive way slowly and it's now when my pulse catches speed.

I can't believe I'm really doing this.

It's so crazy for me to travel *hours* away from my home—away from my doctor and the love of my life. It's fucking insane, but honestly? This is what I want right now. I really, really want this. I can't keep denying myself happiness. Maybe John will finish the competition early and he can fly there too…

I sigh.

What the hell am I thinking? That would never work.

I'm hoping once John hears my voicemail, he'll understand and won't overreact. I hope he accepts my reasons once I get the chance to explain.

I look at Max as he talks nonstop about the places we'll explore and the things we'll eat and the fun places he's heard about. I smile at him. He's making this happen. He should be proud.

We check in at the airport and board our plane, settling into first-class seats.

My phone rings as I place my tote bag on my lap and I fish it out. It's John.

"Excuse me, ma'am, but we need all cellphones and electronic devices off or on airplane mode. We're about to take off." One of the flight attendants touches my arm, smiling kindly as she looks from my phone, to the tubing in my nose, and then into my eyes.

"Oh. Yes. Right. Sorry. I'll shut it off right now." I put the phone on airplane mode then tuck the phone away in my bag so the attendant can walk away.

"Come on, Shakes." Max slouches back in his seat. "Tell the hound you'll talk to him in a couple days. This time is all yours." He thinks John already knows I'm on this trip with him.

I look at my phone again and a new message is there. Must have come through before I hit airplane mode.

> John. What the hell are you thinking, Shannon!?
> PARIS??? Do NOT go on that trip!

I breathe evenly through my nostrils as best I can, turning the screen of the phone off as the flight attendant walks past me again.

I turn to look at Max. His eyes are already closed but as if he feels my stare, he reaches over to place his hand on top of mine. I glance down at his hand, how his skin is about two shades lighter than mine.

I look back up. He's already looking at me, his eyes gentle, his body lax. He leans close to me and murmurs, "Don't let him change your mind about this."

"I'm trying not to." My face goes blank as I look out of the window, watching the ground move below the plane. We're about to leave. There is truly no turning back now.

When we're in the air and the thick clouds pass by us, I close my eyes, gripping the arms of the chair, realizing that going on this trip with Maximilian Grant may not be the wisest thing to do right now.

I mean, I know it isn't and I've always known it, but this is Paris we're talking about. *Paris.*

No matter how I feel, I can't regret this. I have to remember to live, even if that means temporarily upsetting the one man who would do anything for me.

TWENTY-FIVE

The plane ride wasn't so bad.

Max had no choice but to get first class seats so I had plenty of space. Other than his mild snoring, it was okay. I don't know how he slept at all because I couldn't.

It was hard to get through. One minute I was excited and the next I was panicking. It'd been a while since I'd flown on a plane. The last time I did was when John and I flew to Colorado to spend the weekend at the mountains.

John...

He's all I've been able to think about. I'm sure he's tried calling me dozens of times. I have to remember to call him first thing as soon as we get to our hotel. Fortunately, I upgraded my phone plan for international calls and text.

When we land and exit the plane, the airport is crowded. Max pushes through the swarm of people with my arm hooked in his, our bags strapped around us.

"This is fucking insane," he says over his shoulder as we finally reach a set of glass doors. For a moment I think we've finally hit a clearing, but I'm wrong. Outside the airport is a flood of people waving their arms in the air, flagging down cabs.

Max pulls his arm out of mine, whipping out his cellphone. "I'm going to call an Uber."

I'm glad it doesn't take long for our driver to arrive.

"This way." Max turns to the right, pushing through the crowd and walking across the busy street. When we're away from the people flagging down cabs or hopping into their personal vehicles, Max makes his way toward a bridge. "You okay?" he asks me, looking over his shoulder, prepared to stop.

I nod my head, continuing the walk. "Surprisingly, I'm okay."

"Good." We cross the steel bridge where a car is already waiting. The driver greets us in French and Max says something back to him, which makes the man laugh.

"Since when do you know French?" I ask as we get in the backseat of the car.

He smirks. "I picked up a few words before coming."

The driver asks where we're going in English and then we're off, driving through the busy city.

"We made it here. What do you think so far?" Max asks as I stare out of the window in awe.

"So far? That it's such a lively, beautiful mess," I breathe, adjusting my tubing.

"And that's just coming from the airport. Imagine what it's like around the Eiffel Tower."

"What are we going to do first?" I ask, facing him.

"Well first, you're going to get some rest. We'll check in at the hotel, you can freshen up and eat—whatever you wanna do, but we can't do too much. I feel like that was already too much walking across the bridge to get to the car, plus the plane ride was exhausting, I'm sure."

"Are you kidding? I'm fine. Look at me?" I hold my hands out.

He reaches across, picking up one of the tubes. "I don't want you to do too much too soon. You barely slept on the flight. You don't have to pretend with me, Shakes."

I chew the corner of my lip. "Fine. I'll eat, rest some, but then the adventures begin."

He laughs. "Okay. That I can work with."

I pull out my phone from my tote bag, holding it up for a signal. "Damn it," I hiss.

"What's up?"

"No signal," I murmur.

"Wanna try mine?"

I frown up at him. "Yeah, right. So John can ask whose number I'm calling him from? I don't think so."

"So, you *didn't* tell him you're with me?" He looks amused by this.

"I didn't really get the chance. He's been busy in Vegas."

He nods, but I can see in his eyes he's made up his own scenarios. "What about Tessa? I'm sure she'd like to know you've landed safely."

"I'll call her when we get to the hotel." Something occurs to me and I straighten my back, tilting my chin to meet his eyes. "You booked two rooms, right?"

Max frowns. "Um, no."

"What? Max, you're joking, right? We *need* two rooms. We can't share! Are you crazy?" My heart jumps to my throat, imagining Max walking back and forth in the hotel room, a towel hanging off his waist, no shirt, showing three by two rows of perfect abs. Or even me, getting in the shower as he sits in the bedroom. My skin crawls, and I hate that it's not in a bad way.

"Why not? We'll hardly even be in the room," he says, shrugging.

My eyebrows glue together as I focus on him, loathing his careless attitude. "This is not a joke." I pull out my wallet. "I guess I'll be using my credit card to book my own room then. What's the name of the hotel?" I ask, already opening the web browser on my phone. Of course, it doesn't work because I still have no signal. Damn international plan.

"There are two rooms, Shannon! Chill! I was just kidding!"

I look him over. "Promise."

"I booked two rooms, I promise you. I'm not ignorant. Come on, you know me better than that."

I swallow hard. "Well, shit, Max, I thought you were serious—"

"I know you did." He drops his head to look down at me. "Do you really think I'm *that* selfish? To the point that I would leave you stuck in the same hotel room as me?"

I don't say anything. I can't, really. I know Max can be selfish, but he knows I am married and has respect for that. I guess this trip really is just for me.

I look up and the driver is looking through the rearview mirror at us. I snatch my gaze away, looking down at my phone screen, hoping for a signal to appear. Nothing.

The car finally comes to a stop in front of a gorgeous white building and Max opens his door and climbs out of the backseat. I follow suit, stepping out as Max rounds the trunk for our suitcases.

For a moment, I forget about the conversation Max and I just had, taken aback by the building before me.

It's exquisite. Breathtaking. It's the French dream. It looks just like the pictures I used to stare at as I scrolled through Pinterest. The rectangular windows, the arch railings that lead to the entrance. The pointy roof, making it appear as if it's some fancy castle. The revolving crystal doors. The smiling bellhop with his smooth, clean face.

"Holy shit," I breathe. "This place is perfect." I already feel like royalty and I haven't even set foot inside yet.

The bellhop greets us with a heavy French accent, asking to collect our bags. Max hands them over, tips him, then walks inside, my arm hooked through his.

We meet at the front desk, where a ginger-haired woman greets us and Max offers his name.

"Maximilian Grant, correct?" she inquires.

"Yes." Max finally releases my arm, pulling out his wallet and handing her his ID. She looks over it, handing it back and then giving him a few papers to sign. Once that's done, she hands us two room keys with a wide smile on her lips. "Your bags will be up shortly. I hope the stay is very romantic for the two of you," she says as he takes the keys.

"Oh my gosh, no. We're just friends," I say quickly.

"Oh!" She places a hand over the heart of her chest, her face turning cherry red. "My apologies, madam!"

"No worries at all." We turn for the elevator and Max has a smile on his lips. "What's funny?"

"You." He shakes his head. "It's not like anyone here cares whether we are a couple or not."

"Yeah, well..." I shrug as the elevator chimes. He has to know this is just friendly. I'm a married woman and he doesn't need to have any ideas in his head.

Once we're out of the elevator, we walk down the corridor, our shoes clicking along the marble floor. Our rooms are right beside each other.

I take my key and stick it into the lock, turning the doorknob and giving Max a swift glance before walking in. He does the same, but doesn't say anything. He just walks in, allowing his door to shut behind him.

I shut mine as well, locking it and walking in with a sigh. He chose well, I can admit. The room is fresh, the sunlight bright and rich as it pours through the windows. It warms my skin as I walk over to open one of them. But what's even better, I realize, is that across from us, several miles away, is the Eiffel tower.

Aw, Max.

He did this.

He knew I'd want to wake up to this view in the mornings. I'm so grateful that he still knows me. His heart was in a good place when he decided to bring me here. I can appreciate that.

I turn around, admiring the fluffy white and gold sheets and pillows, the white calla lilies in a vase on top of the nightstand beside the large canopy bed. I run my fingers over the sheer white curtain surrounding the bed. Everything in this room is so elegant, so beautiful—way better than I imagined.

"So what do you think?"

A deep voice sounds behind me and I gasp, spinning around and facing Max. He stands in front of an open door, leaning a shoulder against the wall, fingers in his pockets.

"What the hell, Max?" I walk up to him, looking through the door behind him. In there is a room identical to mine. I then look up at him, narrowing my eyes.

"I said we had two different rooms. I never said they weren't connected."

"Wow. Well, I'm locking the door," I inform him, walking to my bed and sitting.

"Do as you please." He dangles the key in his hand. "I have a key, though. Someone has to keep watch over you."

He sits beside me, quiet a beat, looking at the view of the tower. "Do you like it?" he asks.

"Max, I love it. Seriously. This room and this view are incredible."

He looks down at me, his eyes shimmering in the sunlight. "I'm glad you like it. I wanted the best for you."

"Well, you did great." I look down at his hand and how close it is to mine. We've been way too close lately and it's unsettling. Max, he's always going to want more from me. He's going to want to be near me, to touch me, but I can't allow it. I stand, walking to the window to look out of it and to create some proximity.

A knock sounds on his door and he looks back at it, and I'm relieved instantly. "That's probably our bags," he says. "I'm gonna hit the shower. I'll be back to see what you want to eat. I'm starving."

I nod as he walks through the connecting doors to get to his room. He answers his door, takes the bags, pays the bellhop again, and then brings my suitcase to my room.

He's gone again, clicking the connecting door shut behind him.

I sit on the bed, sighing. Grabbing the handle of my tote back, I dig through it until I pull out my cellphone.

"Finally," I breathe when I see there's a signal.

My phone buzzes just as I'm about to call John. He's calling me. He must have been calling constantly. My heart jumps to my throat, but I tap the green button anyway, bracing myself for the backlash.

"Hey, babe," I answer.

"No," he snaps. "Don't *hey babe* me. What the hell are you thinking, Shannon? Fucking Paris? I leave you for a few days and you do something as crazy as that? Don't tell me Tessa got into your head about this!"

"No, John. This was *my* decision. I wanted to come here."

"Why?" His voice breaks. "Why couldn't you just wait until I got back?"

"John, listen, I know you're upset," I murmur, standing and walking to the window. "But I am fine and like I said in the voicemail, Dr. Barad said it was okay."

"I know. I called him and chewed him the hell out about it," he grumbles. "I'm cancelling the rest of my trip here in Vegas and flying out there. I should be there with you."

"No." My voice is abrupt. "Just…just stay there, John. Stop worrying about me so much, okay? Please. I'm not even staying here for long. I will be back before you even leave Vegas. It'll be like I never even left."

"I can't believe this," he grumbles.

"Do you trust me?" I ask.

"What?" My question has clearly caught him off guard.

"Do you trust me, John?"

"Of course I trust you. It's Tessa I don't trust you out there with. I know she's your sister, but she pushes you too close to the edge sometimes, Shannon."

I hesitate on how to respond. He should know I'm not with Tessa. I can't have him thinking that this whole trip.

"John…you should probably know that I didn't fly to Paris with Tessa."

He's quiet for so long I think he's hung up. "Jesus, Shannon. Please don't tell me you went to Paris with that Max guy."

I don't even know how to respond to that. I just close my eyes, waiting for him to take my silence as an answer.

"Are you kidding me? No—fuck that! This changes everything! I'm leaving right now to come and get you!"

"No, John! You cannot do that! You don't even know where I am! I told you I'm fine! I want this!"

"Was this his idea? Huh?"

"No. I wanted to go," I state, refusing to allow the opportunity for John to lay any blame on Max. "And I'm already here."

"I cannot fucking believe this. I ask you not to do anything crazy and you fly off with *another* man to *another* country!"

Wow. When he says it like that, it sounds awful. But Max is a long-time friend. We've been friends for years, despite the differences we had in the past.

I hear John huffing on his end of the phone. "What are you doing?" I ask.

"Going back to my room to pack."

"John, you cannot come to Paris. You have a competition." I try keeping my voice calm, hoping it'll calm him.

"I don't give a damn about the competition! My sick *wife* is in Paris. She's not safe!"

"I'm perfectly fine, John!" I snap, and I don't intend for my voice to be so loud, but it is, and I can't help it. "I'm fine and will be seeing a doctor every single day while I'm here who will make sure I'm alright. I will sightsee, I will take my time, I will live in this moment because, damn it, I deserve it, okay? I'm sorry that I can't live in this moment with you, but this was a once in a lifetime opportunity for me, John. You wouldn't have taken me to Paris in the condition I'm in—I know you. You wouldn't have dared, but Max was willing to take the risk so that I could live for once." I choke on a sob and close my eyes, but it does nothing to mask the pain, or stop the tears from falling.

"You're sick, Shannon. This is not good for you and you know it," John says, but his voice isn't as strong as it was before. "I—I only want the best for you."

"Well if you want the best for me, you'll let me enjoy my

time here. You'll hold back your anger for now and let me have this. You can yell at me all you want when I'm back home, but I told you I need this, so please, John. Let me have it."

He makes a noise and I can tell he's hesitating on what to say next. I sit in the cushioned chair in the corner, dropping my face into one of my palms.

"If something happens to you..."

"Nothing will happen to me," I say back.

"I don't know that."

"I don't either, but I believe that nothing will. I believe that I will come back home to you."

"Fuck, Shannon," he groans, and I hear the anguish in his voice. This is cutting my husband deep.

"I'm sorry, John," I whisper.

He doesn't say anything to that. I hear whimsical noises in his background and men chatting. Someone pounds on my door, startling me, and I look up at it.

"Open up, Shakes! I'm hungry!"

"Who is that?" John murmurs.

"Max. He wants to take me to get something to eat."

John sighs. Nothing more.

"I'll call you in a few hours, okay? Just please don't worry —I mean, you can worry, but please know that I am okay and I am being as careful as I possibly can."

"Yeah, Shannon. Okay."

"I love you," I whisper.

"Yeah. Love you."

He hangs up and I lower the phone as it beeps, staring down at my screensaver—a photo of John and me kissing on our honeymoon cruise, fireworks going off behind us. Right before everything went to shit.

The door clicks and in walks Max with his key in hand.

"See, I knew these connecting rooms would come in handy."

"I'm not hungry right now," I mutter, avoiding his eyes.

"Well, you have to eat," Max says, exasperated with me already. "Come on. There's a café right downstairs. They've been rated five stars. You'll love it. My treat."

I climb off of the bed and go to my suitcase. I feel terrible for being here—guilty, even. Am I selfish for coming here? Am I wrong for doing this?

"Give me a minute to get dressed."

"Okay." Max clearly takes my mood into consideration because when I look over my shoulder, he's gone. I go to the bathroom, which is made mostly of white marble, and get dressed. When I'm freshened up, I walk out and Max rounds the corner, looking me over in my jeans and yellow tank top.

"I was thinking we could make a little stop after we eat," Max offers. "Unless you're too tired."

"No. I'm okay. A quick trip sounds nice."

"Okay, good." He smiles way too hard, like a child with a secret. "There's something I want to show you."

"Okay, but you should know I'm really not that hungry, Max." I put on my shoes, then grab my jetpack, room key, and cellphone.

"Okay, that's fine. Just chill with me while I grab a bite then because I'm starving."

"Sure." I smile, leaving the room with him and heading for the elevator. Silence surrounds us a moment.

"You talked to John, I presume?" Max asks when we're in the elevator.

"Yeah. He's not happy."

"Of course, he isn't. He's worried."

"I know."

Max is quiet again, looking down at the tips of his basketball shoes. "Well, like I said before, don't let him change your mind about this. You're here now, living the dream. You might as well enjoy it, right?"

"Yeah." I force a smile. "You're right. I just worry about him."

"I know." Max wraps an arm around me, hugging me in an awkward sideways position. "But, like I promised, you'll have a good time."

TWENTY-SIX

PAST

It was a hot day in Charlotte. Hotter than usual, actually. The sun was blazing with no breeze or cloud in sight to cool anyone down.

This kind of weather was great to me. I loved a hot summer day. My hair was pulled up into a bun, a round, dark pair of sunglasses on my face. I had my favorite blue bikini on and a French magazine in my hands as I lay on a lounge chair at the pool in Max's complex.

Max climbed out of the pool and walked my way, dripping with water. Picking up his towel, he wiped most of it away, his chest and abs flexing as he moved. I swear I was never going to get tired of looking at him.

"What's that?" he asked.

"A magazine about Paris," I answered, lowering the magazine.

"You're telling me Paris lives inside that magazine?" He sat down beside me and then took the booklet from me.

"Hey!" I squealed as I sat up and reached for it back but he kept moving his long arms further away so I couldn't get it. "Max, come on. I wasn't done reading it!"

"What's so interesting about it?" He scanned the pages.

"Well, if you give it to me, I can show you."

He handed it back with a cocky grin. "Okay. Show me."

I watched him carefully. He seemed serious enough. He was still smiling, but he was a goofball that way. This was as serious as he was going to get right now.

"Well, Paris has a lot to explore. A lot to do. A lot to eat."

"I love that last part," he teased.

"See—look." I pointed at a picture of the Eiffel Tower. "I would love to see the Eiffel Tower up close one day. People say the pictures don't do it justice. You have to actually be there to experience the true beauty of it. It's first on my bucket list."

Max nodded. He was listening.

I flipped the page and smiled. "And this bike—I want one so bad, but they are so damn expensive. I would love to just go to Paris, ride around on one of these bikes, and breathe in the city air. It would be so amazing. They rent the bikes out, you know?"

"Wow. You really want to go to Paris, huh?"

"Yeah." I bit a smile. "You should take me one day. Will you?"

He looked up at me, a subtle smile on his lips. Tilting his head and taking the magazine from me, he moved closer, cupping his hands around my waist. He placed a kiss on my cheek and then my temple.

"My girl gets whatever she wants. When I take over my dad's club in Wilmington, I'll make sure I save up enough money to take you one day."

"I would love that." I tipped my chin, and his lips were only inches away from mine.

"I bet you would."

"What if I decide I want to live there?"

"Then I will be there with you," he said.

"No you wouldn't," I giggled.

"Yeah I would," he swore. "Wherever you go, I go too, babe."

"But what about the club?"

He winked. "I can manage."

"Say you promise to take me then?"

"I promise to take you one day. I will give you whatever you want. No questions asked." His face turned serious, and not before long his warm, smooth lips pressed to mine.

I sighed as I melted in his arms. As if it weren't hot enough, he was surely cranking up the heat.

"I hope you are a man of your word, Grant."

He smirked, gave me a swift kiss, and then stood up from the chair. A sly grin took over his face as he picked me up in his arms and marched toward the pool.

"Oh my gosh, no! Max! Put me down!" I squealed, clinging to him.

But it was too late. He threw me in the water and jumped in right after and we were both in the cold water. While we were under, I could see him smile at me, and I couldn't help smiling back.

When we resurfaced, I swam to him and he murmured how much he loved me as he cupped my ass in his hands.

I wrapped my legs around his waist, sighing as I kissed him.

I loved him so much. He simply had no idea.

TWENTY-SEVEN

We catch lunch in the café downstairs, as Max mentioned. This café serves some of the best coffee I have ever tasted.

I've just had a cream cheese filled pastry with chocolate drizzle on top of it while Max practically ate like a pig, devouring pastries, sandwiches made with baguettes, macarons, and even a rigatoni pasta with tomato sauce. For someone so tall and slender, he has a real appetite on him.

After going back and forth about it while we ate, we decide to go for our first siting. Unfortunately, we get lost a few times along the way, so by the time we reach our destination, the sun is setting.

"I could've sworn we were on the right train," Max says as we walk down the sidewalk. We pass several pedestrians, some of whom are couples, holding hands, and smiling at one another. I purposely keep my eyes away from them, focusing on my surroundings, the paved roads and flats.

We stop in front of a shop, and Max tells me to wait. Less than a minute later an older man is walking out of the shop behind Max with the handles of a bike in his hands. The bike is a robin egg blue, the handles silver, and a brown basket on the front of the bike with a bouquet of pink peonies placed neatly inside it.

I gasp at the sight of it.

"Well?" Max asks as the man hands the bike over to him. "What do you think?"

It's one of the vintage bikes I've always wanted. Granted, I can't really ride the damn thing right now, but wow. It's so stunning I want to cry.

"It's beautiful, Max." I run my fingers over the leather of the seat.

"I hate that today was a waste of a day," he sighs. "Otherwise I'd take you on a ride."

"No." I smile at him. "Today was nice. I saw more than I thought I would."

Max nods, pushing my brand-new bike through a garden, his fingers wrapped around the handles.

"I just thought about something," he says.

I stop walking. "What's that?"

"How in the hell are we gonna get this bike back to the U.S.? International flights are a bitch. I can only imagine the shipping."

I laugh out loud, grabbing one of silver handles of the bike with one hand and running my fingers across the shiny blue paint with the other. "That's what you're worried about?" My shoulders lift carelessly. "I won't really be able to use it once we're back anyway. John wouldn't even let me touch this thing if he saw it."

"John, John, John." Max looks me dead in the eyes, a glint in his. "Have you realized just how many times you've mentioned him since we've landed? I'm starting to think you'd rather him be here than me."

"That is not true!"

He doesn't look assured at all.

"I mean…" I huff. "Do I miss him? Of course, I do. But this trip is a gift from you. You promised it to me and I'm so thankful for it."

"Aw. That's so touching." He grins and the sun makes his teeth sparkle, the wind blowing his cologne past my nose.

I start to grip the bike handles with both hands, but a sudden wave of nausea hits me and I grip the strap of my backpack, staggering a bit.

Max's face turns hard, his brows immediately stitching together. "You okay? Need to sit?"

My head bobs, and to avoid any conflict or cause a scene, I walk to the nearest empty bench with Max. Once seated, I absorb as much of my surroundings as I can, waiting for the nausea to fade.

"I can't believe I'm actually in Paris," I breathe. It's always best to change the subject.

Max gives me an odd look as he parks the bike next to the bench. "I honestly didn't think you'd come." He sits next to me, watching people walk by too. "There's something I've been meaning to tell you and I hope you don't take it the wrong way."

"What?" I give him my undivided attention and when his face changes and he's no longer got his easy-going smile in place, I frown, placing my hand on his arm. "Max, what is it?"

"This trip wasn't exactly all-planned for you." He lifts his head, looking me in the eyes.

"Oh." I nod. "I get it. It's not supposed to be *me* sitting here with you. It's supposed to be some other girl, right?"

He frowns. "What? No, Shannon." He busts out laughing. "No. This trip was supposed to be for me only. No one else."

"I don't get it…"

"This was a one-way trip but I pushed it ahead and

booked another seat so you would be able to join me. I was going to live here, start fresh once you...well, you know." He pauses, and I swallow the brick in my throat. "I thought for a while it wasn't going to be possible to bring you with your disease and everything. I figured why not move somewhere where I'll never be able to forget you...you know?"

"Oh." My lips press together and I lower my gaze. "Wow."

"Not that I would have forgotten you at home either," he states, immediately backing himself up. "It's just that I still can't believe it sometimes." His voice is much lighter, not as deep as usual. "I just can't believe that it's *you* I'm going to lose. Out of everyone in my life, I hate that it's you and I know you don't want to hear that, but I can't keep those words to myself anymore. It's not fair."

"You won't lose me. I will always be here, Max. I will always be right there." I point at the heart of his chest.

He struggles to put on a smile. "How can you take this so lightly?"

"I guess I've just gotten used to the idea of not being here anymore."

A flash of pain runs across his face, like a quick shadow. He tries hiding it but I spot it as clear as day. "I haven't."

Our eyes lock, only briefly. Then I look away, down at my lap. The nausea has faded now.

"Uh, listen." He points to the bike, changing the subject quickly, and I'm glad. "I know you can't ride that thing so what do you say we pretend to be E.T. and Elliot. I pedal and you ride this baby to the moon."

"That is a very odd scenario," I giggle. "But okay." I clasp my hands together, standing as I adjust my jetpack. "Let's do it!"

The corners of his mouth quirks up as he grabs the bike handles and steadies it. After helping me sit, he orders me to hang onto him as he grips the handlebar. I climb on behind him and clutch him around the middle, way too giddy for this ride.

"Ready?" he asks over his shoulder, excitement laced in his deep voice.

"Yeah, I think so." I look around. People are leaving the garden now. "I think they're closing," I say, but he totally disregards me, pushing off and pedaling forward.

I yelp, clinging tighter to him as the cool breeze rushes by me, blowing through my hair. Max zigzags through the garden, riding right by tourists, laughing heartily as we whiz past boxed hedges.

"Hey!" A security guard calls after us.

"Oh shit!" Max pedals faster as the security guard starts to run in our direction. I squeal as he makes a large loop and zooms through the perfectly trimmed grass, hurrying for the exit.

"Oh my God!" I shout, laughing as I look over my shoulder. Max speeds through the park exit, pedaling until the security guard stops and waves a fuming fist at us, huffing rapidly.

Glancing over his shoulder, Max breaks out laughing, riding the bike casually for about two minutes until we come to a stop in front of a museum.

I hop off the bike, exhilarated and laughing so hard my chest hurts. Max kicks the kickstand down, glancing back once more to make sure we aren't being followed.

"That was insane!" I shout.

"I guess we were riding too fast, huh?" he laughs.

"Way too fast. You're insane!"

"Still a rebel," he says with a shrug. His eyes soften a touch as he looks me over briefly. He then points his line of sight to a museum across the street. "I heard Mona Lisa's smile is in the Louvre."

"Yeah. We have to go see her. Tomorrow morning, please?" I beg, turning to face him.

"Tomorrow it is, Shakes. For now, I need to get you back to the hotel for some rest."

My chest heaves and Max grabs my hand, eyebrows lifting with concern. "Ten minute check?"

I hold two thumbs up. "All good. I feel the OPX kicking in."

"Okay. Good." He brings me forward by the shoulders, his eyes turning soft. "I think that's enough excitement for today, though. Let's go."

He pushes the kickstand back, grabbing the handlebars and walking with me at my pace. He doesn't make me feel weird or awkward about how slow I'm going.

Even as people pass by us, walking swiftly, ready to explore the next big thing, he doesn't mind it and I have to admit, this feels nice. The sun is beneath the horizon now, the moon taking its wake. The city night lights are on, twinkling like stars. I smell pasta and tomato sauce and coffee and bread. So many aromas, yet somehow it all blends to perfection.

Max talks about the security guard as we walk and I tease him about how he could have ended up in jail somewhere. Our mix of laughter and chatter continues, even in The Metro and during the train ride back to the hotel.

When we get back to the hotel, I hang out in Max's room for a while. We watch funny French movies and chow down on macarons Max ordered from the cafe, not having a clue what in the hell the shows are saying.

Around 2 a.m., I'm yawning and ready for bed.

"You need your rest. It's been a long day," Max murmurs.

"Yeah. I think I need to switch out my OPX bag too."

Max doesn't hesitate to pick me up in his arms and take me to the door that connects to my room. He walks through the threshold, placing me on the center of the bed and then going for my suitcase, pulling out one of the plastic bags.

He grabs my silver device next, unlatching the hook, taking out the nearly empty bag, and applying the new one.

I taught him how to do it at the airport while we waited, just in case I was too tired or too weak to do it myself.

When he's all finished, he slips out of the room, allowing me to change into my pajamas. I call for him when I'm done, sliding beneath the cool, puffy sheets and snuggling with the pillows.

"All good?" he asks, one eyebrow piqued.

"I might need the pink pill." He squints his eyes at me, confused. "It helps me relax." I point at the vanity and he looks back, going for the case of pills on top of it. He pulls out one of the pink pills, digs in the fridge for a bottle of water, and I down the pill, smoothing the swallow with a swig of water. "Thanks."

"No problem. You all good now?" he asks for the final time.

"Yes," I whisper, revealing an innocent smile as I curl beneath the blanket. "All good."

"Okay. Well, goodnight, Shakes." He walks to the connecting door again, flipping the light switch as he passes it. "I'll see you in the morning." The room darkens, but there are wisps of light seeping in through his room. He's not gone yet.

"Max?" I call.

"Yeah?"

"Today was great. I didn't mind getting lost with you."

He laughs softly. "I didn't mind getting lost with you either, Shakes."

I'm quiet for a moment and he remains in place, unsure if he should proceed to his room or stay.

So, I give him a choice. "Do you think you can stay in here with me for at least an hour, monitor my breathing?"

"Oh—right." He shuts the door, walking back to the bed. "Tessa told me about that. Just listen, right?"

"Yeah. But don't be like Tessa. She runs a finger under my nose to feel my breath every five minutes."

We both laugh. "Alright. You got it." He takes the cushioned chair beside the bed.

"You can turn the TV on if you want. I don't mind."

He picks up the remote, flipping to a comedy.

I listen to him laugh and make smart-ass remarks about the shows until, eventually, I'm asleep and his laughter blends with my dreams.

The dreams are delightful at first.

A man is whispering to me as he stands behind me. His voice is deep and warm and comforting. I turn and the man is holding me in front of the Eiffel Tower, his arms wrapped around my waist while mine are wrapped around the back of his neck.

The man is Max. Our eyes are locked. We're too close together but it doesn't feel wrong.

John appears during the dream, searching the city for me, asking everyone if they've seen a woman who looks like me. He finds me and when he does, I'm kissing Max in front of the tower.

John calls my name and I gasp. Then he charges up to Max, ready to tackle and fight him, but before he can make it, Max vanishes into thin air.

I wake up, panting heavily, looking at Max who is now asleep in the chair, slouched with his head slightly turned to the side. The TV is still on. He hasn't left my side.

Tucking my hair back and controlling my breathing, I grab the remote control, turning the TV off and relaxing again. I take off my tubes and flop back down on the pillows, blowing out a steady breath and staring up at the canopy sheets.

I shift around constantly, which eventually causes Max to wake up and reach for me. "Hey." His voice is thick, groggy. "You okay?"

"Yeah. Fine. Just can't sleep."

"Uncomfortable?"

"No. I'll be okay. You don't have to stay in that uncomfortable chair all night. You can go back to your room if you want."

He sits back in the chair, lips twisting, his body adjusting in the dark. "I'll stay until you fall asleep again."

"Kay." I cuddle with the blankets, listen to the clock ticking on the wall. "Max?"

"Yeah?"

"Think you can sing that song for me? The one you used to sing when you spent the night at my place?"

"Aw man." He laughs and I grin. "Okay. One sec." He sits up, grabbing my hand and stroking the back of it as he starts to sing *I See Fire* by Ed Sheeran.

Don't get me wrong, Max has a horrible voice—it's all crackly, deep, and awkward—but it has always comforted me.

He sung it one night during karaoke at a bar that had two dollar drink night. It was great. Since then, this was the song he'd sing whenever I needed a pick-me-up or a good laugh.

While he sings, I drift to sleep again.

I dream, but this time it's a peaceful dream. I'm surrounded by the people I love.

John.

Tessa.

Danny.

Max.

My friends from Capri.

Even Grandma Lane, Aunt Jessie, and my father, Abraham Hales. The only thing is I'm not actually there. I'm gone already, but in my heart, I'm glad to be gone. Instead of weeping at a funeral, they're celebrating the fact that I'm no longer suffering while they cradle mugs of coffee or hold plates of cake.

They're celebrating the life of Shannon Hales-Streeter... celebrating me.

They're smiling. Dancing. Sharing funny, beautiful memories.

It's lovely—so lovely I feel Max rub my back to partially wake me out of my sleep. I hear a whimper escape me, but I can't pull myself out of the dream.

It carries on. Big smiles. Laughter. Cake. Drinks.

When I finally wake up, the warm stretch of horizon sun is kissing my skin. Max is no longer in the chair next to my bed.

The room is empty, so I take all the time I need to cry.

TWENTY-EIGHT

When the sun is higher in the sky and my tears are gone, I go to a clinic where Dr. Barad's colleague, Whitney Monroe, a beautiful African-American woman who reminds me of Kelly Rowland, gives me a quick lung and body check.

"Have fun, but don't do anything too extreme," Dr. Monroe insists after the checkup. "Make sure you continue your OPX as well. As long as you do, you should be fine, so long as you are careful."

"I will," I say, smiling as I sling my bag over my shoulder and meet Max by the door. "Thanks for squeezing me in. Have a great day, Dr. Monroe."

"You as well, Mrs. Streeter."

After I'm finally free, Max and I are on our way to the Le Louvre to stare Mona Lisa right in the eyes.

"Look how she smirks," I murmur, staring at the painting. "She looks like she's up to no good…or like she knows *we* are up to no good."

Max laughs way too hard, catching the eye of a few

annoyed people who turn their noses up at us when we look at them. "What makes you think we're up to no good?"

"Maybe she doesn't appreciate how I just skipped off with my damn ex to another country like it was no big deal."

"Hmm…I don't know. She seems like the type who can appreciate a girl taking a risk," Max says, shrugging. He has a point.

We continue exploring the museum, taking in each delicate painting and sculpture. When we're done and have caught lunch in a nearby restaurant with the best spaghetti, Max leads the way to the exit, looking up at the gray clouds as we step outside.

"Looks like rain is coming."

"Damn." I poke my bottom lip out, watching the clouds bundle in grey masses.

Max pulls out his cellphone, checking a weather app. "Thirty percent chance. I think we're good for now. A little rain won't hurt anybody. If it starts, we can go somewhere until it passes. What do you wanna do next?"

"Oh! I read something in a brochure this morning about a flea market around here. They say you can find some really nice antiques if you're lucky."

We search the name in our web browser and once Max finds it, he leads the way to the streets to catch a cab.

When we make it to the flea market, Max asks, "What exactly do you expect to find here?"

"I want to get something for Tessa and John. Something they'll remember me by." I step under one of the tents that has baskets full of trinkets, paintings leaning against the walls, and books on a large shelf to my right.

Max reaches up and takes down a vintage looking tennis racket, swinging it like a maniac. The man behind the counter gives Max a stern look over his newspaper, and Max presses his lips and lowers the racket.

"You'd better stop before he grills your ass," I say, laughing.

"Yep. Putting it back now." He hangs the racket back up and then steps beside me as I dig through one of the baskets. I notice something bright and glossy in one of the baskets in front of me and sift it out, only to discover it's a glass angel. It's pink with a chipped wing, but despite the damage and scratches, it is exquisite.

I run my fingers over it, rubbing off the collected dust and smoothing out some of the scrapes. I wonder why something so remarkable and easy to break is in a basket full of metal and steel objects. Maybe it was misplaced.

"I'm gonna go check out the shop over there," Max tells me, pointing out of the tent.

"Sure. I'll meet you there when I'm done."

I watch him leave before turning and looking at the man, asking, "How much for this?"

"I will give it to you for five euros." His accent is heavy as he holds up four long fingers. I walk up to the counter and wrinkles form around the older man's eyes as he smiles.

"Five euros for this? That's all?"

He nods as I hand it to him. "Beautiful isn't it? But damaged." He lifts it up, and then reaches in his back pocket for a handkerchief.

After wiping it off carefully, he places it on top of a gift wrap sheet and wraps it for me, tucking it neatly in a brown paper bag.

"It's gorgeous," I tell him, taking the bag. "I was wondering why it was stuck in a bin with the heavy stuff."

"Ahh, you should not let this beauty fool you. That is very

strong glass it is made of. Very hard to break. As you saw, there is only one small chip of the wing."

"How is that possible?"

"Let's just say, I know the person who created it." He points at the bag. "And you want to know a funny thing?"

"What's that?"

"He told me that he would put it in that basket with those heavy objects and said to me that if someone finds it and wants it, that it will be meant for them to find. The person who takes it with them will be a courageous, humble, and strong individual." He studies the tubing connected to my nose, a wave of sympathy running in his eyes. "He said that whoever finds this will appreciate that his glass doesn't break because the person who sees it believes in its durability and it's beauty, and for that, the person who buys it is just as durable and just as beautiful."

"Wow," I breathe. "That's really lovely. Now I'm really going to cherish it." I dig in my backpack for the money, but he shakes his head, waving a hand. "Never mind that. It is yours to keep. Take it."

My heart swells. "Are you sure? I would like your friend to be paid for his work."

His face saddens. "My friend is no longer with us, but he'd be happy to know his work is being carried around, I'm sure." He smiles, and I can tell it's a genuine smile.

I swallow hard, my eyes burning. Blinking my tears away and stepping away slowly, I stare down at my bag before looking up at the man once more, thanking him graciously before turning and walking out of the tent.

I step to the side, drawing in a much needed breath, and then take out the angel in its brown wrapping paper. It really is beautiful, so carefully detailed.

In a way, I can relate to this angel. I may seem weak and fragile, but I am still strong. I have the strength to get through anything. This angel is flawed and full of imperfections, just like me—able to give out at any given moment, but not knowing when, like me.

Max walks out of the tent across from me with a bag in his hand. "You okay?" he asks.

"Yeah." I hold up the angel to show him. "I bought this for myself."

He presses his lips, looking it over. "That's...cool."

"It's an angel, weirdo." I roll my eyes. "It's nice, right?"

"Yeah. I like it." He digs in his bag, pulling out a vintage gold locket. Opening it, he says, "Got this for ten euros. Not really sure what I'm going to put inside it though, or who I'm giving it too. Guess we'll see."

"Aww, Max."

"It's fucking corny, I know."

"No, it's not. Stop it. It's thoughtful. You'll make some lady feel very special with it one day."

I wrap my angel up as we continue strolling through the flea market. We spend at least an hour here, searching for the perfect gifts for Tessa and John.

John is easy. I buy him a case of vintage cutting knives and wooden spoons. There's no way he'd be able to cook with them, but they would look nice in our kitchen for a display.

Tessa is a little tougher to shop for, but when I finally come across the right gift, I gasp, pulling it out slowly.

"Oh my gosh." I hold up the roman-numerals clock, grinning from ear-to-ear. "For the girl who refuses to ever be late for anything!"

"The girl who is always on time." Max groans. "Man, I

used to hate when she'd call you thirty minutes in advance just to make sure you were picking her up on time."

I laugh, collecting the black and beige clock and checking out at the counter.

We catch the bus back to our hotel, laughing and bragging about our finds. Max goes on and on about how his is more important than mine. I tell him that if he were there to hear just what the man had to say, he'd realize just how important mine actually is—that it was meant for me to find this glassy pink angel.

What that man said, those words are still stuck in my head. I will never be able to forget them. They gave me some sort of peace, like maybe I was meant to come to Paris all along. Don't get me wrong, I still feel guilty as hell about John and making him upset, but I can't lie and say this doesn't feel right.

I'm supposed to be here right now. Enjoying this moment. Holding this angel. Standing next to Max. How can anyone feel bad about this?

My smile never fades, even as I look at Max, watching as he points across the street at a building, saying he's heard of the place and how we should go there tomorrow. It's been so long since I've seen him so calm and collected. *Years*, honestly.

Max, he's stronger now and he has every reason to be because his past was difficult. To this day, I know the tragedies haunt him.

I tried keeping up with him in the past, especially when reality would hit him hard. I tried fighting his demons with him, but he only pushed me away.

What many don't know is that Max abandoned me for a short period of time while we were together. Even though it was brief, it felt like a lifetime and, to this day, it still kind of hurts to think about.

I can forgive him now for all of it because I know that some demons are really hard to fight. But back then, it was so hard for me to forgive him because my love for him was so unconditional, and I couldn't accept the fact that his love for me wasn't the same.

TWENTY-NINE

PAST

Max and I had planned a trip to Hilton Head Island for Fourth of July weekend. I could picture it before it'd even happened. It was going to be so romantic. Large ocean waves and the bright bold sun to bask in. It would be peaceful, relaxing.

It was the first time Max wasn't going to spend the 4th with his parents. This, to me, proved we'd made progress in our relationship. He wanted to be with me, and I'd felt like the luckiest girl in the world. It'd been a year and two months for us now.

His mother, a beautiful woman with high cheekbones (that Max clearly got from her) and rich brown eyes, hugged him tight. She was a petite woman and, standing in front of Max, she looked like a child hugging a tree. It was so cute I laughed.

"Hey now," she said, looking at me with a playful smile, "don't you laugh. Come here! You get one too." My lips broke into a soft smile as I walked to her, falling into her tight embrace.

She made a noise as if she didn't ever want to let me go. It was weird feeling this kind of affection from someone else's mother. I'd never really received that kind of love, but it felt nice and warm and comforting.

Max's mom invited me over for dinner often. We even went shopping together here and there, just me and her. We bonded quite well. We'd shop and splurge and laugh and then grab pretzels from Auntie Anne's along with their delicious strawberry lemonade.

Finally releasing me, Mrs. Grant stepped back and Max gave her a swift kiss on the cheek. "Love you, Mom. We gotta go," Max said, grabbing my hand and leading the way to his car.

I slid in the passenger seat, clipping my seat belt as he brought the engine to life.

"Be safe!" The Grant's called as they stood on their porch.

Max waved a hand out of his open window, hollering, "I love you!" When we were out of the neighborhood, he laughed and said, "My parents will never let me grow up."

"They're wonderful people," I said. "I'm sure it'll be different for them this year since you won't be with them. They'll miss you."

"Yeah, I know." He grabbed my hand and squeezed it. "They adore you, you know?"

"I adore them too."

With the traffic, the ride turned out to be a four-hour drive. I dozed off a couple times, awaking to a nudge on the arm here and there from Max who asked me several times if I was hungry or needed a restroom break.

I stayed awake during the final hour of our ride, singing

some tunes by Maroon 5 and The Foo Foo Fighters with him.

I was giddy by the time we pulled up to the hotel. Max popped the trunk open, pulling out my suitcase and then his before slinging a backpack over his shoulder.

"I don't think you're ready for this weekend, babe," he said as I shut the passenger door.

"Are you kidding? I've been anticipating this trip for weeks. I finally get to relax, have a couple drinks. This is so rare for me."

His brows lifted as he rounded the car. "I'm glad you get to enjoy it with me."

He started for the hotel door and I walked in with him. His phone rang as we met at the check-in counter and he sighed, rustling around in his pocket as the woman behind the counter waited patiently.

"Apologies," he murmured, smiling at her. I forced a smile at her too, then quickly looked away.

Max still had a smile on his lips as he flipped the phone over and checked the screen. But as he read over whatever message was on his screen, his smile slowly faded.

"Max? What's wrong?" I asked.

"Uh—just give me one minute." He dropped the bags, causing them to thump on the ground, and then turned away to call someone. The phone was glued to his ear as he walked to the lounge area.

"Max?" I called again, stepping up to him. His face was paler, his eyes darker. What the hell was going on?

"Yeah. I'll be there." He lowered the phone, staring at the walls made of glass ahead.

"Max?" I said his name in a smaller voice. Something was definitely wrong.

"We have to go back."

"Back where?" I asked, but he didn't answer me. Instead, he went back to our bags that he'd dropped in front of the counter and snatched them up.

"Max?" I hissed as he slung them over his shoulder. "What is going on? Talk to me."

"I'm sorry to do this, but can you cancel our reservation?" Max requested, focused on the receptionist behind the counter.

"Um...sure. Maximilian Grant, correct?"

"Yes. Thanks."

Max turned and hustled for the exit and I scurried after him. Dumping the bags in the trunk and slamming it closed, he hurried to get behind the wheel of his car. I climbed in the passenger seat again, staring at him.

"Why did you cancel the reservation? What the hell is going on?" I demanded.

He didn't look at me, just stared ahead, eyes distant, no emotion whatsoever on his face. He was starting to worry me now. I'd never seen him like this. Speechless. Unmoving.

"Max?" I pleaded, placing my hand on top of his. "Max, please," I begged in a whisper. "Tell me what's going on. Tell me what happened. You're scaring me."

Finally, he looked my way, and when he did, a slow tear made its way down his cheek.

His voice cracked when he finally said, "My parents..."

"What about them?" I insisted.

"They...um...they were just in a car wreck. There was a crash." He swallowed hard, looking through the windshield again. "That was a cop calling me. He said they...that they aren't going to make it." I gasped and he finally looked me right in the eyes. "They're gone, Shannon. My parents... they're gone."

I kept my hand on his arm, but I was at a complete loss for words.

Gone? As in...dead? But...how? Why? We'd just seen them, just hugged and kissed them goodbye. How was this possible?

"Oh my God, Max." I had no words. Truly, I had none.

Max's gaze dropped and then his body shuddered so hard I thought he might break. His hand wrapped around mine and squeezed and it hurt, but not as much as the hurt in my heart.

How the hell had this happened? *Why* did it happen?

"I'm so sorry," I whispered, bringing his forehead to mine. "Oh, I'm so sorry, baby."

He sobbed harder, his thick tears landing on the middle console.

"Here," I whispered. "Let me drive back."

It took a while, but I managed to get him to move to the passenger seat and as soon as I did, I entered the address in the GPS on my phone and drove away from what was supposed to be a special getaway for us and back to our hometown. The getaway didn't matter anymore. Nothing else mattered but getting Max back to Charlotte.

The ride was already overcome with gloom, but what made it worse was the rain that had started on our way back. I looked over and Max's forehead was pressed to the window as he cried harder.

We finally made it to the city, parking at the police station where Eugene was already waiting in the parking lot with a cigarette pinched between his fingers.

"Fuck, Max," Eugene said when he saw him. "I'm so sorry."

Max ignored him, walking right past him and marching into the station. A detective was called for him and Max was sent to the back. I stayed in the waiting area. This felt too personal and I didn't know if he wanted me there.

As I waited, Eugene told me everything. The driver that'd hit Max's parents was driving an eighteen-wheeler truck and was intoxicated. It was raining and somehow, he clashed with Max's parents, veering into their lane.

Eugene pointed to a man with a brown hat on, a confederate flag on the front of it. Brown hair hung below the hat, and the man looked greasy...and also unapologetic. The drunk truck driver sat cuffed to an officer's desk, ignoring the questions being asked of him.

Once Max found out who the man was, things got really bad. We all knew Max had a temper, but I'd never seen him get so angry. And I mean, blood-boiling angry. He stormed through the police department and toward the driver, shoving chairs and objects out of his way, his face red.

The truck driver noticed Max coming, looked him over, and then laughed. He was lucky a cop was there to intervene and stop Max before he could get his hands on him, but it didn't stop Max from spewing hateful words, to which the truck driver laughed even more, and even began taunting him by calling him and his parents' names—*rude* names that no white man ever should have said to a black man in such a moment of grief and despair.

The police officers finally got control of Max and had no choice but to handcuff him and send him to a back room until he calmed down. I couldn't believe this was happening.

I waited three hours for Max to be released and, fortunately, the cops held nothing against him. I saw him come out of the station as I sat on the hood of his car and my heart raced, a light shining inside me. But that light inside me rapidly faded when he came my way, his shoulders sagging and his face blank.

"Max," I whispered. "Baby, are you okay?" I tried to hug him, but he pulled away from me.

"Where are my keys?" he demanded with his palm up and his hand stuck out.

I blinked hard, then dug in my pocket for them.

"I'm taking you home," he grumbled when I dumped them in his palm.

He moved around me, climbing behind the wheel of his car and slamming the door behind him. The slam made me flinch and I froze for just a moment.

He cranked the car, which prompted me to get in. "Max, I'm so sorry about—"

"Just stop, Shannon. Seriously. Just don't," he bit out, avoiding my eyes. He put the car in Drive and drove away from the police station.

I didn't say anything more for the rest of the ride. Hell, I couldn't even look at him. He had every reason to be upset right now. His parents had just died, and a racist man had just laughed in his face about it.

Max dropped me off at my apartment and didn't even bother coming up or allowing me to comfort him with a departing hug. Instead, he pulled off as soon as I'd made it to the sidewalk and my heart cracked as I watched him go, his tires skidding and burning the road.

As I walked up to my apartment door, I couldn't help but think that maybe he was putting some of the blame on me too. If I hadn't offered to take the trip to Hilton Head, he would have gone to the lake with his parents, like he did every single year. Was it my fault? Did I create this?

Three tears slipped down my cheeks when I stepped in front of my apartment door, but I swiped them away, and it was then that I realized I didn't have my keys. I'd left them in my bag, which was in Max's trunk. Luckily, Emilia was home and she let me in, answering the door with a wide smile on her face. As soon as she saw me though, her entire demeanor changed.

"Shannon?" She closed the door and then stepped in front of me. "What's wrong?"

I told her everything, dumped it all right on her.

Things changed that night, I can admit. I expected to hear from Max that same night or even the next morning, but I didn't. I called and even went by his apartment, but there was no answer and when I used the key he'd given me, I saw that he wasn't home.

The day after that, still no call. Not even a text. I figured he needed space and time alone to grieve. I sent a text to Eugene to ask him if he'd seen Max, and he said he hadn't, which worried me. Other than his parents and Eugene, he had no one else, so where was he?

I don't know how many times I'd called Max, but I do know I'd left enough voicemails that his voicemail box eventually became too full to take anymore.

A solid week passed and there was still nothing from him. His parents' funeral was that Saturday, and Max was not answering anyone's calls. Eugene had to take initiative earlier in the week to make the proper arrangements for his brother and sister-in-law since Max was a no-show.

Max didn't appear at the funeral either. And that? That was troubling. What had he done and where had he gone? He couldn't have been far, could he?

I tried thinking of all the places he could be, but other than his parents' house, nothing rang a bell. Eugene and I had even checked their house and there was no sign that Max had been there.

Two nights after the funeral, I began to feel ill. My head was pounding, and I vomited all night long. I slept all day the next day, and when I finally felt the urge to crawl out of bed, I felt even more fatigued than before.

It was dreadful, and even worse, I was still without Max. He was the only person I wanted to be around but there was no sign of him.

After spending four nights going through the same vomiting and fatigue stages, I paid a visit to a doctor. It wasn't like me to suddenly get sick. I knew my body well and I hardly ever got sick...before Onyx Pleura anyway.

The doctor ran every test that could lead to a stomach virus but it turned out it wasn't a stomach virus at all.

My doctor came in, handed me a sheet of paper and said, "Shannon, Congratulations! You're pregnant." He beamed at me, but I stared at him with wide eyes.

"Pregnant? What? *How?*"

"Well, I'm certain I don't need to explain how that happens," he said, teasing. I didn't bother smiling when he did and he cleared his throat, clearly seeing I wasn't in the mood for laughs. "You're about five weeks along now."

"Five weeks," I said. I couldn't believe this. How had I missed this? My head spun, my mouth suddenly too watery. I jumped off the table, rushing for the trashcan in the corner, heaving up the half of the blueberry muffin I had guzzled down that morning.

The tears started as I crossed the parking lot to get to my car and became heavier when I got to my apartment and buried myself beneath the comforter.

Oddly, I wasn't afraid. I wasn't worried. I was just... confused. I was confused because I wasn't sure what to do with the news. I wanted to keep the baby, but at the same time it felt like the wrong time to bear the child of someone who didn't even want to see me.

I called Max again. Then once more. Around the fifth

time, he actually answered, and I was surprised. The sound of his voice made my heart beat faster.

"Max?" I breathed. "What the hell? Where have you been? I've been trying to get in touch with you for days!"

"I'm sorry." He didn't say anything more.

"Are you okay?" I asked, sitting up with my back against the headboard.

"Fine I guess."

"Where are you? What's going on with you?"

He was quiet a moment. "I'm in a good place. Don't worry."

I wasn't sure how to accept that statement. He was still grieving apparently, which was fine, but why was he avoiding me?

"My parents have a condo in Wilmington," he said, and I was glad he at least told me that. "They rent it out as an Airbnb here and there. I've been here a while."

"Oh." Relief washed through me. "Okay. Good."

The line went quiet.

"I have something to tell you," I said, filling the void.

"What?"

"Well, I've been feeling kind of bad the last couple of days. I wasn't sure what was up so I finally went to the doctor to get checked…"

"And?" he urged.

"And, well, I still can't believe it but…" I laughed a little, some joy finally present, "I'm pregnant, Max."

Max, who I expected to respond eagerly, didn't respond at all. I waited for him to say something—anything.

"Did you hear me?" I asked.

"Yeah. I heard you."

Silence again.

"So…what do you think?"

Another stretch of silence. It was killing me. He'd never been this quiet on the phone with me before.

"Max?"

"I'm thinking right now is not a good time for you to be pregnant, Shannon."

His statement made my heart sink to my stomach. I shut my eyes briefly, fighting tears, trying to put myself in his shoes, but I just couldn't.

This unborn child that I'd just found about? He or she was a blessing. He was right about it not being the right time. We were young and had just started at this boyfriend-girlfriend thing, but I knew deep down we could make it work. We always made things work…or so I thought.

I assumed the news of my pregnancy would wake Max up a little, bring us closer together—even heal Max in a way. A tragedy leading up to a blessing.

"What do you mean?" I asked, my voice barely a whisper.

"I just…" He sighed. "You know what? I don't know. Just do whatever you want, okay? Just know that I'm not ready for a kid, but if you want it, keep it."

Selfish. That's what he was. A selfish asshole. Rage sparked in me and I sat forward. "Max, I understand what you are going through, but I think you're forgetting that you aren't the only person who has lost someone before! I lost a parent too, okay? I know how it feels! It fucking hurts and nothing will ever be able to replace them, but what I've just shared with you—this is real life, okay? This is happening so you can't just say shit to me like that! I'm not ready either, but I'm willing to talk it out and make something work!"

"Your father's death is different, Shannon," he muttered. "Plus, I lost two parents. You only lost one. It's not the same."

Wow. I couldn't believe this. "Are you fucking serious?"

My voice cracked and I hated the betrayal of it, "Why are you being like this? *How* can you be like this to me?"

Max didn't say anything. Not a single word, and I waited for it, but I knew he wasn't going to speak again. So I hung up and I cried even harder than I had the days before.

Later that night, Max called again. It was nearing midnight and though I was tired, and my eyes were tight, I couldn't sleep.

"What?" I answered.

"I was only being honest with you earlier, Shannon."

"Sure, Max."

"Why do you want this? You know having a baby is going to throw everything off for you."

"You don't know that," I mumbled.

"No, I do know that, and I know right now that you're living in a fantasy world. Shannon, you work two fucking jobs just to provide for yourself. What makes you think adding an extra mouth to feed will help? I'm still in school myself. We're young as hell and have so much going on."

My eyes burned. I closed them, pressing the phone harder to my ear.

"I want kids one day, and I know you do too, but this just isn't the right time, Shannon, and you know it."

"There is never a right time when it comes to my life, Max! Okay? I have *never* had time on my side, but somehow I always make a way."

"Shannon," he groaned.

"No," I snapped, sitting up on my elbow. "You know what? Fuck you, Max! *Fuck. You!* Just grow the hell up already and stop only thinking about yourself for once!"

I hung up again, tossing my phone across the room and crying so hard that my stomach and ribs began to physically hurt.

I thought about every single thing—from the trip to Hilton, to the moment he answered the phone. I thought about my past—my mother and my father. Tessa. Aunt Jessie. Grandma Lane.

But mostly, I thought about how Max was right. And I couldn't stand how right he was and how little I felt in this big, angry world. I had no idea what Max wanted out of me or what my purpose was in his life, but I knew one thing: keeping this child was only going to tear us apart and bring more struggles.

I had to choose between the man I loved, my life, and the unborn child growing inside me. This was a person I could create. Someone I could get to know from day one and love unconditionally, until the ends of the earth. Love like that was so hard for me to come by.

But I was struggling. I was weak. Hell, I still drove a shitty car that could hardly make it from point A to B. I could barely afford my rent.

I knew what I had to do...I just hated that I had to do it.

Two days later, I laid on a bed that was cold and not at all comfortable, my legs spread apart and thick tears rolling down the side of my face.

When the operation was over, I drove home, crampy, muddled, and depressed and I hate saying this, but I instantly regretted my decision.

Even when Max showed up the next week to try and comfort me, I couldn't look him in the eyes without crying because the truth was right there—he didn't want the baby.

That fucking crash, it ended us way before we completely gave up on each other. To this day, I hate myself for not fighting for us, but I really hate myself for giving up a child that I know would have changed my life for the better.

Some women long to have their own baby, beg and pray to become pregnant, and I just tossed that dream away—got rid of it like it was nothing.

Perhaps this is why I'm dying. Because I tore a life out of me out of despair and fear and loneliness. Out of *selfishness*. This is probably why God is punishing me, making me suffer a slow and painful death. He is not pleased with me or my decisions. He gave me a chance, and I botched it.

Maybe if I'd heard the heartbeat…maybe if I'd seen it there inside me, my decision would have been different. But it's too late to think that way now. The baby is gone, and I am a shell of that woman now.

Max apologized plenty of times for everything that happened after the crash, but his apology meant nothing to me back then. I acted like I forgave him, of course, simply because that's who I was. I still loved him. I still cared about him, but deep in my heart, I knew we weren't meant to be.

We could hardly get through one of the hardest parts of our relationship, so how were we going to get through something much more intense? How were we going to care for a child?

It was terrible, but obviously it was meant to be this way.

It was meant for me to leave Max behind for good. Meeting John was proof that I was supposed to move on from Max.

Max wasn't mine then. He never was. I just wanted him to be. I think about it now and I constantly forgave Max, not because I was still in love with him, but because he begged me so much. Even though he went missing for nearly three weeks, I forgave him.

Even when he flirted with other girls and his ex-girlfriend had a key and I didn't, I forgave him. Even when he got drunk and mouthy with me, I forgave him. Even when he was grieving and angry and said hurtful things, I forgave him.

Why? Because I was lonely, and with him I felt loved and seen in some way.

What I realized with Max after the crash was that he wasn't the type who could handle suffering. Maximilian Grant always had it easy—always had it made—but the death of his parents took a serious toll on him.

If I could go back and change things after the crash, with the baby, the abortion, with Max...I don't know if I would.

Maybe God was testing my faith back then and I failed him. It's no wonder he's taking me away. After all of that, I don't deserve his mercy.

THIRTY

Three hours later, after putting on a fancy red and white halter-top dress that Tessa had no problem helping me pick out from my closet, me and Max are standing in front of the Eiffel Tower.

It's way bigger than I expected, and even more beautiful up-close. The photographs and movies don't give this metal tower justice. It stands tall and firm, built on solid slabs of cement. It's miraculous, breathtaking, especially as the sun sets behind it.

"It's so pretty," I whisper.

Max steps to my side, placing a hand on his hip. He's wearing black slacks and a white button-down shirt with the sleeves rolled up to his elbows.

He points up and says, "If you think it's nice down here, imagine having dinner *inside* of it."

I gasp, meeting his eyes. The brightness of them glimmers from the sunlight. "Wait…are you serious? Is that what you told me to dress up for?"

He puts on a simple smile then holds out an elbow. "Damn straight. Come on."

I hook my arm through his, smiling way too hard, and he leads the way. We enter an elevator with a few other tourists after paying, and as I look out of the windows, my excitement cannot be contained. I can't believe he booked dinner inside the *Eiffel Tower* of all places. How can anything top this?

Before I know it, Max is leading the way to a door where a hostess awaits, greeting us in French.

She seats us at a table by the window with a magnificent view. My heart flutters when I realize how high up we are. The cars are like ants and the people like specks. The sun has set even more now, only a sliver of it peeking over the horizon.

"So?" Max says, looking around. "What do you think?"

"I love it, Max. So much. I can't believe you set all of this up."

"Well, I had to. I figured you needed to experience one of the best views in the city." He picks up his menu and I do my best to contain my excitement, picking mine up as well.

A waiter greets us, Max orders a beer and I request a glass of water, and when the waiter is gone Max looks at me with a small smile on his lips.

"What?" I ask.

"You look great, Shakes. Happy."

"Thanks. Tessa helped me pick my dress out." I tuck a few loose strands of my hair behind my ear, fighting a blush. I straightened my hair. It's thin, but nice. "I tried my best to *not* look sick," I add, then pick up my backpack. "But this fella right here kinda prevents that."

He chuckles, warm and deep. "Nah, I dig it. You made it work."

My laughter fills the space around us.

"So listen," he says, sighing. "I know we promised not to bring up the past or anything, but I can't help myself. I mean, we have this view right in front of us, I'm spending time with one of the most amazing women I've ever met in my life." He looks up, stopping mid-sentence. It's like he's waiting to see if I will stop him from talking, but I don't. This has been on my mind as well, I've just done my best to avoid bringing it up. "I wanted to talk about what happened with us. I feel like we never gave ourselves closure…"

"Okay." I run my palms over the lap of my dress. "How about we talk about it once we order."

"Good idea."

The waiter returns several minutes later with Max's bottle of beer. I reach for my water and sip as Max does. Once we've ordered our food, the waiter takes off with it, leaving me and Max at the table by ourselves again.

"How did you even get a spot here?" I ask, hoping to smooth out some of the tension. "I'm sure this place is always booked."

"I know a guy who knows a guy. He didn't mind hooking me up."

"Well, it's perfect. You did a great job."

"I knew you'd love it." His eyes lock with mine, warm and soft. I look away, down at the flickering candle in the lantern on the table.

Max doesn't move for a long time which causes me to worry, so I look up, only to find him already watching me. He reaches across the table with his long arms, the backs of his fingers hitting my cheek and rubbing downward.

"Max." I shake my head, pulling back. "Don't."

"All this time I've spent with you, Shannon," he murmurs, "I just don't understand."

"Understand what?"

"How I was foolish enough to let you go."

My heart thumps hard in my chest. I don't blink or speak.

He pulls his hand away, looking down at the dark tabletop. "What's crazy about all of this is that you'd think I would be happy, you know?" He folds his fingers on top of the table. "I mean, I'm running my own club in Wilmington. I have a nice home and nice cars and I eat well. There is never a day where I go hungry, never a day when I can't provide for myself...but even with all of that, it feels like something is missing." He studies my eyes. "At the end of a long day, I realize that I'm alone. And when I'm alone, I end up thinking about you and even when I try my hardest, I can't stop."

I pull my eyes away and look out of the window. He can't do this. Not right now.

He huffs. "I know you don't want to hear it, Shakes. Trust me, I know."

I side-eye him.

"Can I confess something?"

"What?" I ask, turning my head a little more to look at him.

"I was afraid to come back to Charlotte and see you."

"Why?" I whisper, and my guard has lowered all over again.

"Because I didn't know how I would handle it. With my parents gone and then knowing that one day you might be gone...it was a lot to digest and I didn't know if I was ready. You deserve better than what you're going through right now."

"This is my life, Max. It's okay. This is happening and I've accepted it."

He blinks through a pained expression. "I know you have." Sitting against the back of his seat, he looks from me to the window. "There isn't a day that goes by that I don't think about what I said to you—what I led you to do."

"You didn't lead me to do anything," I state quickly. "I made the decision. It was my choice." My throat thickens.

"But it was because of me that you did it, Shannon. I pushed you away during my grief instead of bringing you closer to me and opening up to you about my pain. I was fucking stupid and I regret it so much. If I could do it all over again, I would." He leans forward and I swallow hard, shaking my head. I can't listen to this right now. Why is he doing this *now*? "Don't you ever think," he murmurs, "about where we could've been if you'd kept the baby?"

I close my eyes, but it doesn't stop a tear from escaping me. "I think about it every day."

"I know you regret it. I can tell you regretted it when you'd told me you'd done it. I should've been there for you. I should've just manned the fuck up and been there for you. You didn't deserve to go through that alone."

"Don't say that," I murmur. "Don't. You can't beat yourself up because of your grief. You needed that time to yourself to try and heal."

"But that time to myself is what made me lose you."

"You never lost me, Max."

He blinks slowly.

I go on. "Now that I'm sick and will probably never carry a child, I do wish that I'd kept the baby. I wish that I never would have gone to that stupid clinic and let them take that baby away from me. I wonder every day if it would have been a boy or girl, what I would have named him or her." The tears are thicker and hotter now. "Trust me, I wish I could go back to that day and do it all over again too, but I can't, and neither can you. It's just something that I have to live with now. Just like this disease, I have to accept it."

He nods, dropping his head and twisting his lips. "Did you and John try for kids?"

"Not really," I breathe, shaking my head. "I found out I was sick during our honeymoon. My disease came and went, but either way we made sure to stay safe. Now that all of this has happened, I realize it would have been bad to try and create a baby through all of that. Too much stress."

"Damn. I'm so sorry."

"It's okay." The classical music fills the silence that drops between us. "Can I ask you a question?" I sit up straight, putting on a smile.

"Oh, boy," Max groans, sitting up as well. "By that smile I can tell I'm not going to enjoy answering whatever question you have."

I smile. "Why didn't you ever try and find someone else after me? Why remain stuck on being with me, even when you knew I'd moved on with John?"

He thinks on that a moment, and then sighs. "I guess I wanted to win you back. And I guess I also thought that you loved me so much that you wouldn't choose him over me."

I nod and he taps the edge of his beer bottle with his fingers. "You seemed happy," he says in a quieter voice. "Seeing the engagement pictures of you and him on Facebook and Instagram made it clear to me. I'd never seen so much light in your eyes. Even when you talk about him now, I see it."

I look him over before looking away, unsure of what to say to that.

"The one thing I have always wanted," Max says, finding my eyes again, "was for you to find happiness again. Even if it wasn't with me. And you did. And you deserve that. I'll admit, I know how I am, and no matter how hard I try, I don't think I can make you as happy as he does."

I can't even see him clearly because he's a blur behind my tears. I wipe the tears away and bob my head, smiling like an idiot.

"You're such a great human, Shannon."

"And you're an amazing soul, Max."

He picks up his beer and takes a swig of it. I pick my water up and sip it. Moments later and our meals arrive.

I devour my pan-fried fish and asparagus, downing the croissants that come along with it. Max finishes his filet mignon and orders another beer to wash it all down. By the end of dinner, he's full of nothing but laughter and I love seeing this look on him—the happiness and the joy in his eyes.

"I think you may have drank just a little too much beer," I say, fighting a smile as he plays with his fork.

"Yeah right. I'm good. I feel good. Wish you could drink though."

"Ehh." I shrug. "I'm alright. To be honest, I don't really miss drinking."

"You were pretty fun when you were drunk—not that you're no fun now."

"Yeah, yeah. You only liked me when I was drunk because I always said yes to everything."

"Bingo!" he chimes.

I laugh, picking up my water and taking a small sip with a playful roll of my eyes. As I set my glass down, a new song plays and Max's eyes broaden, as if he has some magical idea.

He slides out of his chair and stands, walking to my side and holding out a hand.

I frown, looking up at him. "What are you doing?"

"I want you to dance with me." His eyes are gentle. "I promise I won't ask you to do a jig for me this time."

I drop my head and laugh. "Okay. Sure." I grab the hand

he offers, picking up my jet-pack with the other hand and tossing it on my shoulder.

He helps me put it on all the way then one of his hands goes to my waist, the other holding my left hand. I sling my arm over his shoulder, tilting my head as he waltzes to the middle of the floor and begins a slow dance.

Most of the guests have left. Other than two couples eating, we're practically alone and I'm curious to know how long we've been here now.

Max's eyes leave mine. He holds me close, breathing softly. I ignore the way my heart races at our proximity, the way I feel in this moment. I can't deny that I feel alive. While we slow dance, I feel like a healthy, normal girl. I'm a girl dancing *inside* the Eiffel Tower. What a dream.

"I don't ever want you to forget this night," Max whispers in my ear.

He brings his head back enough so he can press his forehead on mine. My breath catches. Max's eyes drop to my mouth and I can tell he wants to kiss me. He even begins to lower his mouth, bringing it closer to mine, but I back away.

"Max," I whisper. I pull away, removing my arms from his shoulders.

"Shannon," he pleads, and regret instantly pools in his eyes. "I—I'm sorry. I didn't mean—"

I look at my surroundings. The view of the city. The lavender sky. The candle lights and the kissing couples. What is all of this?

What the hell was I thinking?

I shake my head swiftly. "I'm sorry—we can't do this."

His hands drop to his sides, face going blank. I walk closer to him, looking up and into his eyes.

"Max," I plead. "We *cannot* do this."

"I know." He closes his eyes. "Fuck, I know. I'm sorry. I knew this would be a bad idea."

"No—listen." I grab his hand and squeeze it. "Don't blame yourself, okay? This is—this is my fault. When I decided to come to Paris with you, I was being completely selfish. I didn't think about how it would make you feel, I just thought about myself." I try blinking my tears away but it's so hard. "I didn't think about *John*." Max's gaze darts away, going any direction other than mine and I hate that I have to tell him this out loud but, deep down, I know he already knows this. "Trust me, I have had so much fun here with you. You've done for me something that not many would do. You took a risk with me, and I will never forget that. You are a great person and I of all people know that, but when it comes to this"—I point back and forth between us— "well, we just have to face it, Max. No matter how hard you try, or how much I may think about you or miss you, even, we're just not meant to be together."

"Oh, wow." It takes no time for the tears to pool in his eyes again. "Fuck." He blinks and his tears fall. They hurt my heart to see.

"I love you to *death*, Maximilian Grant, I do. But I found happiness and peace and security with John. John picked me up and pieced me back together again. He made me accept my childhood and the darker parts of me. He made me realize that life can be beautiful if you make it beautiful, and those are only some of the reasons I fell so hard for him. I love you so much, but I love my husband more, okay? And I'm sorry it's this way, but it's the truth and I refuse to lie to you about that."

"Yeah. I understand," he murmurs. His throat bobs as he swallows. I release his hand, taking a look around. The other couple is leaving now. There's a man standing at the bar, sipping wine.

"I'm so sorry," I say, pleading. I really don't want him to hate me for speaking the truth.

"Don't be sorry. I understand where you're coming from, Shakes. Trust me, I know it. *I get it.*" He shrugs. "So maybe you're not meant to be mine, but I know one thing. My love for you will never change."

All I can do is nod at that statement.

He smiles, then flicks his wrist to check the time. "It's almost ten," he says with a sigh. "We should probably go before they kick us out."

"Right."

We walk back to the table and Max picks up his beer, finishing it off. He then calls for the waiter and asks for the bill and as he waits for the waiter to return, our eyes connect.

He smiles. I smile.

This is okay. He's okay…I think.

Once he has paid, we're out of the Eiffel Tower. The night is cooler, and it envelops us as we step outside. When we're far enough away from the tower, I turn and look up at it again. It twinkles with bright gold lights, a smattering of stars behind it.

I whip out my cellphone, turning my back to the tower, snapping a selfie, and then sending it to Tessa. She replies with *Lucky bitch!*

I grin and turn around, but someone bumps right into my shoulder, knocking me down on the ground. My phone falls and I feel something crack behind me.

"WATCH IT!" the man shouts.

"You…you fucking watch it," I wheeze. I turn on my side, reaching for my phone. I want to curse him the hell out, but I can't seem to find the breath to do so. I'm winded now, and it takes me several seconds to gain some sort of composure and realize what the hell is happening.

It was my jetpack. It did crack. There must be a hole. I'm losing oxygen.

"No, motherfucker! You watch it!" Max barks. I look up and he's rushing up to the man, gripping him by the collar of his shirt and squeezing tight.

I scramble for my cellphone that slid on the ground. The screen is now cracked.

"No, Max." I breathe harder, clutching my phone in hand and pushing off the ground. "It's fine. It's whatever. Let's just…let's just go."

"No, it's not fucking fine." Max's voice is full of anger. "You aren't walking away until you fucking apologize to her. You just knocked her on the ground, man! What the hell is wrong with you?"

I slide my phone into my backpack and then turn to where Max is having a showdown with the burly man. The man is nearly bald with a large beer belly and greasy skin. He's drunk. That much is clear.

"Fuck off! She should watch where the fuck she's going then!"

"Fuck you! How about you watch where the fuck you're going! That's a lady, man!"

"Max!" I yell.

"Does it look like I give a shit!?" The man can't be from here. He has to be American by the accent.

"Max!" I call again as people begin to slow down to watch him and the drunk man. "Max can we just go please?"

I rush for him, ready to grip his arm and drag him away from this place, but before I can reach him, the man gives him a hard shove on the chest and then swings a large fist at him.

Fortunately, Max ducks and the man misses, and Max takes a swing back. The man shoves Max again, causing him to bump into me, knocking me down once more.

I land straight on my ass, yelping in pain. The ground is hard and cold, and suddenly I can't breathe at all.

My chest feels tighter. My breathing irregular. *Fuck, I can't breathe.*

Max and the man are on the ground, some of the by passers gasping while others laugh and record on their phones.

"Max!" I try and scream his name, but my voice is barely a whisper. "Stop! Max!"

Fuck, I can't breathe.

And Max doesn't stop. I'm not even sure he's listening to me right now. Him and that temper. It's so bad. It's too much sometimes. He won't stop until he's won, or until someone has ripped him away from the man.

The fight seems to slow in speed. Everything around me is a blur, from the fighting men in front of me, to the twinkling lights on the tower beyond.

My heart is slamming in my chest, working harder, harder. I hear my pulse in my hears, *th-thump, th-thump, th-thump.* I try and say Max's name again.

I can't.

I'm dizzy now. Losing breath.

I try to say his name one more time. "Max!" I croak, but that's all that's left in me. I fall sideways on the ground.

"Oh my God! Is she okay?" I hear a woman scream.

"Shannon—oh, no. *Fuck!* Shannon!"

Th-thump, th-thump, th-thump.

This is it, I think to myself. I'm about to die. Right here in front of the Eiffel tower. I guess there's a sweetness to that.

"Shannon!" Max calls again, and I feel a pair of large

hands cradling my head. "Someone call an ambulance! Please!"

I lift my head up to the sound of Max's voice.

"Max?" I whisper. "Max... what's...what's happening?"

"Nothing's happening. I'm here," he murmurs. "I'm right here."

I try to say his name again.

"Don't speak. Relax." I can hear the panic in his voice. He knows I'm going to die too.

Feebly, I reach for Max's face and for a split moment, my vision isn't so blurry. I can see him. I can feel him, my upper body now cradled in his large arms. His eyes are watery.

"It's okay, Maximilian."

"No. No, no, no, no." Max says the word hurriedly, rocking me in his arms. "Fuck, this is my fault!"

I close my eyes and my arm falls gently from his face. The last thing I see are the lights of the Eiffel Tower. So bright. So beautiful. It's not such a bad view to go out to.

The last thing I hear is Max shouting Tessa's name. *Tessa?* The last thing he says is, "Well, you have to! We have no choice! Call John. Tell him something happened. I—I fucked up, okay? I really fucked up!"

"*That's it.*" I hear a voice in the back of my head as my eyes seal tight and darkness consumes me. "*Close your eyes. Just let go, baby girl.*"

The voice sounds just like my father's. They're the same words he used to say when he took me and Tessa swinging at the park every Sunday. Back when things were sort of okay.

Ice cream.

Swings.

Laughter.

Sunlight.

We always had so much fun with him.

"*Close your eyes. Feel the breeze. Imagine you're flying when I push you on this swing. It's nice, right? That's all you have to do. Just fly.*"

I feel my lips quirk up to smile.

The real voices are an echo now, *fading, fading, fading.*

"*Close your eyes. Let go. You'll be okay. I promise.*"

THIRTY-ONE

Darkness.
   Light.
   Darkness.
   Light.
   In and out.
   I can't seem to stay awake, but there are voices around me and they're familiar.
   "John! Just calm down!"
   "No! Don't tell me to fucking calm down! I knew this would happen! I warned her!"
   Tessa and John. They're arguing.
   "I thought she would be okay," I hear Max say. "She told me it was okay. I understand your anger, but she was fine until last night. She fell and the jetpack cracked. I got her to a hospital as soon as I could."
   "You shouldn't have brought her here at all! You see what you did, right? You got into her head! You fucked this all up and now she might just die because of you!"
   "John, if you are going to blame anyone, blame me," Tessa

pleads. "I was watching her. I shouldn't have let her go, no matter what the doctor said. I could have convinced her to stay."

"Yeah, well, it's too fucking late for that, don't you think, Tessa?" John growls. "Goddamnit!" A door slams shut seconds later.

"Fuck, Max," Tessa whimpers. "I told you I wasn't sure about this. I mean I wanted her to experience this, but look at her. I didn't want this!"

"I'm sorry. I didn't think this would happen. We were supposed to be on a flight home right now."

"You better hope she pulls through." Tessa's voice is thick with tears. "You better pray to God or I swear I will never forgive you for this, Max. I forgave you once. I won't do it again."

Another door slams shut. Or maybe it's the same door.

Monitors beep.

Darkness consumes me again.

THIRTY-TWO

MAX

I can't sit in this waiting room for another minute. My ass is sore. My body hurts. I've been here for over a week now and Shannon still hasn't woken up without crying out in pain. She's hurting so badly and her cries are killing me. They don't think it'll get any better. To calm her down, they sedate her. I don't like admitting to it, but I think this may be the end.

I look to my right, spotting Dr. Monroe rushing out of Shannon's room and heading toward the café. It's four in the morning and she looks exhausted. Shannon is getting worse, is what I heard her tell John while eavesdropping.

Apparently, the blackness is spreading even more on one of the lobes on her lungs, basically eating that part of it alive. No amount of OPX will help at this point. All they can hope for is a miracle.

The Hound is still in the room and I know he won't be

leaving anytime soon, so I take this opportunity to talk to Dr. Monroe myself.

John has threatened me to stay way from the room, which at first resulted in a nose-to-nose confrontation. Unfortunately, I was kicked out by the security guards. He's lucky he has the advantage of being her husband.

Tessa told me I didn't have to leave the hospital, but that I had to stay out of the room and respect his wishes.

I don't mean to disrespect the guy, but she's one of my only real friends. I've known her longer. I care too much about her to just leave and sit around in my hotel, waiting for a phone call that may never even happen.

Fuck that. I want to be here as soon as she opens those big brown eyes of hers again, for good this time. Because she has to. Shannon is strong. She has to pull through.

I push out of my chair, following Dr. Monroe down the hallway. When she's inside, stopping at the coffee station, I grab a cup, pretending I'm in need of a caffeine boost too.

"Hey, Dr. Monroe," I sigh.

She whips her head up, meeting my eyes and then forcing a smile. "Oh, hey, Max. Still hanging in there?"

"Yeah. I guess." I force a wary smile.

She pours some coffee into her cup, then pours some into mine. "Can I help you with something, Max?" she asks.

"I wanted to ask you about Shannon. Is there no one here who can help? No donor or anything anywhere?"

She gives her head a sad shake. "None, Max. It's going to be hard to find a healthy, matching set of lungs with her blood type."

"But it's just one part of her lung that's really bothering her, right?"

"Yes, her right lung is the most infected, but for a better

outcome, we'd likely do a double lung transplant, just so the mass doesn't spread to the other lung."

I drop my head, defeated. "Damn. I see."

I can feel Dr. Monroe's gaze on me. She places her cup down on the table, folding her arms across her chest. "You should go rest a little, at least until Shannon wakes up. There isn't much you can do for her right now."

"I don't want to leave," I mutter, looking away.

"Yes. I understand that, but you are exhausted, and Mr. Streeter is clearly not going to let you back into the room unless Shannon is awake. You can't expect to sit in the waiting room forever, can you? Something tells me Shannon wouldn't want that."

My lips press, and I hate how much she's right. Shannon wouldn't be happy about it. She would tell me to pull my shit together and go clean my balls, or some silly shit like that.

"You're right," I whisper. "Well, do you think you can tell Tessa to call me if she wakes up. I won't be gone long."

"Sure thing." She smiles, so warmly it fucking hurts. How can she be so content? I know she doesn't know Shannon all that well, but shouldn't this hurt her too? Knowing someone she's caring for is about to die? Or is death just a normal occurrence for her?

I don't bother asking any of those questions. Instead, I turn away and walk down the hallway to get to Shannon's room door. I don't go in, but I do take out the jewelry box that's in my pocket and place it in the drop box at her door. It's the gift I was going to give her on our walk back home from the Eiffel Tower—before I foolishly got into that dumb brawl.

Why can't I just control my fucking temper? The slightest things piss me off, and it's gotten worse since my parents died. I shouldn't have paid that man any attention. I should have ignored him and went for Shannon first thing, but I let my rage blind me.

Stupid. So fucking stupid.

I turn away from Shannon's door, walking back down the hallway and exiting the hospital.

I jump into the car I rented, slamming the door behind me and resting my forehead on the wheel. My heart slams in my chest the longer I think about everything that happened.

This trip? It was a fucking mistake. I should have just let her stay home where it was safe and came here by myself like I had planned. I never should have brought it up to her. Now look at her, so close to death I'm sure she can smell it.

All I wanted was to show her a good time. I wanted her to know that I still love her and that I care and will never forget about her, even after she's gone. I guess I've fucked that up too.

I crank the car, peeling out of the parking deck and hitting the road. I drive furiously to my hotel, passing the lights and disregarding stop signs.

"Fuck!" I bark, slamming a palm on the steering wheel. What hurts the most is that this will be just like how it was with my parents. She'll be gone. I'll be weak. I will never forgive myself.

It took me so long to accept the fact that it wasn't my fault my parents passed, but with Shannon? It's different with her. She was never supposed to leave me. She was never supposed to be diagnosed with something so rare—something so fucked up.

She's supposed to be here forever.

Until my last breath…right?

I don't realize I've zoned out. My mind is elsewhere, focused on memories of us. How she used to kiss me. How I used to hold her. How I used to make the sweetest love to her.

How I hurt her.

How I broke her.

How I made her cry.

How she always found a way to forgive me until, one day, she just couldn't.

I never should have skipped town. I should have tried harder for her. I never should have left her. She deserved so much more than I gave her.

I've done Shannon so wrong, and yet she constantly forgives me. She never forgets about me, even while married to a man who I know is so damn good to her. I can't even hate him because he is exactly what she deserves.

Someone good. Someone *there* for her. Someone who cares. I envy his love for her.

Something crashes and thuds in front of me and I curse, slamming down on the brakes, but it's too late.

BOOM. CLACK. *SKERRRKK.*

My windshield shatters.

My body rolls and I feel a sharp pain in my neck.

It hurts. And the car...*fuck*, the car is closing in around me. Glass is still breaking.

The car is flipping, and I swear this doesn't feel real. It's like some out of body experience, only I'm here and I feel it all.

I realize after the car has flipped for the final time, slamming right into the thick trunk of a tree, that I'm not dreaming.

I'm in pain now. So much pain. My mouth tastes of hot

copper. The steering wheel is broken. How the hell is it broken?

My legs feel numb, and my abdomen...*shit*. I can hardly breathe. I try and talk, but liquid falls out of my mouth and I weakly lift my hands, studying my palms. They're wet and stained red.

People are shouting. Lights from emergency vehicles emerge. They're bright. They hurt to look at, but I can't blink.

I can't blink because they're not there anymore. My eyes are closed now.

I feel cold. Empty. The pain is vanishing, morphing into a feeling I can't quite explain.

"Shannon," I whisper.

I love her so much.

Yes. I love Shannon Hales and I will love her forever, even as I take my last breath.

THIRTY-THREE

Light. *So much light.* I wasn't expecting this.

A scratchy groan fills my throat and I shift on the stiff bed, only to feel as if something has stabbed me near the ribs.

"Ow." I whimper, clutching my side.

"Holy shit. Shannon!" Tessa's voice rings and is loud. It makes my head throb. I turn my head to look at her and she shoots out of her chair, her eyes rapidly filling with tears.

"Tessa," I croak. Damn, my throat is so dry. I need water.

"John!" she calls. "She's awake! Oh my God, she's awake! It worked!"

"W-what? What worked?" I wince, confused. And I still need water. "Tess, can you get me some water please?"

"Oh, yes! Of course! Oh my gosh, I'm so sorry." She rushes for the pitcher on the counter, pouring me a quick cup and then spinning around to hand it to me.

The bathroom door swings open as I gulp the water down, and as Tessa pours me more, John walks out of the bathroom. His face is pale, the scruff around his mouth and along his jaw like a shadow.

"John," I call, my voice a near whisper.

He's at my side in an instant, breathing my name, and wrapping his fingers around the nape of my neck. I hold my water close to me, feeling some of it spill onto my chest from the embrace.

He inhales deeply, sighing with what seems to be relief before kissing my forehead. "Damn it, baby, I thought you were...*shit*. I thought you were gone."

"Should we call the doctor in?" Tessa asks, giving John a worried look.

I wince again, dropping my gaze and spotting blood on my gown. I frown and with minimal energy, begin to lift the gown but Tessa reaches down rapidly to stop me. "I wouldn't do that," she says, and then she takes my cup and places it on the table next to the bed.

"What the hell is going on? What happened to me? Why am I so sore?

"You're okay, Shannon," she assures me, a smile spreading across her lips. But just as quickly as that smile appears, it vanishes, and her eyes are cloudy. "Oh my God."

"What?" I ask.

"I—I can't do this." She chokes on a sob. What the hell is wrong with her? "I thought I could—that I should be the one to say something when you woke up but...shit. I—I can't." She steps closer to me, kissing me on the cheek. "I'm glad you're awake, Shanny. I'm going to get the doctor."

"What the hell is going on?" I demand, and I really don't care who I get an answer from as long as I get a damn answer. They're both acting so weird right now.

Tessa looks at John. I switch gazes between both of them.

"Go ahead," John finally says to her, and she spins around, hurrying for the door and fleeing, but not before giving me a quick glance over her shoulder.

"John." I push up, but the pain is so much worse that way, so I slouch back down. John helps me relax, adjusting the pillow behind my head. "What is she talking about? What happened?"

He pulls a chair up to the bed and sits. "I will explain everything," he murmurs. "But first I need to know how you feel."

"I'm fine." I look from him to my device in the cubby in the wall. "I ran out of the OPX. I thought I had more." And then it hits me. The reason I'm here. The person I came with. "Max?" I gasp. "Max! Is he okay? Where is he?"

John immediately lowers his gaze but grabs my hand to squeeze it. "Max is still around."

Oh thank God. "Okay. Good." I notice the words on the wall are in French at the top and translated to English at the bottom. We're still in Paris.

John flew all the way here? He must be furious me with. I am the worst wife ever. "Oh, God, John, I'm so sorry," I whisper, the emotion thickening my throat. "I—I should have listened to you. I did something crazy when I said I wouldn't. I just really wanted to come here before I died and—"

"Stop." John lifts a swift finger, cutting me off. "Don't apologize to me. You needed this trip with him."

My eyes narrow, and I swipe at the corners of them. "You aren't upset?"

"Of course, I'm a little upset," he says through a ragged breath. "I was pissed when I heard what had happened to you and I flew out here first thing. Nothing mattered except being here with you."

My lips press, and I focus on my fingernails. They've gone some, the pink polish chipped.

Raking his fingers through his hair, and sighing, John lifts his head, and his eyes are hard on mine.

"Shannon, there's something I need to tell you."

Oh, Jesus. He's scaring me. Is he going to leave me? Demand a separation? Is he going to ask for a divorce?

My heart catches speed and the monitor by the bed beeps quicker. John glances at it. "Is it because of this trip? Are you going to leave me?" I ask, feeling tears creep to the rims of my eyes. "If so, I mean I guess I understand. I'm dying and I didn't listen to you."

His eyes drop to mine. "What? No! Nothing like that, babe. I would never—" He stops talking immediately, then sighs. "I love you, Shannon. I will *never* leave you. Calm down. It's okay."

My pulse settles, and the beeping of the monitor slows to a steady rhythm. "Okay...so what is it then? What do have to tell me?"

His lips twitch, and his mouth is prepared to speak, but he stops when Dr. Monroe and Tessa walk into the room.

"There she is!" Dr. Monroe grins as she walks my way, holding her hands out as if she is truly happy to see me. I return a wary smile. "You had us all scared there for a minute. It was a long seven days."

"Seven days?" I gasp.

"Yes, but don't you worry. You are okay now." She's still smiling. "How are you feeling?"

"Good I guess."

"How is your pain?"

"On my side?" I ask, touching it.

"Yes. On a scale of one to ten, how would you rate it?"

"Hmm...maybe a six or a seven."

"Okay, good. I'm glad it's not too severe. The fentanyl is clearly doing its job after such an intense surgery. In the mean time, let me do a quick vital check, make sure all is still well."

I chew on my bottom lip as she steps closer my way with her stethoscope. As she does, I notice John and Tessa are both staring at me and for the first time they are smiling. Hope swims in both of their eyes.

"You mentioned surgery," I murmur, looking up at Dr. Monroe. "What was it for? What happened to me?"

"A miracle is what happened, Shannon," Dr. Monroe says with a warm smile. "There was a match that came in for you. Same blood type as yours and all. A female with the same height and build. Her lungs were strong and in perfect condition. It's unfortunate we lost her, but we are grateful that she was a donor, otherwise you would not be sitting here right now."

I swallow hard, my eyes rounding. "Are you for real?"

"Yes," she responds, elated. "As of two days ago, I am pleased to tell that you have been cured of Onyx Pleura, Shannon. You have a new set of lungs now. You're going to be okay."

I gasp and then immediately cup my mouth. *Oh my God. I'm... fucking speechless. This has to be a dream or some kind of twisted, sick joke. I must still be in a coma, wishing something like this would happen because this cannot be real.*

As if she's read my mind, Tessa says, "Trust me, Shannon, this is happening." She sobs and laughs at the same time. "You're better, sis! You're going to be okay!"

"I can't believe this," I breathe. I want to rejoice. I want to shout and scream and run until I can't run anymore, just to test these new lungs out, but perhaps that's a little overboard.

I draw in a deep breath and tears sting my eyes. I can breathe clearly. Evenly. I don't feel any pinches or pain as I breathe. It's smooth. Easy.

"I suppose you've already been told about the unfortunate

event with your friend Max too?" Dr. Monroe's voice fills the room again, and I whip my head up, my shock transforming to confusion.

"What are you talking about?"

She looks down at me after checking the monitor and her smile evaporates. Stepping back, she folds her fingers in front of her and clears her throat. "Oh, I um…I apologize. I had assumed you were already informed."

Her eyes move over to John and Tessa, as if seeking backup. John shakes his head. Tessa closes her eyes briefly before opening them and looking down.

"I will tell the nurses you're awake and to deliver some food. I will be back later to do another check on you, then we'll perform a few breathing tests." She walks out of the room so fast that her white coat is like a blur.

"What is she talking about?" I look between my husband and my sister. Both of them have these guilty looks on their faces. Neither of them can look me in the eye.

"Tessa?" I whisper, my voice cracking. She looks away, turning for the sofa and dropping her face into her palms. I put my focus on John. "John?"

"Yeah, babe?"

"What is she talking about with Max? What unfortunate event?"

John sighs and looks down at his lap. I can feel my heart thundering in my chest now. I need answers, and they are all stalling. "John, what the hell happened to Max?" I demand.

"He got into a wreck!" Tessa shouts abruptly, and then her face is in her hands again and she's sobbing. "God, Shannon, it was bad. So bad." Her voice is muffled in her hands, but I hear every word.

"A wreck? H-how? How did that happen?"

Tessa's face is completely covered by her hands now. I

know she won't say anything again for a while, not through those tears, so I look at John for answers.

He slides to the edge of his chair, grabbing my hand, kissing my knuckles. Not once do his eyes meet mine.

"Max got into a wreck leaving the hospital two nights ago." He pauses, swallowing hard, still avoiding my eyes. "He didn't want to leave the hospital the entire week you were in and out of consciousness. I told him he couldn't stay in the room with us—that he had to wait in the waiting room if he was going to stay. I...*blamed* him—told him it was his fault that you'd passed out and for putting the idea to travel to Paris in your head."

"God, John," I breathe.

"I know," he whispers, his thick hair falling to his forehead when his head drops. "I'm sorry, Shannon. I was just so pissed that he was here with you. It hurt me to know that." He shakes his head. "Anyway, he um...he finally left two nights ago. Dr. Monroe said she recommended he go and get some rest. Two hours later, Dr. Monroe came back into this room and told us Max had been rushed to the ER."

I gasp, and Tessa finally drops her hands and sucks in a breath, standing from the sofa to meet me at my side. She sits on the edge of the bed and rubs my back.

"Is he okay?" I manage to ask.

"He's not okay," John murmurs. "When he crashed a, um...a pole got lodged in the tip of his spine. Dr. Monroe says it struck the stem of his brain. The crash was so bad that he broke twenty bones. His legs were crushed and basically obliterated by the impact. She says he may never walk again." John looks up. Tessa sobs silently, shaking as she clings onto me.

"But he is okay, right? He's fine? He's alive?" Hope. I need hope.

"He is alive, yes." Sweet relief. *Thank God!* "But," John continues, and my relief is washed right away in an instant. "He is not okay, Shannon. Max has been considered brain dead. His lungs are still working, his heart is still beating, but that's only because of the life support. His brain has given no response and the doctors think it never will at this point."

"Oh my God," I whimper, and there's a crack in my chest, widening with each breath. "A-are you serious? Please. Please tell me this isn't for real."

"This is serious," Tessa whimpers. "Eugene is here now. He got here this morning."

"Eugene?" I turn my head to meet her damp eyes.

"He's next of kin. He will decide whether to pull the plug or not."

The plug? No. No, this can't be happening.

"No! I—I have to see him!" I start to hyperventilate, wishing my lungs would fucking give out on me right now so I can pass out again and not think about all of this. "This—no! No, this can't be happening. Max has to be okay. He has to! I was the one who was supposed to die, not him! I'm the one who's supposed to leave this world, not him! I'd finally come to peace with that! Where is he?" I demand.

"Three floors up," Tessa whispers.

"Well, I have to go see him! I can't just sit here. I have to go!" I start to peel off the tape that is connected to the IV in my hand, but John grabs my wrist before I can take it out. "John. Let me go! I have to see him! You don't understand!"

"I understand that you care about him, but you can't go yet. Not while you're still healing. He will still be here, I'm sure. Tessa told his uncle that you'd want to see him before he makes a decision."

I watch his eyes for several seconds, my vision blurring. I

then snatch my gaze away, covering my mouth and dropping my line of sight. "I can't...I can't believe this."

"There is something else you should know," Tessa says.

"What? What more could there be?" I snap. I'm pissed. And hurting, and I feel suffocated. My chest feels so tight, my body full of raw, ugly emotions.

"The woman's lungs they donated to you, she was a result of the crash Max was in."

I peer into her eyes and I swear my heart drops to the pit of my stomach. *"What?"*

"A city bus hit Max. Totaled his car. The cops told Eugene the impact was strong because Max was most likely speeding. From what witnesses were saying, Max's car flipped a total of six times before it stopped. During one of those flips, the car hit a woman. She, apparently, was walking home from work."

The tears have free-fallen now, streaming down my face. I shut my eyes, imagining a poor woman being trampled by a flipping car. I imagine Max, and how terrified he must've been while it all happened.

How is this my life?

How did this happen?

It seems my health has been traded for his life, but if I had a choice, I'd choose dying over losing him because I can't handle this. Losing him is losing a huge part of what made me who I am.

"How many days do I have to wait?" My voice cracks. "To see him. How many days?"

"At least wait one more day," John says, stroking my forearm. "If you want, we'll take you up ourselves. Get you a wheelchair and everything." He stands from his chair, exhaling slowly as he cups my face in his hands. He tries to get my eyes on his, but I can't look at him—not because I don't want to, but because I was so, so wrong.

If I'd stayed home, I could have died there. Max never would have gotten into that wreck—never would have been hit by a damn city bus.

"I know you're hurting," John whispers in my ear as he wraps his arms around me. "And I know you want to drop everything and go now, but please, Shannon. Just stay here. I will make sure you see Max before we are out of this hospital. You have my word."

I bury my face in his chest. I'm fighting like hell to fight my tears and to not break down right here, right now, but I can't help it. So much has happened within the last two weeks. So much that I could have controlled and changed, but I was too stubborn and selfish to do so. This is all my fault. This is the curse I carry. Everyone I love ends up dying or hurt.

John sits on the edge of the bed and continues holding me. His tight embrace is warm, but it's not enough and it's not what I need at this very moment.

I won't feel complete until I see Max. I won't feel okay until I can look at him and see the damage for myself. I need hope.

He can't be gone. I refuse to believe that one of the strongest men I know is about to lose his life right now.

THIRTY-FOUR

Many people have experienced personal losses. To lose someone who is close to your heart is like losing a piece of yourself. You'd do anything to get that person back. You'd fight like hell and walk through flames to find them again. You'd sacrifice whatever you have as long as you get to see that person smile at least one more time.

I have lost many people I love over the years—hell, I lost my father and was left with a mother who couldn't give two shits about me.

It was hard to recover after losing my father, and to this day I constantly wish he were still here to see how his girls grew up, but losing *Max?* Losing Max is earth shattering. I know there will be a permanent shift in the air once he's taken his last breath, and I know it will break me.

I won't say he is my soulmate, because he isn't. John is, and he always will be. But Max was a friend—a very close friend—and he was honest and true, and he had so much good in his heart that he constantly failed to see it in himself.

Yes, he made mistakes, and he always reacted before

thinking things through, and maybe we shouldn't have said or done certain things to one another in the past, but at the end of the day, we were meant to cross paths.

Just like me, he'd lost so much, so to know that he is losing his *life*...well, I just can't stomach the thought of it. It's not fair.

That's why I have waited until 3:30 in the morning to do what I'm about to do now.

I carefully took out my IV less than an hour ago. My hand is sore, and my body is still a bit drugged up from the meds, so as I climb out of bed, I stumble a bit, but I gain my footing, despite my legs feeling a little weak.

John is sound asleep on the sofa. He has to be exhausted. He's snoring, and he only snores when he's dead tired. I guess since I'm awake now he's found some peace.

Tessa took off to a hotel around the block. She has a room booked and the only reason she is there is because John is taking up the couch. She promised she'd be back by morning.

Before she left, though, she gave me a gift from Max. A gift that I really wish she'd waited to give to me because seeing it broke what was left of my heart after the news.

It was the locket he bought from the market. I thought for sure it was a mistake—that it belonged to him—but then I opened it and saw the pictures inside it.

There was wedding photo of me and John on the right and on the left, a rare candid of Tessa and Max. It was taken back when we were dating. I remember taking the picture on Max's phone, teasing them both about how they'd one day become siblings-in-law as we ate lunch. They pretended to hate each other, but I knew deep down they both had love for one another. In a way, he was like the big brother she never had.

Fighting like cats and dogs, but also getting along when need be.

He must have saved the photo of him and Tessa and gotten the one of me and John from my Facebook. This gift gives me all the more reason to go to him.

I pick the locket up from the bed and clutch it in hand, then I tip-toe across the cool floors, making my way to the door. Fortunately it doesn't creak. It swings open with ease and when I'm halfway out the door, I glance back.

John is still snoring. He won't wake anytime soon. I peer down the hallway, looking left and then right, making sure the hall is clear.

It's clear enough so I make my way to the elevator, pressing the button and walking right in when it opens. My room is on the second floor which means he's on the fifth. Three floors up.

I press button 5, jamming my thumb down on the close button to speed up the process.

The elevator spits me out on floor five and I turn right, following the signs that lead to the ICU. It doesn't take me long to find a room with the name Grant on it.

This is him.

Seeing his name makes this all the more real. My heart beats just a little bit faster. I take in a ragged breath, pressing my palm to the hard oak, briefly shutting my eyes.

Then I grip the door handle and push the door open slowly. It's mostly dark inside, minus a dim gold light shining from the middle of the ceiling. It shines right down on Max, and when I see him, my heart skips a beat.

The machine to his right beeps in a steady rhythm. A loud, windy noise moves through the room and I look to the left, noticing the machine with tubes that are connected to his mouth. It's the only thing keeping him alive.

I stop in front of his bed, choking on a sob as I stare at him. He's bruised and battered, and his eyes are sealed closed with tape. Even from here, I can tell the life in him is gone.

"Oh, Max," I cry in a whisper, rubbing his leg. I walk around the bed and lean over him, and despite the pain I feel in my body, it can't even compare to the pain I feel in my heart. "Oh, I'm so sorry." I stroke his face, his smooth skin, sobbing again.

I sit on an empty space on the bed, watching his chest rise up and sink down. Breaths in and out, in and out, but they aren't his.

"Why did this have to happen to you? It was supposed to be me, not you." I grab his hand and it's cold. Despite it, I squeeze it and hold it in mine. "I want you to know that I'm sorry about everything. About the past. About the *baby*. About all of it. I'm so, so sorry. I really love you. I love you so much."

I don't know why I expect him to respond. I watch his face, study it for some kind of change, some sort of reaction, but there is nothing. No sound from him. Just forced breaths. A beeping machine.

I drop my forehead to his chest, bringing my hand down to entwine our fingers. I cry, listening to his breaths, taking note of the ticking clock on the wall behind me. I apologize over and over again. Even though this isn't my fault, it feels like it is. One life for another. It isn't fair. Life is never fair.

I turn my head, sniffling, eyes tight and wet, and look out of the window, watching wisps of sunlight slowly spill over the horizon. The sky is filled with splashes of pink, orange, and yellow. The clouds are stretched, parting for the sun to make its breakthrough.

"Look, Max," I breathe. "It's beautiful. You always loved a good sunrise." I smile, gripping his hand tighter, a warmness sinking through me. "Remember that Kings of Leon concert we went to? I wanted to go so badly, and you got me tickets." I huff a laugh. "I was so damn excited the night before that I couldn't even sleep. It was my first concert. I remember staring out of the window the entire time while you slept. I watched the sun rise and I kept thinking to myself that it was the most beautiful sunrise I'd ever seen." I pause, stroking his cheek. "But I take that back now because this right here? A sunrise in Paris? Nothing will ever top this." I laugh softly, grabbing his hand again. It's warm from mine now. I wish he could squeeze my hand back.

His chest rises and sinks. Rises and sinks. No noises. No words. This is not Max.

"Oh, I love the locket by the way." I sniffle, picking it up from the table beside the bed. "It's beautiful. The pictures are thoughtful."

My eyes prick with tears as I open it and look at the photos again. Max is smiling. Tessa is trying not to smile as he has his arm thrown around her shoulders.

The breathing continues. The monitor beeps. I study Max's face—every single feature of it—and it dawns on me even more. My friend is not here. He's not coming back.

I swipe the back of my hand over my face to rid myself of the tears, then I bring the blanket on top of him to keep him warm. I'm not sure if he'll feel the warmth, but his body is cold.

As I watch him, the door swings open and Eugene walks in with a cup of coffee in hand. When he spots me, his eyes stretch with surprise.

"Oh, Shannon," he says. "I wasn't expecting to see you yet."

I swipe my eyes, forcing a smile. "Hey, Eugene. Yeah, um, I'm not supposed to be here. I snuck out."

"Typical Shannon," he jokes, placing his cup down and then moving closer to the bed. His smile fades as he looks at Max, and his eyes immediately glisten. "I can't believe I'm about to lose him too."

I climb off the bed carefully. "You don't think he has a chance?" I ask and I can feel my bottom lip trembling.

Eugene sighs, walking next to me. We both stare down at Max and I want to scream for him to wake up, to move—to do anything to show us a sign of life. But he doesn't. He won't.

"Shannon," Eugene says in a soft voice. "Look at him and tell me what you see."

I study Max, how his chest elevates while the rest of his body remains perfectly still.

"I see a man I don't recognize," I whisper.

"Yeah."

"If this happens, I'll never get to see him again, Eugene. Neither of us will."

"I know, but it's what he would want. Max wouldn't want to be a vegetable."

He's right, but I argue anyway. "Yes, that's true, but who knows?" I shrug, forcing a wary smile. "Maybe he'll come out of it one day and slowly build himself back up again. Anything could happen? Hell, I thought I was going to die and now I have a new set of lungs and another chance at life."

Eugene shakes his head and his eyes start to water again. The sunlight makes his tears sparkle, and when he finally makes a move, he rubs the back of his head and exhales.

"You want to know what I think?" he asks.

"What?"

"I think deep down Max wanted something like this to happen."

"What do you mean?"

"All he could ever talk about was how he wished he could help you—how he wished he could donate his own lung and save your life. He even said he'd die for you, and you know what? I believed him."

"But that...that's not fair. I would never have asked that of him."

"He knew that." I hate that he's already talking about him in the past tense, so I snatch my gaze away.

"Max wouldn't have been able to cope with losing you if you'd died, Shannon. I don't know why the universe works the way it does, but all of this clearly happened for a reason."

Sorrow floods every single part of my frail body. It takes over, but I nod, keeping my head up, because it's true. I turn to Max again, running my hand across his bruised cheek.

Eugene is right, but I hate that I'm losing someone else. I hate that it's Max of all people. It seems my life comes with a big price tag over it. If I don't bargain, I don't survive.

"I know," I whisper.

Eugene rubs my upper back. "I'll give you some time with him."

I know what he's really saying. He's telling me without actually telling me that once I leave this room, he's going to have them pull the plug.

Max is going to be gone for good and the next time I see him, it will probably be when his body is in a casket or an urn.

Eugene is out of the door before I know it and as soon as he is, I lay on the bed next to Max, draping my arm across his middle and holding him close. I shut my eyes and weep quietly, and I can't ignore the memories that come to surface.

I remember it all, from the very first day we met in Capri, to our first kiss in the parking lot of my apartment complex. I remember the first time we made love. The first time we argued. The moments we laughed and even the moments we cried.

I remember each beautiful and heartbreaking moment. Every touch. Every breath.

Everything.

Every time I close my eyes, I will think of Maximilian Grant. Every time I think of club Capri, drink pink moscato, or do a quick *shoulder jig* to fast-paced music, I will think of him. Max will never be forgotten. My memories of him will forever be cherished and that brings me some sort of comfort.

When the sun is higher in the sky, I sit up and kiss Max on the forehead. One of my tears drops on his cheek. I wipe it away carefully.

I guess it's time.

"Thank you for everything, Max. For putting up with my craziness. For loving me despite all of my flaws and all of my trauma. For taking risks with me and being a complete goofball with me when I needed it most." I sob and laugh, shaking my head.

"You can rest now, okay?" I stroke his forehead with the pad of my thumb, then lean down once more, kissing the apple of his cheek. "I will love you always," I whisper. "And I will always remember you, even when the time comes and I'm taking my last breath."

EPILOGUE

TWO YEARS LATER

I've dreamed of traveling the world so many times before, but I never thought I'd actually be able to go anywhere after being diagnosed with Onyx Pleura.

For the last two years I have been checked every single month for OP, but on this twenty-fourth month, I don't have to go back until every three months for a routine check. I have never felt more blessed.

It has been tough dealing with my losses, but I have moved forward. I am feeling much better, and now that things are picking up with me and John, and Tessa has gotten married, I couldn't ask for a more perfect life.

Today I am really happy though. Why? Because me, John, Tessa, and Danny are in Dubai.

Fucking Dubai!

This happened because John was given another chance to compete in a cook off in Vegas. All the chefs surprisingly wanted to do another competition after they'd heard about why he'd fled the competition two years ago to go to Paris. The competition took place five months later, during the winter.

It was great. Really great. The thing is, John actually had a clear head and I was able to go this time. I sat in the front row and cheered my adorable husband on.

John came in second place in Vegas. The chef that came in first place was a Japanese professional with three chain restaurants and, apparently, he's a big deal. For John to come in second place to him was incredible.

It was such a close call that dozens of reps came to John, offering him many golden opportunities to travel the world, create new dishes, and put his name out there even more.

Of course, he took most of the opportunities. We did have to move from Charlotte to Miami when he opened up his very own restaurant, but it wasn't a bad move and his restaurant is thriving.

This is why we're now in Dubai. I'm sitting on the edge of the king-sized hotel bed. The room is gorgeous, full of the warmest colors. Browns, burgundies, beiges, and accents of gold.

I put my dangly gold earrings in one by one, staring absently at the shimmering ocean through the picture window ahead of me.

When I'm done placing my earrings in, I stand and walk to the window, and as I stare out at the ocean water, how it shimmers and the waves clash, I can't help but think of Max.

Max and I never went to a beach—well, we tried to, but due to certain life changing circumstances, it didn't work out. There was a lot we left unsaid and a lot I wish I could go back and change, but when I think about it all, I am at peace with it now.

Max and I were complicated from the start, our back and

forth wishy-washiness some sort of child-like game we secretly loved. I actually smile when I think back to the time he saved me from losing my job.

I wonder sometimes what his last words would have been to me. After Eugene had the doctors pull the plug, I always wonder what he would have said.

About two weeks after his death, we'd finally returned home. I was healing and had the green light to go. John got me home and settled in. He'd checked the mail the next morning and brought a letter up to me.

It had a stamp of the Eiffel Tower on the top right corner and my name and address were scribbled on the front of the envelope in Max's handwriting. I knew his handwriting very well. There was no return address. He probably did that on purpose. He knew I'd know his handwriting.

I'd ripped the envelope open and read it right away.

Shakes,

So, while you were sleeping and I was monitoring your breathing, I was watching this sappy-ass movie about a chick who is heartbroken over some guy, and how some other guy cares deeply for her, but she doesn't know it. He wrote her a poem and stuck it in her mailbox and left his name, and she really appreciated it. I thought it was kinda cool how he won her over with that—not that I'm trying to win you over or anything. And not that this is a poem, but... yeah. It's something. I know you're a word girl, so I thought I'd give it a shot too. Check it out...

People come and go.
Sometimes they leave us sooner than we'd like them to.
They may be gone, and yes, it will hurt at first, but the memories will never fade.
They will be there when you need them most.
During the darkest of hours, in the sanctity of time.
That's what we as people should hold onto; the joy we shared.
The life we created. The countless memories.
Because those memories can be powerful, and they can last infinitely.

You might think it's kinda shitty, but it took me <u>HOURS</u> to come up with so you better enjoy the hell out of every word. Frame it if you have to. LOL.

Love you, Little Shakes.

Max

Thinking about the letter brings tears to my eyes. Hell, when I had first read it, I was a blubbering mess, but when I think of it now, it makes me smile. Max never realized just how thoughtful he was.

When I hear the bathroom door open behind me, I blink my tears away and smooth down my dress.

"Babe?" John's deep voice fills the room.

I glance over my shoulder. "Yeah?"

"Has Tessa called to let you know she's ready yet?"

"Not yet."

John is quiet a moment, but I can feel his gaze on my back. His footsteps are quiet as he steps behind me, and I reach back, grabbing hold of his hand, entwining our fingers, and placing his palm on my belly.

"What's bothering you?" he murmurs in my ear. "Is it the baby?"

"No," I breathe, breaking into a full smile. "Not at all. She's fine." I turn in his arms to look up at him.

"Tell me what it is," he pleads, his hands going to my waist.

"I was just thinking about...well, I know you get really tired of me bringing him up." I force a laugh, dropping my gaze to his black tie. "I just think Max would have really loved this place."

John smiles, his head tilting, and then he wraps me in his arms, sighing in my hair. It's not as easy as it used to be to hug him. This six-month belly of mine stands in the way now, a clear reminder that this little girl inside me will cause a big change in our lives.

"I don't get tired of you talking about him, Shannon," my husband says. He releases me, and when we're face to face again, he plants a soft, warm kiss on my forehead.

"I know he's happy for you right now. He was a good guy, I know. Don't think you can't talk about him with me because you can. I'm here for you. I know how much he meant to you."

"It doesn't bother you?" I ask in a quiet voice.

"Not at all."

"But that night when I snuck out of the hospital room to see him...you weren't upset about that?"

"No. I knew where you were. I saw that empty bed and knew exactly where you had gone. Getting your final words in with him was personal and I had no right holding you back from that. You knew him the most."

I'm so glad to hear this. John and I hardly talk about that night. After I came back to the room with puffy eyes and a runny nose, he didn't say anything. He just helped me get back into bed and stroked my hair until I fell asleep.

He knew where I'd been. He knew there wasn't much he could say or do because it wasn't going to make a difference.

All he could do was be there for me, and I'm so grateful that he was. He's an incredible husband, despite having a sometimes-shitty wife. To this day, I still don't feel like I deserve him.

The hotel phone rings on the nightstand. It's most likely Tessa calling. John pulls away to answer it, telling her we'll be right down.

He hangs up and turns back around to look at me and a slow smile spreads across his lips.

"What?" I ask, laughing.

"Nothing," he says quickly, waving it off, but he keeps smiling.

"No," I giggle. "What? Tell me."

"Well, I just…" The apple in his throat works up and down. "I never thought I'd see this day. You, carrying my baby. Both of us in another country. Healthy. I was so afraid about not getting the chance to fulfill my life with my one true love but look at us now? It's just so surreal."

My teeth sink into my bottom lip. "Aww, John. You're going to make me cry."

"Please don't. You just did your makeup and we don't have time for you to do it again," he chuckles, and I break out in a joyful laugh. He wraps his hand around mine and we walk to the door. "Come on. Let's go meet your starving sister before she bites her husband's head off."

I laugh as we leave the room, so ready for us to take on this night. John hasn't been like this since the day we met. To see him so happy, well it completes me. Even if the OP were to sweep through my lungs again one day, at least I'd know that our baby will be well taken care of.

They say people come into our lives for a reason. Some don't believe that saying, but I do. I believe I was with Max in the past to learn and to grow. And I believe I met John so that I could learn to be loved properly, cared for, and to heal from all the trauma in my past.

Both of these men were so close to giving up in their lives, but I was there to help pick up some of the pieces. I of all people know what it's like to constantly lose—to feel like you've hit rock bottom at every turn—but I also know how to keep going.

If it weren't for either of them, along with my sister, I don't know where I'd be now, but I am here. I am happy. I am healthy. I have a new start and I'm even carrying a new life.

I will cherish it all.

Every second.

Every breath.

Every laugh.

I will take this chance and do it right. For Max. For my father. For my baby.

I will do it all, and nothing will stop me or break my spirit because I have so much to live for. I have *always* had so much to live for.

This is the life I have been given.

I am strong.

Powerful.

Empowered.

Renewed.

Every moment counts now, and I will make sure that the

rest of this life I've been given is worth every single sacrifice I have made.

The End

Thank you so much for reading *Until the Last Breath*. I truly hope you enjoyed this story and the rollercoaster of emotions. I know some hearts may be broken, but I hope I can make it up to you now by letting you know that I wrote an exclusive bonus chapter in Max's point of view! It's when he first talks to Shannon in club Capri! If you'd liked to read it, click here!

Max's Bonus Chapter

FOLLOW SHANORA

Feel free to follow me on Instagram under the username @reallyshanora! I am always eager to chat with my readers there!

Join my Facebook Fan group! Just search for **Shanora's Queendom**

Join My Newsletter for exclusive updates at this link: shanorawilliams.com/mailing-list

Visit www.shanorawilliams.com for more book information and details.

MORE BOOKS BY SHANORA

WARD DUET
THE MAN I CAN'T HAVE
THE MAN I NEED

CANE SERIES
WANTING MR. CANE (#1)
BREAKING MR. CANE (#2)
LOVING MR. CANE (#3)
BEING MRS. CANE (#4)

NORA HEAT COLLECTION
CARESS
CRAVE
DIRTY LITTLE SECRET

STANDALONES
COACH ME
TEMPORARY BOYFRIEND
MY FIANCE'S BROTHER

DOOMSDAY LOVE
DEAR MR BLACK
FOREVER MR. BLACK
INFINITY

SERIES
FIRENINE SERIES
THE BEWARE DUET
VENOM TRILOGY

Most of these titles are available in Kindle Unlimited.
Visit www.shanorawilliams.com for more information.

Made in the USA
Middletown, DE
12 February 2023

24727439R00166